THE FORBIDDEN

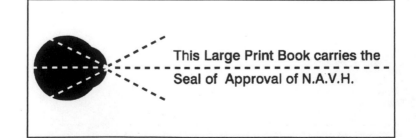

This Large Print Book carries the
Seal of Approval of N.A.V.H.

THE FORBIDDEN

BEVERLY LEWIS

THORNDIKE PRESS

A part of Gale, Cengage Learning

Detroit • New York • San Francisco • New Haven, Conn • Waterville, Maine • London

GALE
CENGAGE Learning

LIBRARY OF CONGRESS CATALOGING-IN-PUBLICATION DATA

Lewis, Beverly, 1949-
    The forbidden / the courtship of Nellie Fisher series #2 / by
Beverly Lewis.
        p. cm. — (Thorndike Press large print christian ficiton.)
    ISBN-13: 978-1-4104-0492-3 (alk. paper)
    ISBN-10: 1-4104-0492-7 (alk. paper)
    1. Amish — Fiction. 2. Lancaster County (Pa.) — Fiction.
3. Large type books. I. Title.
PS3562.E9383F67 2008b
813'.54—dc22
                                                                2008005383

Published in 2008 in arrangement with Bethany House Publishers.

Printed in the United States of America
1 2 3 4 5 6 7 12 11 10 09 08

DEDICATION:

*To John and Ada Reba Bachman,
my dear uncle and aunt.
With love and greatest gratitude.*

PROLOGUE

Winter 1967

I dreamed of Suzy last night. In the dream, it was deep winter and heavy snow fell as we walked to the barn to feed the calvies . . . little sisters once again. The whistle of a distant train, its sad, haunting sound, hung in the dense, cold air as it echoed through our cornfield. Yet why was the corn still tall and thriving in the dead of January?

All of this was crammed into a dream that lasted only a few minutes at most. My friend Rosanna King says dreams are like that, tantalizing you with a mixture of puzzling things that don't make a whit of sense.

Even so, I awakened with the knowledge that I must be moving beyond my initial grief. *Jah,* I long to see Suzy again, to talk with her and feel her gentle breath on my hair as she sleeps, sharing our old childhood bed. Sharing our lives, too. But something has changed in me. Maybe it helps to know that *Dat* and Mamma believe Suzy's in heaven, even though she died before she could join church. So terribly bewildering, as this idea goes against the grain of everything we've always believed.

Following her death, I didn't dream very often of my sister, though I'd wanted to. Now it's like going from a drought to a torrential rain. The floodgates have opened and she and I are together nearly every night as young girls . . . as if the Lord God is permitting a divine comforter to fall over me.

I daresay it is a comfort I sorely need, what with the six-month anniversary of Suzy's death having come and gone — December ninth, which my oldest sister, Rhoda, says was not long after Pearl Harbor Day. Another sad anniversary — the start of a world war decades ago. *Ach,* such strife between our country and another, and now a terrible clash is going on in a place called Vietnam, according to Rhoda.

She brings up the oddest things relating to the modern world. I see the look of surprise in Mamma's eyes nearly every night at supper. Dat is more stoic, slowly running his fingers up and down his black suspenders as he quietly takes in Rhoda's remarks.

My sister Nan's disapproval is evident in the jut of her chin and the way her blue eyes dim as Rhoda chatters about the foreign things she's learning while working for the Kraybills, our English neighbors who live half a mile away on the narrow, wooded section of Beaver Dam Road. She works every weekday, snow or not, and sometimes on Saturdays. At times I wonder if she'd be willing to work Sundays, too, given the chance.

Rhoda's not the only one working extra hard these days. Dat has been busy, as well. The bakery shop — called Nellie's Simple Sweets — will soon be home to three cozy sets of tables and chairs, about the size of those in the ice-cream parlors *Englischers* frequent. Three customers will be able to sit at each round table, and if some want to squeeze in, then four. Oh, such gossip that will fly. I must be careful lest I hear things not meant for my ears, especially from fancy customers.

Mamma's returned to working with me just recently. Nan still helps some, too, but only when things get real busy. Otherwise, it is my mother and me tending the store and, oh, the interesting tales she tells of bygone days — like a tomato-growing contest she won as a girl by supporting the tomato with a hammock of netting, and raising pigs with her younger brother. Like *Mammi* Hannah Fisher, Mamma has a knack for describing past doings.

My beau, Caleb Yoder, has only dropped by the bakery once, but he won't be doing that at all now — not if he wants to receive his inheritance of nearly a hundred acres of farmland. His father has forbidden him to court me, but Caleb has promised we'll see each other secretly . . . somehow.

Already three weeks have passed since he revealed the startling news and we held each other before parting ways. Ach, but it feels like forever. There was no word from him during Christmas, so he's abiding by his father's wishes. No matter this temporary silence, I trust him to know what to do to gain his *Daed*'s approval of me. Surely word has reached David Yoder's ear that I have not gone to Preacher Manny's church a second time — nor do I intend to. I'm not walking the "saved" path that has enticed a good many families in our church district already.

My staying put has caused an awful rift in the house, especially on Preaching Sundays when my family and I go our separate ways. I to the old church, and my parents and Rhoda and Nan to the new.

Plenty of folk are at odds on this issue. There is even a growing division amongst those in the new church — some have still stronger leanings toward the world, desiring electricity and cars, of all things. My parents won't hear of that, so we continue to drive horse and buggy and bring out the gas lamps and lanterns at dusk.

There's a hankering for light on both sides of the fence. For some this breaking away has required a quick decision, as Uncle Bishop has decreed a ninety-day grace period on excommunication and shunning for folk who want to leave the old church and join the new. The incentive is mighty strong for those already baptized into the Old Order church, since there are only a few short weeks to decide for or against the tradition of our ancestors. A right sobering thought.

Knowing that this new way was Suzy's belief makes it strangely appealing. But as curious as I am, I won't risk my future with Caleb Yoder, even though I am still in *Rumschpringe* — a running-around time sanctioned by the People. The old church is where I belong, with my beau. Dear Dat and Mamma don't realize I've already decided against embracing their faith — Caleb and I would stand no chance if I were to be baptized into the New Order. How can I think of doing so, when marrying him is my very best hope for happiness?

The smallest seed of faith is better than the largest fruit of happiness.

— HENRY DAVID THOREAU

CHAPTER 1

Nellie Mae Fisher loaded her newly baked goods onto the long sleigh and covered them with a lightweight tarp before tying everything down securely. She slipped her outer bonnet over her *Kapp* and breathed lightly as she pulled the sleigh through the backyard, toward the bakery shop behind her father's farmhouse. The January air was frosty, and she pushed the woolen scarf into place to protect her nose.

The expanse of land beyond Nellie's Simple Sweets lay buried beneath a blanket of snow, the unfruitful cornfield of last summer now as white and perfect as any neighboring field. A ridge of tall trees to the west stood stark and forklike against the sky, and only a handful of stray leaves still clung to the maples near the barnyard. Closer in, a few scraggly remnants of cornstalks remained, their reedy stems silhouetted brown against the snow.

Our first Christmas and New Year's . . . without Suzy.

Nellie Mae sighed, struck by the way the sky seemed to hold back the daylight behind a barricade of gray-white clouds, hoarding it away, depriving the earth of direct sunlight. She'd heard her father compare the icy ground to iron, telling Mamma quietly that even death itself was not as hard as a field of frozen ground. With recent heavy snows and continuous arctic air, Nellie was certainly glad to have rescued Suzy's diary from the earth well before this cold, long month.

There had been times as children when she and Suzy would wade through waist-deep snow, unbeknownst to Mamma, who would've had a thing or two to say about it had she known. They'd longed for summer's glow during the dark months of the year, just as Rhoda and Nan had. All four sisters had used this selfsame sleigh over the years, pushing through the snow on foot, in search of spring's greenery. Even the sight of dull green lichen on a tree trunk gave cause for rejoicing.

Oh, for spring to hurry!

Nellie opened the door to the snug shop and began unloading the sleigh of the day's inventory of goodies. Immediately, though, she sensed something was amiss, and when she moved behind the counter, there was nineteen-year-old Nan crouched with her best friend, Rebekah Yoder, Caleb's older sister. They rose, streaks of tears on each girl's face, and Nan quickly sputtered, "Ach, but it's just so unfair."

Confused, Nellie shook her head. "What is?"

"Rebekah's father . . . well . . ." Nan glanced at her friend, who was clearly as upset as she.

Instantly Nellie knew why the pair had been hiding.

Rebekah dabbed her face with a handkerchief. "I'm not supposed to be here," she admitted and sighed loudly. "What with the split between the People, my father's not in favor of certain friendships."

Certain friendships?

Unable to divulge her own predicament, Nellie simply nodded as Rebekah revealed that her plight was "all the family's, truly." She didn't go on to explain what that meant, but Nellie presumed she was speaking for herself and her brother Caleb, as well as Rebekah's mother, who until these past few months had often given Nellie's mamma rides to and from quilting bees.

Nan suddenly reached for Nellie's hand. "Would it be all right, do ya think, if Rebekah and I met here sometimes to visit?" Nan's eyes were pleading.

Nellie forced a smile. *Will I get myself in further trouble with David Yoder, harboring Caleb's sister?*

Nan groaned. "Oh, I don't understand why this has to be."

Rebekah's face was taut with worry. "Me neither."

"Even the bishop said no one's to be shunned for followin' Preacher Manny and the new church," Nan reminded.

"Well, you don't know my father, then," Rebekah said. "He'll shun if he wants to."

Nellie's spirits sank like a fallen cake.

"Come." Nan reached for Rebekah's hand and led her toward the door.

Nellie watched them go, not knowing who had her sympathy more — Nan and Rebekah, who were most likely scheming about future ways to visit — or her beau, Caleb.

She turned on the gas-run space heater in the far corner and then removed her coat, scarf, and mittens. Rubbing her hands together, she waited for heat to fill the place. As she did, she walked to the window and stared out at the wintry landscape. *Why didn't Caleb send word during Christmas?*

"How much longer till he gets his father to see the light?" she blurted into the stillness.

Deep within her, she feared Caleb's longing for his birthright. One hundred acres of fine farmland was nothing to sneeze at, and his father's land was ever so important to him. To her, as well, for it would provide their livelihood as Caleb cared for her needs and those of their future children. He had worried something awful about this when they'd met unexpectedly at the millstream — their last time together. She'd heard in his voice then the hunger for his inheritance. Soon she would know where things stood. After all, Caleb was a man of his word. He'd asked her to marry him and she had happily agreed, but that was before his father had demanded they part ways.

Why should David Yoder keep Rebekah and Nan apart, too?

Having witnessed Rebekah's misery, she worried that David Yoder had more sway over his son and daughter than she'd first believed. What with Rebekah busy working as a mother's helper for another Amish family, she had less opportunity to be influenced by the world than Nellie's sister Rhoda did working at the Kraybills' fancy house. No, Rebekah would most likely join the old church and stay in the fold, just as Nellie would when the time came. Doing so meant Rebekah would also eventually comply with her father's wishes and choose a different best friend, which would hurt Nan terribly.

Turning, Nellie took visual inventory of her baked goods — an ample supply of cookies, cakes, pies, and sticky buns. The bleak reality was that there had been few customers willing to brave the temperatures this week. She'd thought of asking Dat if she ought to close up during the coldest weeks as some shops did in Intercourse Village, although many of those were not Amish owned. Yet Nellie had hesitated to ask — her family needed the extra income from the bakery more than ever this year, due to last summer's drought.

"Right now we look as good as closed," she murmured, eyeing the road and the lack of customers. It was safe to head to the barn to see how Dat's new tables and chairs were coming along.

On her way, she noticed Nan and Rebekah now walking side by side toward Beaver Dam Road, Rebekah's hands gesturing as she talked spiritedly.

Rebekah knows her own mind. At twenty, she would be marrying before long — if not next fall, then the following year. As far as Nellie knew, Rebekah had no serious beau, though, of course, that didn't mean anything. Courting was done secretly, and most couples kept mum.

Glancing over her shoulder, she looked back again at Caleb's sister, graceful and tall even next to willowy Nan. Nellie couldn't help but wonder what the two girls were cooking up, the way they leaned toward each other. For now, at least, their tears had turned to laughter.

Nellie opened the barn door and headed to the area opposite the stable. Her father had carved out a corner there for his business records and occasional woodworking handiwork.

His back was to her as he appeared to scrutinize one of the chair legs, his nose nearly touching the oak. "Hullo, Dat," she said quietly so as not to startle him.

He turned quickly. "Nellie Mae?"

"Not many customers yet . . . well, none at all, really. Thought I'd drop in." She paused, aware of his pleasant smile. "Just curious to have a look-see." She pointed at the unfinished chair.

"Two tables are done, but, well, I'm a bit behind on the chairs, as you see." He set the chair down. "You discouraged 'bout the winter months, with so few customers?"

"The pies sit, is all."

He nodded slightly. "Seems winter's got sharper teeth this year, jah?"

She couldn't remember such a long cold snap. "I daresay we'll be eatin' more of those baked goods ourselves if . . ." She didn't finish. No need to say what Dat knew.

It wasn't merely the cold that kept folks away. Here lately they were seeing fewer of the families who held steadfast to the teachings of her father's older brother, Bishop Joseph. *Uncle Bishop* Nellie had always called him — a term both of endearment and reverence. Though the bishop himself had instructed the People not to shun one another because of the church rift, the truth of the matter was clear in the dropping number of customers at Nellie's Simple Sweets. Never had it been so quiet.

Nellie wondered if she'd have to start working for worldly folk, as Rhoda did, upsetting her father even more. Doing so would bring in extra money and help make up the difference for the family in the long run, though it would further jeopardize her chances with Caleb.

"Saw David Yoder's girl over here," Dat spoke up.

Nellie nodded, unwilling to say anything.

"Seems odd, ain't?"

"Jah." She sensed his meaning.

"We'll reap what we sow . . . sooner or later."

She inhaled slowly. "'Spect so."

Dat winced openly. "It's a new day in many ways, and there's no tellin' folk what to do. You and I both know that."

She said not a word, for she was unsure now what he was referring to. She suspected he might've had his ears filled with David Yoder's disapproval of Preacher Manny's teaching on "salvation through grace." More than likely that was a big part of it.

Sighing, she figured if Dat suspected Caleb's father of keeping her and Caleb apart, he'd be all for encouraging them to continue courting. Dat was like that. When it came to love — the kind you married for — she was sure he would err on the side of the couple's choice.

"Like I said, people will embrace what they long for, Nellie Mae."

She caught the perceptive glint in her father's eye. *He knows I have a beau. . . .*

CHAPTER 2

Rosanna King wasn't surprised to see Kate Beiler around midmorning on Friday. Her cousin had been faithfully coming once a day to supplement the twins' formula following their release from the hospital five weeks earlier.

Kate liked to coo at the babies, kissing the tops of their fuzzy little heads. Since New Year's, Rosanna had noticed Kate was visiting more often than simply to be a wet nurse. But today she looked tired, and Rosanna wondered if she might stay for only a short time.

Making a beeline for tiny Eli, Kate picked him up from the playpen. "Ach, look at you." She stroked his rosy cheek. "You're catchin' up to your sister, seems to me." She held him out a ways, moving him up and down, as if weighing him in a scale of sorts.

"He's eating right good," Rosanna spoke up.

"Every four hours or so . . . like the nurse at the hospital said?"

"Jah, and if one baby doesn't awaken and cry for nourishment, the other does, and soon they're both up. They're well fed, I'd say."

Kate turned back to Eli, who was bundled in one of the crocheted blankets Rosanna had made.

Meanwhile Rosanna reached for Rosie, whose soft fists were moving for her open mouth. "You need some love, too, jah?" Cuddling Eli's twin, she walked the length of the kitchen, pondering her feelings. Why was it every time Kate arrived, she felt like declaring, "The babies are mine, too"?

Lest her brooding show on her face, Rosanna sat down at the table and smiled down at Rosie. It was clearly time for the babies' feeding, and she ought to be glad for the break in the near-endless bottle-feeding routine. There were instances when she had to resort to propping up a bottle for one twin while holding the other. When that happened, she'd burp the one before switching babies for the second half of the four ounces of formula.

Helpful as Elias tried to be, her dear husband obviously had more on his mind than assisting with the twins, although it was plain he was partial to baby Eli.

Truly, Rosanna was getting plenty of motherhood training with her double blessings, both of them precious gifts from the Lord. She glanced over at Kate, still cradling little Eli in her arms, and pushed away the peculiar thoughts that beset her today.

No need to worry. . . .

She lifted Rosie to her face, burrowing her nose into her warm, sweet neck. "You ready for somethin' to eat?" she whispered, loving the smell, the feel of her.

"You go ahead and take care of Rosie while I tend to Eli here," Kate directed. "Not sure I'm up to feeding them both today."

Rosanna felt some surprise at this, though she knew it was time for Kate to be done nursing the twins altogether. In all truth, she had been looking forward to this day.

Eli let out a howl and Kate began to undo the bodice of her cape dress. "Mamma's here," she muttered, never looking Rosanna's way as she offered her breast.

Rosanna's heart caught in her throat. *Maybe Kate's not the best choice for a wet nurse.*

Now Rosie was *rutsching,* nuzzling for nourishment in earnest. Put out with Kate for her comment to Eli and for always placing his needs before Rosie's, Rosanna stood to warm her daughter's bottle, swaying back and forth and making soothing sounds as she did so.

She recalled Kate's unexpected decision to nurse the twins after their birth. Kate had never conferred with her cousin about this, though Rosanna had assumed she wanted to give the premature babies a good start. Despite her intentions, the recovering Kate hadn't had enough milk to keep up with the minimum six feedings a day per baby, so after a week, she'd nursed each of them only once daily, returning to the hospital for the feedings after being discharged herself. With the debt of gratitude Rosanna felt she owed her cousin, she had been quickly persuaded that Kate should continue to supplement the babies' formula until they were two months old. What she hadn't realized was how awkward the arrangement would be. *For both of us, probably.*

As she nursed Eli, Kate cooed softly. Then she addressed Rosanna from over her shoulder. "I hear your husband's been spending a lot of time with Reuben Fisher."

"Jah, Reuben — and others — have been a big help to Elias."

"No, I don't mean helpin' round the farm."

Kate frowned. "Your Elias and Reuben are talkin' Scripture, that's what."

For the life of her, Rosanna did not recall Elias mentioning any such discussions with Reuben Fisher or anyone else, although Nellie Mae's father often assisted her husband in mixing feed and unloading it from the silo. "Are ya sure 'bout this, Kate?"

"Well now, I wouldn't make it up."

Suddenly she felt all done in. "Who Elias chooses to work with ain't my business."

Or yours . . .

Kate's eyes widened. "You must not understand. I meant —"

Nodding, Rosanna softened her tone. "Well, I believe I do."

"You're sayin' you don't mind if Elias is listenin' to wrongful teaching?"

"If the bishop's not troubled by it, then who are we to —"

"No!" Kate shook her head. She removed Eli from her breast and put him on her shoulder, rubbing his back. "Flash conversions, Rosanna . . . that's what's going on here. Folk are getting emotionally caught up, talking 'bout prideful things like a close relationship with God. It ain't right."

Secretly Rosanna hoped her husband *was* drawn to the teachings she'd been hearing herself from Linda Fisher. To her, they seemed wonderful-good — not wrongful at all.

Without saying more, she carried Rosie to the rocking chair in the corner of the kitchen, putting some distance between herself and Kate. Rosie lurched forward when presented with the bottle, and Rosanna enjoyed her nearness as she rocked gently, caressing the baby's downy soft hair.

Watching Rosie, she wondered if there was a way to bring milk into her own breasts. She'd heard of it, though perhaps it amounted to an old wives' tale — or something requiring a Lancaster doctor, maybe. *What would it take?*

Kate's voice startled her. "Don't fool yourself about the bishop, cousin. He's mighty troubled . . . yet bein' ever so lenient where Manny and Reuben — well, the whole lot of them — are concerned." Kate coaxed a resounding burp from Eli, then another, and promptly put him on her other breast. "You must not be keepin' up with things."

I'm too busy for the grapevine. If there was something Elias wanted her to be aware of, Rosanna knew he'd tell her come nightfall, when he was so dear to her once the twins were settled into their cradles. Elias was like that, always eager to share with her the things on his mind while they nestled in

29

each other's arms. Eager in other ways, too.

Nellie Mae took care to redd up the bakery shop following a not-so-busy Friday afternoon — less than a handful of customers the whole day. She counted the money and placed it in her pocket, thinking she'd like to slip away to the millpond behind the old White Horse Mill to ice skate. She and Caleb had gone there twice as a courting couple, so perhaps she might catch at least a glimpse of him. She hadn't forgotten seeing him the last time she'd been there — most surprising and ever so nice, till they'd had to say good-bye.

Earlier she'd run to the mailbox, as she had every day for the past few weeks, hoping for a letter. Caleb could easily write her without anyone's knowing if he just left off the return address.

Unless he's ill.

The thought had not crossed her mind before now, although she hadn't seen Caleb at any of the youth gatherings associated with Christmas. She hadn't seen him in church on the Sunday two days before Christmas, either, but that didn't mean he hadn't been there. The house of worship — Deacon Lapp's farmhouse — was so packed full of folk she might simply have missed him.

"Maybe Caleb *is* under the weather." She knew of several families who'd suffered from the flu in the past days.

Glancing around the bakery shop, she eyed the area where she envisioned putting the tables and chairs. If customers could linger and talk, they might purchase more goodies.

She wondered if she shouldn't add sandwiches or homemade soups to the selection of items printed on the small blackboard on the wall behind the counter. But with the nix on their family by many devoted to the Old Ways now that Dat and Mamma and her sisters were attending the new church, Nellie might not get to realize her hopes of that. Besides, most folk wanted to eat next to their own fireplace on a bitterly cold day. Who could blame them?

She turned off the portable gas heater and headed for the door. Leaning into the wind, she picked her way across the snow-covered ground, aware that a substantial amount of ice lay beneath. Friday nights were skating nights at the millpond. If she could just get out of washing dishes later, she would bundle up and go.

With renewed anticipation, Nellie Mae stepped into the house and removed her boots, coat, and scarf. She fairly flung off

31

her mittens, suppressing her giggles as she sent them flying across the summer porch.

If Caleb and I can bump into each other once, why not again?

Delighted at the prospect, Nellie made her way into the warm kitchen for supper.

CHAPTER 3

Nellie's muscles were already stiff from the biting cold, yet she pushed onward. When she rounded the bend on Cambridge Road, she spotted Rebekah Yoder and several of her sisters there. Her heart leapt.

If they're here, surely Caleb is, too.

Merrily she dashed across the snowy banks along the millpond, near the area where she and Caleb had once walked hand in hand. She had never been afraid of the ice, not even in late winter when the pond would begin to thaw in places. She'd always assumed she'd have more sense than to fall in.

Thinking suddenly of Suzy, Nellie realized she hadn't followed through with her hope to find out more about what had happened the day her sister had drowned. Even though the busy days of Christmas had come and gone, she'd had no desire to go in search of Zach and Christian Yoder, two Mennonite brothers who had befriended Suzy. Nevertheless, she was still quite curious to talk to anyone who'd been with her sister on that terrible June day.

Pushing that sad thought aside, she took note of the dozen or more young people presently skating and continued to look for Caleb as she put on her skates. She dared not ask Rebekah or her sisters about him. She would mind her own business and glide out onto the large pond to skate.

The first star of the evening appeared like a pulsing dot of white light. Nellie was so taken with the icy splendor around her, she scarcely even saw Susannah Lapp until she nearly collided with her. Susannah squealed and narrowly missed falling, and Nellie skated hard to the right, trying to maintain her balance.

Ach, not her!

Quickly she chided herself. No reason to view Susannah as a threat any longer. *Caleb's father is my greatest fear now.*

Nellie made another pass around the pond, this time carefully skirting the others. But the longer Nellie stayed, the colder she would be by the time she departed for home. Again she pondered Caleb's whereabouts, and a little panic flitted through her mind: Surely he was not avoiding her.

Still she remained, determined to be on hand in case he happened to arrive late. After all, it was a perfect night for skating, and no doubt he would think so, too. The ice was hard and slick, its formerly rough surface swept smooth by the wind.

A night meant for a girl and her beau . . .

She was gaining speed again, waving and smiling at Rebekah Yoder, when she thought she saw someone standing dark and rigid against the trees on the banks of the millpond, across the way. Was it Caleb?

Not wanting to stare, Nellie forced herself onward, heart pounding with anticipation.

Elias didn't mention Reuben Fisher at all while Rosanna lay in the crook of his arm. She waited and wondered as she thought back to the peculiar things Cousin Kate had voiced with such conviction. Were they true?

Elias *did* have something interesting to talk about between kisses. Maryann Fisher, who lived across the way with her husband, Ephram, had been home alone when her labor pangs began. Elias had stopped by to deliver some tools for Ephram, who'd gone to the town of Cains on an errand.

"Honestly, I thought I might have to help

deliver Maryann's baby while her four young ones looked on."

"Oh, Elias . . . what on earth?"

"Well, I was able to send the oldest boy up the road to the community phone booth — thank the Good Lord for that — and the midwife came just in time."

Rosanna shook her head. "Poor Maryann, she must have been terribly frightened."

"On the contrary . . . said she'd be fine if I would watch her littlest ones, Katie and Becky."

Rosanna couldn't help but giggle. "You must be countin' your blessings 'bout now."

He chuckled. "S'posin' if I can deliver calves, I can help bring a baby into the world." He paused, pulling her closer. "But watching them toddlers of Maryann's and keepin' them out of trouble . . . now, that's another story yet."

Rosanna smiled up at Elias, who quit his laughing and looked at her with a familiar glint of yearning. "Let's not be talkin' of Ephram's new baby, love," he said softly, his face very near.

Let's not talk at all. She wrapped her arms around his neck, impatient for more of his kisses.

The shadowy figure was a man, but not one

young enough to be Caleb, Nellie decided as she cast another furtive glance. He inched his way toward the pond, and she could not tell if he was watching any skater in particular. Even so, the man was clearly observing them, and his presence made her uneasy.

Who is it?

She wondered if other skaters had noticed the man. It was obvious from his appearance he was Amish. Otherwise, Nellie would have been even more concerned.

She sped twice more around the pond before stopping to wait for Rebekah on the side nearest the trees. When Rebekah spotted her and waved, heading that way, Nellie motioned her over. "Don't look now, but there's a man standing there . . . watching us."

Rebekah dug in the blades of her skates, spraying ice as she came to a stop. "Oh jah, I know." She laughed softly. "It's my father, come to take us home . . . when we're ready."

Nellie felt silly. "Seeing a man there scared me." She paused. "Well, just a little."

"I'm not surprised." Rebekah acted a bit sheepish. "He's overseein' us, I'm guessin'."

Giving a quick squeeze of her hand, Rebekah headed off around the pond again, catching up with her sisters.

Nellie Mae was now so cold her toes were numb. *I should head home.* She clumped to the bank, where she leaned against a tree to remove her skates, wishing for the wrought-iron bench where she and Caleb had sat and talked, his strong arms around her when she began to shiver.

But the bench was on the other side of the millstream, and she dared not try and climb down to it, not when her feet felt like clubs. She wondered if her toes were frostbitten and attempted to wiggle them beneath her thick socks as she worked on her snow boots. Then she took the long way around the stream to a footbridge, moving toward the road.

Forcing her feet forward, she looked up at the sky and at the many stars of the Milky Way, pondering the fact that while a good many of Caleb's family were present this night, he was nowhere in sight.

Squeezing her eyes tight, she fought back tears. *I miss you so much, Caleb.*

After a time, she heard the *clip-clop* of a horse and buggy slowing down behind her.

"Nellie Mae!" Rebekah Yoder called. "Come, get in the buggy with us."

Fatigued, she had not the strength, nor the gumption, to refuse. She turned and hobbled to the carriage. "*Denki,* ever so much."

"Ach, Nellie, you're limping." Rebekah helped her inside.

"Did you hurt your foot skating?" one of Rebekah's sisters asked from the back as Nellie settled into the front seat next to Rebekah.

David Yoder spoke up before Nellie could respond. "She's a farm girl — she'll be fine." He kept his gaze toward the road.

Is he picking me up so Caleb can't?

"I'm ever so thankful for the ride," she managed to say, not sure how she would ever have made it home with the feeling all but gone from her feet.

Rebekah reached under the heavy woolen lap robe and squeezed her hand. "I did something like this once . . . skated too long and nearly lost a toe."

"What'd you do?"

"Soaked my foot in cool water . . . let it warm gradually." She paused, glancing at her father. "Your mamma will know what to do."

Jah. Bet she'd chuckle if she knew why I went in the first place.

Then, a moment before they crossed the one-lane bridge on Beaver Dam Road, Rebekah leaned over to whisper, "I'll be tellin' Caleb I saw you."

Nellie Mae let out a gasp, her breath twirling into the air. *No question about it. She knows. . . .*

Barely missing a beat, Nellie whispered back, "I'll tell Nan I saw you, too."

CHAPTER 4

Rosanna awakened to Eli's cries early Saturday morning. Pulling on her old chenille robe, she glanced at Elias, in deep slumber.

How does he sleep through such howling?

Hurrying now to the sitting room-turned-nursery, she bent down to pick up Eli. More than Rosie, he was typically impatient to be fed, especially after the midnight hour. She looked at peaceful Rosie and was again surprised that anyone, infant or father alike, could sleep through such hearty cries.

She gripped the stair railing with her free hand, wishing at times like this they might consider moving to the large bedroom on the first floor. Of course, that would mean having the babies sleep in the same room as they, something Elias would not want even at this tender age. She also cherished their time of lovemaking, especially this night. She'd felt quite vulnerable and ever so put out at Kate for calling herself mamma to little Eli. Couldn't her cousin guess how Rosanna might feel about that?

Downstairs, she warmed Eli's bottle, and when it was ready she watched as he worked his cheeks and lips. Later, when he was burped sufficiently and asleep in her arms, she climbed the stairs. Still groggy, she tucked him into his cradle, only to rouse Rosie to feed her next. Tired as she was, Rosanna treasured these nighttime feedings. *Just the babies and me . . . and the dear Savior.*

Rosie nestled her wee face into Rosanna's bosom, which again made her wish she could suckle both babies — not just Eli, as Kate had chosen to do today. Swiftly she removed the second small bottle from the gas-powered refrigerator, shaking it before placing the bottle into a pan of water and turning on the gas stove. Elias had been wise to replace the old woodstove before the twins had come home.

"*Ballemol* — soon," she promised Rosie as she kept an eye on the stove, making sure the bottle didn't get too warm. Rosie burrowed her head into her once more. *Oh, dear little one.* She wondered whether Eli and

Rosie would ever fully bond with her, with her cousin constantly coming around. Did they sense, on some subconscious level, who Kate was?

When the bottle of formula was warm enough, Rosanna sat in the rocking chair, facing the window and looking at the moon — a wide fingernail in the heavens. And she prayed, asking God questions she hoped He might see fit to answer. Their good neighbor Linda sometimes expressed herself in such a way in prayer. Linda had invited her and Elias to attend a "new group" with her and her husband, Jonathan, some Sunday, and although Rosanna was intrigued, she was reluctant to mention it to Elias. But if her husband was discussing Scripture with Reuben Fisher, as Kate reported, maybe Elias wouldn't mind if his wife started praying out loud.

Sighing, she thrilled to the intimacy between her and the daughter she had longed for as Rosie began to relax. "You're my own little darlin'," she whispered. "You and your brother . . ."

Thinking of the day ahead and of missing quilting bees and work frolics, Rosanna did not regret being sequestered in her home with two adorable babies. Presently it seemed she had no need for human interaction beyond that with her husband and children, though there was no chance they'd be left to themselves. The twins' maternal grandmother, Rachel Stoltzfus, had initially come nearly as often as Kate herself, but her interest had seemingly faded in the past few days. Rosanna wondered if Kate's keen attention might diminish over time, as well, particularly once she was no longer acting as a wet nurse.

Feeling guilty at the thought, Rosanna allowed a short prayer to form on her lips. "Lord, help me to be generous with these little ones . . . so graciously given."

Betsy Fisher overheard her daughters talking in Nellie Mae's room prior to Saturday breakfast. They had never before congregated there, at least not that Betsy recalled. Yet they were certainly there now and talking quite loudly, too — loud enough for her to make out every word.

Rhoda's sharp voice rose above the others. "You really ought to go again, Nellie Mae. You seem to think you're better than the rest of us — standin' your ground thataway!"

"What way?" asked Nellie. "That ain't fair to say."

"Sure it is," said Nan. "Rhoda can speak her mind — it's 'bout time someone did."

Nellie fell silent.

"Jah, you should come along on Sundays," Nan said, her tone more gentle. "Why not?"

"I know you'd like me to join you, sisters," Nellie answered, her words less defensive. "But I like followin' the way we were all taught to follow since we were babes. Why's that wrong now?"

"Well, there's nothin' at all wrong with that if you like livin' without electric and cars and whatnot," Rhoda said, worrying Betsy.

"Seems to me you're chasin' after the world, not Scripture," Nellie spoke up.

Betsy touched the small sachet pillow Suzy had made for her — the headache pillow was often tucked inside one of her pockets — and walked toward the door of Nellie's room, her hand poised to knock. More than anything she wanted to put a stop to the senseless conversation. She'd had no idea how interested Rhoda seemed to be in fancy things, other than the necklaces dangling over her side of the dresser of late. Was Nan leaning the same way?

She sighed, folding her hands now. She yearned for her children to know the Savior, not fuss over living in a house with or without electricity. She'd hoped they would catch that insight from Preacher Manny's sermons, or from the Sunday school the new church was talking of starting up soon. The thought gladdened her heart, for she prayed daily that more souls would come to understand the saving grace of the Lord Jesus, bishop's deadline or no.

The girls were talking again, but the conversation had veered away from Preacher Manny's Sunday meetings to the upcoming Singings and other youth-related activities planned for those in the New Order. Feeling awkward about listening in, Betsy knocked on the door.

Nellie appeared, looking well rested, her big brown eyes brighter than usual. "Mornin', Mamma."

"Anyone hungry for breakfast?"

That got a quick response from Rhoda, who rushed past her and down the stairs. Nan followed close behind, but not before giving Nellie Mae a sidelong glance.

Nellie remained, going to sit on her bed. Betsy said no more and simply headed toward the stairs, wanting to give her pensive daughter the room she needed.

Rhoda entered Mamma's kitchen ahead of her sister. Being she was not scheduled to work today, she would attempt to help as much as possible in her father's house . . . her home for the time being. Today she would simply go through the motions again, just as she'd done since first starting to work for Mrs. Kraybill. Preparing breakfast *there* was a joy, what with such appealing and thoroughly modern appliances. Mamma and her sisters would surely succumb, too, if they had the opportunity to see such wonderful-good things as blenders and electric mixers in action.

Jah, they're missing out something awful.

Her thoughts swirled back to yesterday, when Mrs. Kraybill had caught her paging through one of the several family picture albums. Rhoda had closed it right quick, apologizing, but the still-youthful Mrs. Kraybill had not been at all displeased and had even encouraged her to "enjoy whatever you see." Rhoda had relished the look of kindness and even pleasure on her employer's sympathetic face. That moment she turned a corner in her thinking about what she'd always been told was sinful.

What would Mamma think? Rhoda was torn between wanting to shield her parents from her longings and moving forward with her secret plans.

Truth be told, she was itching to immerse herself as much as possible in the Kraybills' wonderfully enticing world — full of not just fancy items but lovely ones. Rhoda craved beauty; she craved travel, too. She dreamed of owning a car and of seeing the country someday, especially the ocean. Other than pinching her pennies, which she was quite happy to do, it might not take much effort at all to realize her dream.

First chance she got Monday, she'd have another look at the Kraybills' newspaper to see how much money a used car might cost her. She didn't feel comfortable going to a used car lot by herself to look around, like some boys in their Rumschpringe were known to do, but she could easily read the classified ads. Who knows? If she had enough gumption to ask, perhaps sometime Mrs. Kraybill would take her car shopping.

Monday's the day after Preaching, Rhoda thought, not knowing why she should plan such outright wickedness after the goodness of the Lord's Day. When did willful disobedience ever pay off?

She shuddered, thinking of Preacher Manny's urgent calls to the youth for repentance . . . and Suzy's drowning came to mind. No matter what Nellie Mae had shown them in Suzy's diary about her surprising turnaround, Rhoda still assumed the Lord God had allowed her youngest sister's death.

Might her own disobedience come to a similar bad end?

Rhoda shrugged. With so many opinions about which way was right flying around Honey Brook, it was up to her to find her own way. Right now that meant letting her enthusiasm for experiencing what she'd been deprived of all these years guide her. *No, I'm not at all ready to join the old nor the new church, neither one.*

Part of Rhoda's hope was to catch a man, fancy or otherwise. *A shiny blue — or even green — car might do the trick,* she thought. Hiding her yearning for a beau had not been easy, but she'd managed to conceal from Mamma and her sisters her dire disappointment at being passed over at Singings and other gatherings. What good were such finicky fellows? She would gladly leave them in the dust and make her own future. She refused to die a *Maidel*.

She pictured herself driving along dressed fancy, her long, uncovered hair flowing in the breeze. She'd find herself some pretty new glasses, too, though she would not stoop to wearing those sleeveless tent dresses or silly-looking halter-top blouses she'd seen in the catalogs on Mrs. Kraybill's coffee table.

She laughed with glee at the Rhoda of her imagination, a Rhoda who would not remain lonely for long. Fact was, if she made the jump soon, she could be married within the year.

Still, I must keep my plan a secret, Rhoda thought. *And I best be careful. . . .*

CHAPTER 5

Christian Yoder had a powerful sense that someone was hovering near his bed. He lifted his head and saw his younger brother, Zach, leaning on the footboard, his shape visible by the light of the moon streaming into their shared bedroom.

"Zach?" He paused. "What's up?"

The room was weighty with silence.

Chris sat up and swung his legs over the side of the bed. His bare feet touched the floor. "Man, it's cold in here."

Zach made a gesture in the dim light. "Sorry. Didn't mean to wake you." He reached up to his bulletin board to straighten a five-by-seven photograph of Suzy Fisher, an enlargement of the only snapshot he had of her. The picture had gone up the week after her untimely death. "I . . . couldn't sleep."

It was hard to see his brother like this. Until last year, most people would have described

Zach as an incurable optimist. "Don't worry about it. I'm awake," said Chris.

Still standing by the bulletin board with its mementos and news clippings, Zach shook his head. "She's with the Lord, right? Isn't that what we believe?"

Chris sat quietly. He understood Zach's grief. Suzy was his brother's first love, and there had been something remarkably special about her, beyond being interesting and full of life.

Or was it Zach's guilt, knowing they were partially responsible for Suzy's death? The guilt dug at Chris's soul, too. She had several sisters, if he remembered correctly, including Nellie Mae, the sister Suzy had talked about most often. It had been his idea to ask Suzy's close sister along that day, an offer she'd refused.

How devastated Nellie Mae — the whole family — must have been. Must *still* be. Great as the gulf was between their way of life and his, he'd wanted to express his utter sorrow and somehow . . . apologize. As if that would make a difference.

"Suzy is more alive than we are . . . don't forget that," Chris said.

"Yeah." Zach wandered from the window back to his bed, where he sat staring out at the moonlight. "I guess we'd better get some sleep." His eyes looked hollow.

Suzy's death had affected everything — even Zach's spiritual life. Not to say he was struggling in his faith, but he'd been shaken to the core, just as Chris had been. Their whole family had felt the loss; they'd all been so fond of the freckle-faced Amish girl with wheat-colored hair.

"Ever think of going back out to the lake?" Chris hadn't planned to say that.

But Zach nodded slowly. "Maybe we should sometime. When do you want to go?"

Chris already regretted making the suggestion, but he couldn't back out now, not with Zach agreeing to it. "Next weekend's good. Too much going on today at church."

Zach glanced at the bulletin board once again, then at Chris. "Sure, guess I can wait."

"Hey, it's already the Lord's Day . . . lighten up." Chris threw his pillow across the room, but Zach ducked.

Reuben Fisher waited for church to begin, killing time in the raw air. He noticed Benjamin, one of his five married sons, hurrying his way.

"'Mornin'," said Benjamin, ankle-deep in snow. "Seems your cousin Jonathan Fisher's bought himself a used car. A '65 Rambler

Marlin — a two-door fastback."

"Ach, but you know a mite too much 'bout this here car business, son."

Benjamin poked at the snow with his black boot. "Honestly, I wouldn't mind gettin' me a good-lookin' car like that. Perty beige color."

Reuben shook his head. Were the New Order meetings merely leading to this? He glanced across the way at his eldest sons — twins Thomas and Jeremiah, both in Sunday black — and wondered how long before they would start such talk. "How is it you're privy to Jonathan's purchase?"

Benjamin brightened. "Saw the car myself while I was over there helpin' in his barn. It's a dandy, I daresay."

Reuben swallowed hard. "A car is the last thing I need . . . or want." Fact was, he'd heard tell of others roaming around used-car lots, asking English neighbors for advice and whatnot. All of them wasting time running helter-skelter.

"What we've got is a split within a split, seems to me." Benjamin moved toward the back of the house. "How many will there be, when all's said and done?"

Reuben recognized the truth in his words and was worried about his own family, and not merely his married sons. Even Rhoda was giving him cause for concern, since she was the only unmarried daughter outside the protection of his roof, spending more time at her employers' place than she did at home anymore.

He paused to take in the landscape, white and crisp. Winter was a time for resting the land, but his body needed some rest, too, thanks to several new foals here lately and three older horses in need of veterinary attention. Come to think of it, his brain could use something of a respite, as well. He pondered now several recent lengthy discussions he'd had with Elias King, just twenty-four. Young, for certain, but what a good head on his shoulders. The young man seemed hungry to talk of the Lord, but not in the way one might expect of a staunch Amishman. Clearly, Elias was searching, much as Reuben himself had been. Longing for the meat of the Word, as Preacher Manny sometimes referred to spiritual sustenance.

Just then Reuben caught sight of his cousin Manny — the Lord's appointed — coming up the lane with his family, all of them waving now, squeezed into the enclosed gray buggy.

"Lord, bless him abundantly for stickin' his neck out," he whispered, waiting to greet Manny and grip his firm hand yet again.

What's Manny think of all the car talk?

Preacher Manny was not a judgmental sort, though he liked to follow the rules. He had not lightly dismissed the teachings of the *Ordnung* on salvation, and he was putting much care and thought into the new ordinance being discussed now. Soon they'd all be back to square one on that as the new church worked to incorporate God's Word, their primary guidebook for living, into the new Ordnung. Meanwhile, those yearning for cars and electricity were already joining up with a nearby Beachy group, whose church met at a separate meetinghouse instead of in houses, and where services were held in English, of all things.

Nellie Mae huddled under her quilts, staring at the bedroom ceiling. *When have I ever been so ill?* She found it ironic that she'd wondered if Caleb was sick, and now here she was, too feverish to get out of bed.

She closed her eyes, well aware she was the only one home on this particular Sunday. For the fast-dwindling Old Order group, today remained a no-Preaching Lord's Day. Her family, of course, had made their way to Manny's church after Mamma had once again invited Nellie to join them. Even if she'd wanted to, there was no way she could go today.

Honestly she was so weak she couldn't think of getting up early to bake tomorrow, as she always did on washday before helping Mamma and Nan with the laundry.

Maybe none of the regulars would notice if the bakery shop was closed. She felt sure she would still be lying there flat on her back come morning, so hot was her brow . . . and nauseated her stomach.

Is it the flu? Or did I eat something bad?

Oh, she wished Mamma had stayed home to warm up some chicken broth or brew a pot of chamomile tea. In her haze of intermittent discomfort and rest, Nellie missed Caleb even more.

When she did at last fall into fitful slumber, she dreamed they were walking along the millstream, only she was on one side and he was on the other, the water rushing between them.

Caleb was telling her she was old enough to make a stand for or against the old church . . . and her family. "What will *you* do, Nellie?" he asked.

She wanted to say that while she was an obedient daughter, she was also ready to be out from under the control of her father. Ready, too, to make a life with her husband someday soon.

"You know how much I despise conflict," she managed to say in her dream.

"Well, who doesn't? Anyway, you haven't said which side you'll be on, if things heat up."

Her mouth felt dry. "You think it'll come to that?"

"Oh jah, there'll be a battle. I'm sure of it." Then he asked again, "Whose side, love?"

In her dream, she hoped it wouldn't mean having to choose. Such things created horrid complications between siblings, parents and grown children, close friends. . . . She'd heard plenty of reports about families here and there leaving the Amish community for the Mennonites and other Plain groups. Yet even in the midst of her very mixed-up dream, Nellie seemed to know that this battle had already taken place, and she was simply reliving the church split that now divided so many.

When she awakened, the anxiety the dream had stirred up lingered, and she hoped Caleb might never goad her in such a manner in real life. She curled tightly into a ball beneath Mammi Fisher's warm winter quilts and pushed the awful dream far, far away.

A while later, thirsty and wishing to know the hour, Nellie crept out of bed and down the stairs, then limped dizzily toward the kitchen. After managing to pour a glass of water, she propped herself up with her arms on the counter and squinted up at the day clock. *Nearly time for Preaching to come to a close,* she thought as she eyed the clock's blurry face.

Her head ached with the effort and Nellie moaned. She should have spoken up and given Mamma a clearer explanation as to why she was staying home. Her family might find it a bit too coincidental that she had begged off attending their church yet again. Certainly Rhoda had seemed to view her resistance to their invitation with some disdain.

Serves me right, their abandoning me, she thought ruefully, slowly heading back toward the stairs.

Then, glancing out at the snow-covered fields and yard, she noticed a tall black shape moving down the road. Inching nearer the window, Nellie tried her best to make out who was there. Could it be she was sleepwalking and merely dreaming?

She leaned on the windowsill, almost too feeble to stand. The man headed straight to their mailbox and stopped in front of it. "What on earth?" she muttered, frowning as she watched.

A wave of nausea forced Nellie back to the

stairs, and she pulled herself up step by step, gripping the railing, until she came at last to the landing at the top, where she fell into a heap on the floor. There was no way she could get out to the mailbox to look inside . . . not in her sick state. The best she could do was edge down the hall and climb back into bed, hoping Dat and Mamma wouldn't tarry at the common meal following church. Hoping, too, that if Caleb *had* risked placing something in the mailbox for her, her family would remain none the wiser.

If, indeed, it was Caleb at all. . . .

CHAPTER 6

Long before dawn Monday, Nan surprised Nellie by coming in and sitting on the bed. "You never woke up for supper last night," Nan whispered. "Mamma tried to nudge you awake several times."

Nellie stretched her legs beneath the quilts, achy all over. "Ach, I slept ever so hard . . . yet I'm still all in."

Nan touched Nellie's forehead. "I'd say you've got a fever."

"Can you . . . would you mind puttin' a sign on the bakery shop?"

"Why sure. But you stay put, all right?" Nan smiled sympathetically. "Seems you've got the old-fashioned flu."

Nellie's head throbbed. "Much too early for you to be up, ain't?"

"Don't worry over me. You're the one burnin' up." Nan rose slowly. "I'll get a cool washcloth for your forehead."

Closing her eyes, she felt relieved that Nan

wanted to take care of her. As much as she desired to get up and bake and go about her regular Monday routine, she simply could not.

Hours later, when she'd awakened again and daylight had come, she heard voices downstairs. Was it her lively niece Emma with her mamma and younger siblings? Normally Nellie would hate to miss a morning's fun with her five-year-old niece and her two younger brothers, Jimmy and Matty. Six-year-old Benny, now a first-grader, would be at school.

Soon Nan brought in another cold cloth to replace the warm one, and Nellie tentatively sipped the cup of lukewarm chamomile tea, sweetened with honey.

"This'll do ya good . . . not too hot to spike your fever." Nan's voice was as gentle as Mamma's might have been . . . or Suzy's.

"Kind of you." Nellie lifted her eyes to Nan, whose blue eyes were ever so bright. Her sometimes-distant sister was being unusually attentive. Whatever the reason for the change, Nellie Mae was grateful.

"Martha's downstairs with the children," Nan said, confirming Nellie's earlier hunch. "Here for a quick visit."

"I'd hate for any of them to get this flu."

Nan agreed. "We'll keep the little ones

downstairs, but I'll be checkin' on you in a bit."

"Denki, sister." Nellie offered her best smile.

Nan left the room, leaving the door ajar.

Once, when Betsy Fisher was in her teens, she'd gone walking along one of the back roads, only to be knocked down by the thunderous boom of a low-flying jet plane. She recalled the sensation of being stunned by the sound and sight of the enormous plane even now as she held her granddaughter Emma on her lap while sitting at the kitchen table. This time, though, the shock had reverberated from a few simple words.

"We're looking into buying a tractor." Had her daughter-in-law really said such a thing?

But clearly she had, and Martha went on to add that her husband, James, and his younger brother, Benjamin, had recently hired a driver to take them into town to talk to a contractor about installing electricity in both their houses.

Ach, what a big can of worms we've opened. Betsy was appalled, knowing even more was sure to come.

Her head spun with the realization that yet another group had obviously exploded forth from Manny's New Order church, this one bent on all things modern. For sure and for certain, the Beachys were much too fancy for her liking.

She suddenly realized she must have been holding Emma too tightly, because the little sweetie protested and slid off her lap. She felt stricken, similar to the way her eardrums had been assaulted years before, although presently it was her sense of right and wrong that was being shaken. Betsy had lived long enough to know that when certain things were set in motion, one simply could not stop the coming change.

Before Cousin Kate was to arrive for the babies' midmorning feeding, Rosanna wanted to prepare two loaves of bread to bake. She'd missed kneading bread dough, missed the feel of the flour between her fingers. There'd been precious little time for either baking or quilting — her two fondest interests — since Eli and Rosie had arrived. Even so, she cherished her time with her babies, holding them longer than necessary, spoiling them at every turn. Oh, the joy of cradling such snuggly wee ones close to her heart, where she had longed for them as dearly as any birth mother.

No wonder Kate offered to be an occasional wet nurse, she thought. *How could anyone resist such adorable children?*

It nagged at her, though, that Eli was Kate's obvious favorite. Rosanna brushed away her frustration and began to measure the sifted flour. Then, setting it aside, she combined the shortening, salt, sugar, and boiling water, mixing them together till the shortening was dissolved. At last she was ready to add a mixture of yeast, sugar, and warm water and thoroughly blend all the ingredients in her largest bowl.

She thought of her mother, deceased now for many years. Oh, what she wouldn't give to have Mamma here, helping to nurture Eli and Rosie, offering loving advice on everything from feeding schedules to how to burp Rosie when she seemed so tense and colicky, tucking her tiny knees up close to her tummy.

She remembered how elated she and Elias had been at the babies' birth — how much more would her mother have delighted in having these unexpected grandchildren, Rosanna's blood cousins. She'd spent hours studying the set of their eyes and the shape of their earlobes, seeking any resemblance to herself and her many brothers . . . longing for even the slightest connection.

She continued working the dough, adding the remaining flour until the mixture was soft and no longer sticky. Now she would let it rise for a couple hours or so.

Moving into the front room, she sat for a time, enjoying the quiet before Kate's arrival, knowing it would soon come to an end. *Maybe today's visit will be more comfortable for all of us.* With that hope in mind, Rosanna began to talk to the Lord, her very own Savior, according to the Good Book. She had Linda Fisher to thank for opening her eyes to this most priceless truth.

It was past ten o'clock when Reuben finished rubbing liniment on several of his older horses' legs. He thought ahead to writing out detailed feeding regimens for his growing colts as he moseyed out to the road to mail a feed payment. Observing the graying sky, he wished for the piece of blue over toward the south to spread this way. The days had been too long dreary. Some steady sunshine would undoubtedly lift the spirits.

Having son James's wife and little ones visit there that morning might be precisely what he needed, though he knew Betsy would enjoy the visit, as well. Thankfully his wife didn't seem so much blue anymore as mighty busy. And a busy person — as opposed to a busybody — was a wonderful-good thing.

Truth was, he was miffed at Cousin Jonathan, getting this whole car-buying thing started. The man who'd been the first among them to talk openly of salvation was now a believer with a car, of all things.

Just what was Jonathan thinking? Didn't he know others would follow? The idea of his own cousin driving a car gave Reuben the heebie-jeebies as he lifted the flag and opened the mailbox. He would have slid his envelope right in but stopped when he noticed a piece of mail already inside. *Has the postman arrived?* He looked down the road a ways, to the neighbors' mailbox. Their flag was still up.

That's odd.

Reuben pulled the envelope out before placing his own letter in the box. He saw what looked to be a personally delivered letter to Nellie Mae. *C. Yoder* was boldly written in the corner, yet there was no return address.

David's boy's courtin' our Nellie?

The idea peeved him. David Yoder was one of the most outspoken, bullheaded men he knew, and although Reuben had shown kindness toward those in his former church, he struggled now with the notion that Caleb might be pursuing Nellie Mae. Surely Caleb hadn't bargained on the letter's being discovered by anyone but Nellie, her being home alone yesterday for no-Preaching Sunday.

He glanced again at the lackluster sky. Disheartened, he decided to let Betsy be the one to deliver the letter to Nellie Mae, tempted as he was to destroy it or return it to the boy. Still, he would not fall prey to David's own tactics. He'd heard from Deacon Lapp himself that David was encouraging an arrangement between one of the deacon's daughters and Caleb, all to the end of keeping the youngest Yoder boy firmly planted in the old church.

Seems David might be a bit late, Reuben thought wryly.

CHAPTER 7

"I hope you and Rhoda don't get this awful bug," Nellie said softly. Nan had come upstairs again after Martha and the children left, and Nellie was glad for the company. The silence of the house now was a stark contrast to the playful noises of her little niece and nephews.

"Ah, well, the flu's missed me the past several years," Nan was quick to say. "I'm ever so lucky, really."

Nellie looked at her slender brunette sister — so obedient and loyal to attend Preacher Manny's services with Dat and Mamma. "Don't you mean you're blessed, not lucky?"

Nan cast a sideways glance. "You must've heard that at the new church, jah?"

"Prob'ly." Now that she thought of it, she had heard it on the one Sunday she'd succumbed and gone.

"If you ever want to borrow our Bible

69

— Rhoda's and mine — just say so." Nan smiled pleasantly. "It's ever so interesting to read for oneself, truly 'tis."

Nellie had often wished she understood the Scriptures read in High German at Preaching service. "In English, is it?"

"Jah. Dat says sometimes it's best to read a verse several times. Let it sink in, ya know."

"Never heard it put thataway."

Nan sighed fitfully and looked toward the window. "There's much that I'm learnin'." She was silent for a moment and a tear trickled down her cheek. Swiftly she brushed it away. "Ach, I'm sorry."

Nellie's heart sank. "Nothin' to be sorry for." Nellie wanted to add, *We're sisters, after all . . . you can tell me what's troubling you,* but she merely reached for Nan's hand.

"I read the Good Book for more than just to learn what's written there," Nan whispered through more tears.

Nellie listened, holding her breath, not wanting this moment of sharing to slip away.

"My heart's in little pieces." Nan pulled a hankie from beneath her narrow sleeve. "Mamma knows . . . but I've never told another soul. Not even Rhoda."

"Aw, Nan."

"Dave Stoltzfus was everything I loved in

a beau, Nellie Mae. Everything . . ." Nan wept openly.

"You cared deeply" was all Nellie could offer without crying herself. This was the first she'd heard the name of the boy who had wounded her sister so.

Nan bobbed her head, her face all pinched up. "I mostly read the psalms. King David endured much sadness, too, yet he could sing praises to Jehovah God in spite of it."

Nellie had never heard the verses Nan spoke of. "I'm glad you're finding some solace."

At this Nan seemed unable to speak, and she looked down at Nellie, whose heart was warmed by this demonstration of tenderness from the sister who'd always preferred Rhoda.

Nellie woke with a start and saw Mamma standing near the bed.

Slowly Mamma sat, an envelope in her hand. "I didn't mean to waken you, dear." She tilted her head, concern in her eyes. "Your Dat brought this in . . . for you."

She'd nearly forgotten about having seen someone near their mailbox earlier . . . yesterday, was it? The indistinct man by the road had become lost in a tangle of confusing dreams to the point Nellie'd felt sure she'd imagined him. "Ach, what's this?"

Mamma said nothing, though she remained. After a lengthy moment, she asked, "How are you feelin' now? Has your fever broken?"

Nellie shook her head. Oh, what she wouldn't give to be free of the fierce heat in her body. She felt hot all over, even to her own touch. Yet despite the fever, she felt an uncontrollable chill and could not get warm. Even now she had to will herself to relax so her muscles wouldn't lock up and become so tense she shivered all the more. She craved a reprieve from the sickness that had plagued her since Saturday night.

Has it been only two days?

Mamma changed the wet cloth on her forehead and had her sip more tepid tea with honey. Then, laying a hand on Nellie's brow, she bowed her own head, lips moving silently.

Nellie felt comforted, yet uneasy, as she wondered if Preacher Manny taught this sort of praying. Truly, she seemed to be learning newfangled things without even attending his gatherings. But she was touched by Mamma's gesture and hoped the prayer might indeed restore her to health sooner.

When Mamma was finished, she opened her eyes. "I pray that the power of the living

God will raise you up once again."

Nellie found herself nodding, although she doubted the Lord God and heavenly Father wished to be bothered with such a small request.

Mamma lifted the cool cloth and leaned down to kiss her forehead before departing the room. Then, and only then, did Nellie dare to lift the envelope to her eyes. The letter was indeed from Caleb.

Despite being so ill, her heart skipped with joy, and she quickly opened the sealed envelope.

My dearest Nellie,

I haven't forgotten you, not for a single minute! Christmas was terrible, not seeing you. And for that I'm awful sorry.

I feel like a bird in a locked cage. And confess that I'm sinning to carry this letter to your mailbox today, Sunday, January 13th, by pretending to have the flu, which is sadly going around. So while my family is out visiting, I'm "sick" in my bed — well, I'll soon be out walking to your house, darling Nellie.

If ever there was a girl for me, it's you. The times when I think of you, even dream of you, are more than I can count. I hope you don't think poorly of me, leaving you without the company of a beau for even a while. For certain I despised doing so.

And now here it is nearly mid-January already, and I still have not solved our dilemma. Daed has demanded that I shun you and your family, yet I yearn to talk with you and be near you once more.

You musn't fear for our future, my dear, dear Nellie. I will know very soon what must be done so that we can be together.

With all my love,
Caleb Yoder

Hands trembling, though no longer from fever, Nellie folded the envelope in half and slipped the letter beneath her pillow. *Oh, Caleb, you risked so much to deliver this. How could I have doubted you?*

She hadn't forgotten his endearing words, the way he held her at the millstream as he kissed her face, though never her lips. To wait was their unspoken courting promise.

Sliding her warm hand beneath the cool pillow, Nellie touched his letter, wishing she might find a way to get word back to him.

While Rhoda dusted the Kraybills' front room, their cat pushed against her leg. Back arched high, he let out a resounding *meow*.

"Ach, you're hungry, is that it?"

Pebbles meowed again. This pet was always looking for a handout.

He followed her across the entryway, then through the formal sitting room, with its high wooden mantel and matching gold overstuffed chairs, and into the kitchen. Opening the bag of kitty chow, Rhoda filled Pebbles's dish and checked his water bowl, too.

Standing there, she watched the black-and-white cat nibble away at his dinner, knowing her father would never allow something as frivolous as keeping a pet indoors. Then, eager to get back to work, she returned to the living room, as Mrs. Kraybill referred to their cozy and well-furnished front room. Rhoda straightened the coffee table, trying not to glance at the magazines stacked neatly there, especially one periodical that seemed to have strayed from Mr. Kraybill's study — *Car and Driver* magazine. She'd noticed the new issue had appeared last week. Her parents would be chagrined if they knew she was coveting the cars featured within the shiny pages, yet she couldn't deny to herself that she was ever so weary of horse-and-buggy travel.

Like some of the church boys surely must be.

Several from the old church had purchased cars and hidden them far from their fathers' houses, sowing disobedience before eventually becoming baptized church members. Some of those same fellows had given her the cold shoulder at Sunday night Singings. Not caring to admit it, even to herself, Rhoda realized she was on a path to show them just what they'd missed.

Even so, she would wait to investigate the pages of the most current car magazine until she knew she was truly alone here — till Mrs. Kraybill, wearing a wine-colored suit and black heels, left for her ladies' auxiliary meeting in New Holland. She glanced at the clock. *How much longer must I wait?* she thought.

Of course, she was expected to thoroughly clean the first floor today, but midafternoon Mrs. Kraybill allowed time for her to enjoy another break, complete with tea and cookies — the latter frequently purchased from Nellie's Simple Sweets.

Rhoda was less interested in the goodies here lately, as she desired to drop a few pounds. She felt sure that a trimmer figure and a pretty car were just the ticket to getting herself a husband.

CHAPTER 8

Nellie Mae felt better when she awakened Wednesday morning. Though her fever had suddenly broken yesterday, Mamma and Nan had covered for her at the shop, baking fewer items than normal, since customers were only trickling in anyway.

Nellie soaked up the compassion offered by her next-older sister, who smiled warmly across the breakfast table as she passed the food directly to her.

Later, after the table was cleared and Rhoda was off to work, Nan washed the dishes while Mamma dried, with both insisting that Nellie simply sit and sip tea at the table.

But it was after Mamma had left the room to go upstairs and have a "devotional time" with Dat that Nan sat down beside her. "Rebekah Yoder was here for another visit," she whispered.

"When?" asked Nellie.

"Yesterday, when you were still in bed." Nan looked troubled. "She told me something awful surprising. Said her mother heard that someone ran an ad in the *Lancaster New Era* to advertise Nellie's Simple Sweets."

"What? You're sure?"

"That's what she said. Seems her mamma was ever so outspoken 'bout it, saying it sounded just like 'them Fishers' to do something that worldly."

Nellie was horrified to think Caleb's mother would talk about their family like that. "Well, who would've done such a thing?"

"Only one I can think of." Nan glanced toward the doorway. "My guess is Rhoda."

Nellie laughed. "But why?"

"Seeing some of the old church folks droppin' off as customers since the split . . . well, it's bothered Rhoda somethin' awful." Nan paused. "Probably she's tryin' to help, is all."

"Ever so nice, really, when you think 'bout it."

Nan agreed. "'Specially since she's been rather aloof here lately." She took a sip of tea. "You know what else?"

Nellie listened as she pushed her teacup and saucer away.

"Rebekah said she thinks the ad's a

wonderful-good idea. She says we'll get more Englischers than we'll know what to do with."

Nellie groaned. "If that happens, how will we keep up?"

"Wait and see. No need to borrow more worry." Nan was grinning to beat the band. "I'll help ya more, Nellie Mae, and Mamma will, too."

"Dat's nearly finished with the tables and chairs," Nellie reminded her. "Maybe that's why Rhoda would pay to publicize the bakery shop — do ya think so?"

"Who's to say? Knowin' her, she might simply have an interest in bringing in more fancy folk." She sighed. "She sure seems to like the Kraybills' house a lot."

Better than ours . . .

Nan rested her face in her hands, her elbows on the table. "I daresay things'll start lookin' up round here."

"For you, too, Nan?"

"In some ways, maybe." Again Nan looked toward the doorway, as if to make sure Mamma was out of earshot. "I'm ready to forgive . . . to overlook my former beau's foolishness. But I can't say I'm ready to put aside my anger toward Rebekah's father. He's got no right keepin' friends apart."

That's the truth! Nellie thought.

"You'd think David Yoder would listen to Uncle Bishop, of all things. He seems so bent on following the old church, it really makes no sense that he won't follow the bishop's bidding 'bout not shunning." Nan rolled her eyes.

Nellie agreed and rose, carrying her cup, saucer, and spoon over to the sink. "Oh, how good it feels to be stronger again. Can't remember the last time I was so sick."

"Well, thank the Good Lord for health . . . and Mamma for her prayers," Nan said.

Nellie didn't share how Mamma had placed her hand on Nellie's forehead while she had prayed right over her. Nan probably knew something about that sort of praying now, too. For sure and for certain, this family was changing — and mighty fast. And if Rhoda had indeed placed the newspaper ad, their older sister seemed bent on heading in a direction of her own choosing.

Chris Yoder stood in the doorway, waiting for his class of boys to arrive. The Wednesday night group had doubled in size since he had begun teaching. Two of the most outgoing boys had invited school friends the same age, and the new kids simply kept coming, bringing along even more friends.

He walked to the windows and leaned back

against the sill, regarding the classroom. He and Zach had given the place a fresh coat of eggshell-colored paint this fall, replacing the former gray. Chris had also purchased a chalkboard with his own money.

He prayed for the impressionable young lives God allowed him to shape each week, whispering their names to the Father. One boy particularly concerned him — Billy Zercher — a loner with dark circles under his wide blue eyes.

"Help me reach him. . . ."

Chris knew he was probably too impatient for results. With high school graduation just around the bend, he was eager to get on with life in general, as well as ready for the divine call. His father had always said it was better to be a moving vessel than a stagnant one . . . waiting for something big to happen. And big was what Chris wanted. Outside grocery stores and along the sidewalk at the local public schools, he and his brothers had passed out tracts containing invitations to revival meetings at Tel Hai campground. While their efforts were met with modest success, he hoped for something even more fruitful, something that might reach more than the two or three stragglers who found their way to the meetings. If he had his way, he would work tirelessly to stamp out the recent "God is dead" nonsense heralded by *Time* magazine and others.

As for his future livelihood, his father's landscaping business was definitely an option. Chris knew the ropes — the appropriate, careful way to handle tree roots during transplanting and the like. He'd effortlessly memorized every perennial unique to this locale. He knew their watering needs, how deep the roots went, and which were blooming plants and which were not.

Lately, though, he longed for something with eternal meaning, some kind of full-time ministry. Hopefully he'd figure that out while attending Bible college in Harrisonburg, Virginia, next fall.

Chris wasn't the only one with grandiose dreams. He knew Zach had his heart set on ministry, too, and had even been praying for his life mate with that in mind, asking for a girl who loved God with all her heart, mind, and spirit. When he met Suzy Fisher, Zach had believed that his future bride *had* been revealed, if perhaps a tad too early. Their next-older brother, along with their dad, had tried to dissuade Zach from falling too hard, too fast . . . especially for an Amish girl.

Chris, on the other hand, had never encountered any girl who turned his head. But Zach was sure he'd found a special love early in life and had confided as much to Chris. He'd decided to ask Suzy to go steady the afternoon of their outing to Marsh Creek State Park. And then in one terrible instant, Suzy was gone, swallowed up by the vast lake.

Chris and Zach had immediately jumped into action, as had their three older brothers, leaving their horrified dates alone in the other rowboats. At first, Chris's terror kept him from filling his lungs with adequate air to dive farther down.

But finally, on his third dive, Chris managed to dive deep enough to swim up with Suzy. Too late — her lungs were already full, her body limp.

She never knew Zach thought that God had brought them together. . . .

Chris believed in God's sovereignty, as did all four of his brothers. Their parents had drilled it into them as youngsters. To think Suzy, so new to their Mennonite church, might have become his sister-in-law had she lived. But now it troubled him to know that Zach was unable to shake the memory of Suzy standing up — then teetering — in the rowboat, her long dress billowing as she lost her balance and plunged overboard. He suffered frequent nightmares, thrashing in his bed across the room he shared with Chris. The dreams and flashbacks kept him on edge all day, and his grades had plummeted.

Even Chris had struggled to concentrate after last June's accident. He recalled going through the motions at the nursery, alongside his dad. When the opening for a Wednesday night youth leader had come, he'd gladly accepted.

The Lord knew I needed this class. . . .

Moving away from the window, he scattered extra Bibles on the large, round table before scanning his note cards once more. But his thoughts stubbornly returned to Suzy Fisher's conversion and sudden death.

To think she might have died in her sins.

He thanked the Lord again for causing their paths to cross, for preparing Suzy's heart to receive Him. He prayed, too, that somehow Suzy's death would not be in vain.

The group of boys rushed into the classroom with a bustle of talk. Quickly they took their seats, forming a circle of eight energetic third- and fourth-graders. Chris hurried to sit at the table with them, wanting to be on their level, like an older brother. "You guys ready for the sword drill?" he asked.

There was a sudden flurry as those who hadn't brought Bibles snatched up the ones in the center of the table. Thumbs poised over the gilded edges, they waited, eyes bright.

"Galatians 6:2," Chris announced.

"Bear ye one another's burdens, and so fulfill the law of Christ," one boy belted out, not bothering to search for it.

"No fair!" another boy piped up.

"Isn't this a *sword drill,* not a memory verse drill?" asked Billy Zercher.

Chris looked at Billy in surprise. "You're right." He smiled. "Want to pick a Scripture?"

Billy turned shy, eyes blinking. He lowered his head and fell silent.

"Let me!" came the chorus of voices.

Chris glanced at Billy. *I won't give up on him. And not on Zach, either . . .*

CHAPTER 9

The moment had come.

His countenance absolutely serious, Daed sat Caleb down Wednesday night and began to outline the future, beginning with his expectations for the initial division of farming and dairy responsibilities, next moving on to the eventual land transfer. "Son, I want you to be in charge of everything — plowing, planting, and working the land, overseeing livestock. For a while, of course, you can rely on your older brothers for some help with that, just as I do now." He ran his thumbs beneath the length of his black suspenders before delving into more detail.

Anxious as he had been for this day to come, Caleb paid mighty close attention. *My birthright, at last!*

After a time, Daed leaned back in his chair and seemed to appraise him. Caleb met his father's gaze, uncomfortable under the unexpected scrutiny.

"Listen, Caleb, I'm proud of you for breakin' things off with that girl of yours. That is, I assume you have."

His father's words filled him with resentment, but he managed to maintain eye contact.

"Don't think I haven't noticed you're not attendin' Singings and whatnot."

Caleb clenched his jaw, saying nothing.

"Now's the time to find a befitting wife. Don't let the grass grow under your feet." His father added, "A deal's a deal. I'll sign the deed over when you've found yourself a suitable bride."

"Suitable?" Nellie Mae was the most suitable bride he could imagine. "Why not Nellie Mae? She hasn't joined Preacher Manny's church, Daed. She's staying Old Order. You'll see for yourself next fall when we're both baptized."

His father grunted. "Way I see it, girls tend to follow their mammas even after marriage. It's a good thing you've let her go."

Caleb opened his mouth to respond but changed his mind. It certainly wasn't Nellie's fault Reuben Fisher had abandoned *das Alt Gebrauch* — the Old Ways — getting caught up in his preacher cousin's dangerous way of thinking about things like studying Scripture. Why should Caleb have to abandon his affection for Nellie Mae because of his father's opposition to Reuben's keen interest in all of that?

Daed continued. "You could marry any number of girls in our church district . . . Deacon Lapp's daughter, for one."

"Susannah?"

Daed's eyes brightened. "She's a strong one — a hard worker. Mighty pretty, too. Even prettier than the Fisher girl." Daed pointed his finger at him. "What I'm saying is, I expect you to marry a respectable girl from one of the families in our church. It's the only way to get your land." By this his father meant no one would do from among either the "saved by grace" folk or those splintering off further yet. Caleb had heard that several of the so-called tractor enthusiasts were already dialing up folk on telephones installed *inside* their houses, no less.

Judging by Daed's flushed face, now was not the time to press further, risking his ire. No, his father was much too caught up in this split, drawing fine lines for his family about who was and was not fit for association. Caleb had wondered if his sister Rebekah wasn't given a similar ultimatum. Yesterday he'd overheard quarreling between the usually calm Rebekah and Daed, and Rebekah had burst out crying, saying she was going to visit her best friend, Nan. "And no one will stop me!"

Clearly he wasn't the only one put out with his father's bias against the Fishers, though it appeared Rebekah was more headstrong than he.

Or so Daed assumes . . .

Daed didn't bother to dismiss him but simply rose and ambled out to the utility room. Caleb couldn't forget this was the same man who had nine years ago railroaded Abe, his older brother, forcing him to marry his pregnant girlfriend. But Caleb's situation was nothing like that of the too-amorous Abe.

Still, he shuddered to think how swiftly he could be pulled into a ferocious tug-of-war between the inheritance he was raised to and darling Nellie Mae. Fact was, all could be avoided if his father saw for himself that Nellie Mae was wholly faithful to the Old Order. If only Daed would just give it time.

Word spread about the newspaper ad for Nellie's Simple Sweets like dandelions gone to seed in summer. Betsy's sister-in-law Anna, the bishop's wife, took it upon herself at the sewing frolic on Thursday morning to point out that it was "just a sinnin' shame" for the Fishers to stoop to such a deed. She said it right to Betsy, who was taken aback.

"Well, it's not Reuben's or my doing," Betsy replied.

"Whose, then?"

"I don't know." No one in the house even read the daily paper put out by Englischers. The only paper they subscribed to was *The Budget,* a Plain publication from Sugarcreek, Ohio, that chronicled the week's activities.

"I daresay some folk will do anything for extra money." Rachel Stoltzfus put in her two cents as if she hadn't heard Betsy at all.

"Had nothin' to do with it, I tell ya." Betsy turned away, peering down at her sewing. This morning's group numbered eight other women, including her own daughters-in-law Esther and Fannie — wives to Thomas and Jeremiah.

Always one to offer a kind word, Esther spoke up on her behalf. "Now, why would ya think such a thing of *Mamm?*"

Rachel harrumphed, keeping her head down, her eyes fixed on a torn seam on her husband's shirt. All of them were mending various items of clothing, gathering for the fun of it as they did several times a year. But today's frolic was proving not to be much fun for Betsy, and she decided to go about her business, stitching up the hem on her oldest dress, hoping to get another month or two's wear.

"Ask your mamma if she's purposely stirring up trouble by bringin' more English
customers into the neighborhood," Rachel
prodded again.

It was daughter-in-law Fannie's turn to re-
tort. "Listen, Rachel, you can speak directly
to Mamma — for goodness' sake, she's right
there across the table!"

"Jah, and you can't say yous don't rely on
outsiders for feed and grain and suchlike,"
Esther pointed out, momentarily setting her
work aside to look at Rachel.

"Feed salesmen ain't exactly outsiders,"
Anna said, re-entering the conversation.

"True," said Betsy, "they're *Mennischte* —
Mennonite."

"But tractor salesmen, what 'bout them?"
Rachel shot back.

Now Betsy was really peeved. "I have
nothin' at all to do with them."

"Oh, but others here do . . . and you know
right who you are, too!" Rachel rose quickly,
marching to the back of the house, where a
small washroom had been added on, similar
to Reuben's addition on the Fishers' own
house.

Silence reigned while Rachel was absent,
though Betsy felt like spouting off but good.
She was being sorely tested here in her
sister-in-law's house, but she was holding

her peace all the same, just as she had the day Reuben's mother had lambasted her. Of course, that had been a different matter altogether.

Well, maybe not so different, come to think of it.

All these insinuations from Rachel and even Anna were directly related to the tension between the church groups. Three of them now — Old Order, New Order, and the Beachys. Truth be told, it was rather surprising that the bishop's wife would have included womenfolk from all three groups at today's work frolic.

Got to give her some credit for making an effort at unity, Betsy mused.

She recalled Preacher Manny's sermon last Sunday on having a brand-new life. Manny had said the Lord would not force His life upon anyone against his or her will. One's will played a big part in coming or not coming to Calvary's cross. That, and the divine calling — the inward drawing and wooing, much as in courtship the lover pursued the beloved. Might Anna and the bishop eventually be drawn to salvation? Might Rachel, too? Betsy faithfully prayed so, just as she trusted for others in her community still in bondage to tradition.

Less than one month before changing

Rosanna wished to goodness Cousin Kate had gone to the sewing frolic instead of staying so long after nursing Eli this morning. That her cousin had entirely given up on nursing Rosie seemed odd, though it was time now for Cousin Kate to be done nursing both babies.

Rosanna's anticipation had nothing to do with keeping Kate away from the babies. But Kate was not at all herself, and her behavior was setting Rosanna on edge. Was it postpartum blues? Plenty of women suffered during the months following a birth, and she, of all people, wanted to be understanding and compassionate. Even so, it jarred her when Kate completely ignored her gentle question about when she planned to stop nursing Eli.

Rosanna tried again. "Two months have come and gone, cousin. Elias and I have appreciated your help, but I'm sure ya have better things to do with your time than make daily visits here."

Even after this, Kate seemingly refused to look Rosanna in the eye. Instead she leaned over Eli, stroking the dimpled arm that peeked from beneath his blanket.

"Such a handsome one, he is," Kate murmured. "So like his father."

Rosanna shuddered at the comment. How would Kate feel in her place? Leaning hard against the doorframe, she tried to see things from Kate's perspective — how very difficult this must be, giving her babies away. She couldn't begin to imagine it.

"Look how his right eyebrow arches ever so slightly," Kate said, tracing it with her pointer finger.

"I've noticed, too."

Then Kate touched her own eyebrow, as if comparing.

Rosanna had to glance away. She could not abide her cousin's coming here any longer.

Inching back toward the kitchen, she wondered if Kate was taking any herbs known to help alleviate depression. Maybe she should simply go through her cupboard and offer Kate some blessed thistle or evening primrose oil to brew for tea. She knew, as many of the womenfolk did, that these would not interfere with nursing. *Though I wouldn't mind that coming to an end.*

Suddenly Kate burst into tears in the next room. "Oh, my precious *Boppli*." She rose from the rocking chair, waking tiny Eli. Then, wandering to the front room, she carried him over her shoulder, stroking his back while he blinked his little eyes at Rosanna.

Ach, is she having a breakdown? Or does she really have so little regard for my wishes?

Then and there, Rosanna decided she'd definitely go to the next quilting frolic, or maybe go visiting and take the babies along. *Let Kate come to call and simply not find us here!*

Nellie Mae suppressed a squeal of delight when she went to pick up the mail before returning to the shop after the noon meal Thursday. Caleb's name and return address were printed in the corner of an envelope for all to see.

Another letter so soon . . . how bold of him!

She ran across the snowy yard to the front porch, where she sat, in spite of the cold, to read the letter from her beloved.

Dearest Nellie,

I've missed you more than I dare to write. I must see you again. Let's meet secretly at our special place.

I will come on foot this Friday following supper. Hopefully it won't be too cold for you. Bundle up, all right?

Counting the hours.

Yours always,
Caleb Yoder

She pressed the letter to her lips. He cared

deeply for her — that much was clear. He had again risked being found out with yet another letter. Of course, there was nothing for him to fear *here,* for her parents were not holding an inheritance over her head.

No, Nellie was free to see whomever she wished . . . to marry Caleb, for that matter. Obviously Dat and Mamma wanted her to join them in their beliefs, but they had not expressed any conditions about whom their daughters might marry.

Even so, Nellie worried for Caleb . . . for them. What would he do if his father refused to change his mind and allow him to court her?

Will Caleb love me enough to bid the farm good-bye?

Nellie knew that Caleb's love for his birthright lay less in the land than in what it meant for his future family. Caleb was not selfish in desiring it. Rather, he showed himself to be prudent and reliable, and for that she loved him all the more. But she could not tell him so before Friday, because she did not dare to write a letter back.

Tomorrow I'll see him!

CHAPTER 10

Friday evening Nellie managed to leave the house only after helping in the kitchen, making small talk with Mamma and Nan. It was imperative, to her thinking, to lend a hand, since Rhoda hadn't yet arrived home, something that was becoming the norm. Nellie stayed as long as she could, risking being late for meeting Caleb.

Had her heart ever pounded this hard before? She hurried now along the snowy road to meet her beau, the air of excitement within more noticeable to her than the bitter cold.

Soon, very soon, we'll be together!

She wished she might have thought to hitch up the horse and buggy. Maybe, just maybe, Caleb was counting on her doing so, though he hadn't suggested it in his sweet letter. Still, she had plenty of layers on and would fare well on foot for a good couple of hours or so, if necessary.

As she picked her way along the road, she longed to lay eyes on Caleb — to see him, talk to him, and listen to the news he had to share with her. To think they had been apart for more than a month. How long would it be till they'd see each other again, after tonight? She would not allow herself to think that way. It was far better to live for this precious moment and be thankful for what time they did have together.

When she rounded the bend of the old mill, she looked everywhere, eager for a glimpse of him. A few couples were already skating on the pond, and their occasional laughter wafted across the millrace to where she stood. She hoped Caleb hadn't brought his skates, since she hadn't carried hers. Feeling awkward, even conspicuous, she scanned the area for signs of her beau, in case he'd decided to wait for her off the road.

She squinted through the trees, looking, but when he did not arrive, she circled the stone mill to check the other side. He might have decided to be careful and hide from prying eyes. She hoped she hadn't misunderstood his letter or arrived too late. Had she lingered too long after supper?

She spied the wrought-iron bench where they'd sat together. The bench seemed to her now a symbol of their courtship, the place where they had shared their first words of endearment and where she had accepted his tender affection. She smiled, recalling the way his gentle kisses had created feathery tickles in her stomach.

Caleb's fondness for her was evident in the genuinely respectful manner in which he conveyed his love, unlike some boys who pushed the limits. Truly her beau was nothing less than a gentleman.

Turning to face the road, Nellie peered into the twilight, longing for Caleb. *Where are you, love?*

Though he disliked admitting to harboring any pride, Reuben took pleasure in not being easily *ferhoodled.* In fact, he was nearly always composed and had refused to be drawn into the too-frequent church debates of late. A good many arguments were flying back and forth between the three Honey Brook Amish groups, despite the bishop's attempt to keep the peace.

This evening he'd slipped out to visit with his son Ephram. The problem, as Reuben saw it, was that Ephram and Maryann had but a few weeks left till the *Bann* threatened any baptized adults who chose to leave the old church. Where would that leave Ephram if he decided to join Reuben and Betsy in the new church *after* the grace period was up? While either group of new church folk would surely welcome him, Ephram and his family would be shunned from the old fellowship, many of whose members were blood relatives. If that came about, Ephram's livelihood would suffer, just as his father's presently did. *Bann or no Bann, there's no denying times are tough.*

Now that Reuben had arrived, he found himself pacing, nervous. "'Tis high time we got things out in the open, son," he said after greeting Ephram.

"I'll never see things your way, Dat." His son leaned against the wall, arms folded over his thick chest. "Save your breath, I say."

Reuben shook his head. "I've held my peace long enough," he said. "I've been praying for ya, son."

"Like I said, Dat, best be savin' your breath."

His heart's closed up. . . .

Lifting his eyes to the rafters, Reuben recalled how unbendable his bishop brother Joseph had been earlier today. Fact was, Ephram and the bishop saw eye to eye — their thinking as skewed as Reuben's had been for all the years of his life, till now.

"Someone's been running a newspaper ad for Nellie Mae's bakery shop in the English paper," Ephram said, abruptly changing the subject. "The grapevine's swinging wide and far about it, wonderin' if it'll show up in next week's papers, too."

"Well, what on earth?"

Ephram's eyes narrowed. "You mean you had nothing to do with it?"

"Why should I?"

"I just thought —"

"That's where you got yourself in trouble, son. You're jumping to conclusions, when you ought to be askin'." Reuben forced a laugh.

"I'm askin' *now.*"

"Folks wrongly assume things all the time. But what's it matter if you or anyone else thinks I placed an ad?"

Ephram's expression turned to one of astonishment. "Matters a whole lot if you're set on bringin' in more and more outside folk to Nellie's bakery shop. Looks bad, like you're too anxious for the fancy."

"Ain't my doin', that's for certain."

"Maybe so, but you've been turnin' the other way for as long as Nellie's run that shop, ain't so?"

Reuben could scarcely believe the tone his son was taking with him. He refused to defend his decision to allow the bakery shop to Ephram or anyone else — plenty of Old

Order families had roadside vegetable stands and the like. No, right now he was beginning to feel like walking straight out of Ephram's barn, lest he fall into temptation and put his hands on his brawny son's shoulders and shake him good. The grapevine was indeed ever present, but the way folk interpreted what they heard from the rumor mill was the real problem.

"Nellie's Simple Sweets does our family more good than harm," he said at last. "And I've never had cause to question the way your sister handles things. You should have the sense to know she'd no more place an ad than I would."

After a terse good-bye, Reuben hurried to the buggy, more aware now of the cold. "A body shouldn't be out in this for long," he muttered to the horse.

He arrived home to Betsy, who was anxious to discuss Nellie Mae. "She's been gone awhile — on foot, no less." She looked up, her embroidery balanced on her lap.

"Meeting a beau, no doubt." He glanced at the kitchen clock.

"Not just any fella, I don't think."

He knew as much. And the worst of it was knowing Caleb Yoder was not likely to shift toward the New Order — not the way his father was shooting off his mouth amongst the old church brethren. If Nellie Mae married Caleb . . . well, it meant a worrisome situation.

"We'll lose her," he whispered. "She'll submit to her beau's way of thinkin'."

Betsy frowned.

"And just when I'd hoped she might be leanin' toward salvation." He remembered her momentary tenderness after she'd gone with them to hear Preacher Manny that once.

"Let God do His work in His way, love." She reached for him.

He bussed her cheek. "You're right 'bout that." He wouldn't admit it, for surely his wife suspected it already, but he'd gladly help the Lord along, and right quick, too, where their children were concerned.

Betsy picked up her embroidery hoop. If Reuben wasn't mistaken, she was repeating a Scripture verse as she worked.

He hadn't removed his coat, since he'd intended to check on his horses. His boots left prints in the icy snow as he trudged toward the barn, where he looked in on the new foals first. When he was satisfied they each had enough bedding straw, he went to the small corner of the barn where he kept files on his horses' breeding records, as well as their veterinary appointments. It was there also that he had put in a good many hours

crafting the round tables and chairs for Nellie's bakery shop.

Perching on his work stool, Reuben thought
again of the grapevine. "Nonsense is right,"
he muttered, tracing a circle in the sawdust
on the workbench. He cared not one iota
who might've paid for the ad. As for bringing it up to Betsy, he'd let her mention it. No
sense making a big to-do.

Going to inspect one of the completed
chairs, he ran his hand over its smooth seat,
then the straight slats on the back. He would
be finished by Monday, perhaps at just the
right time, too, since Nellie Mae was well
enough to tend the store again.

Let the Englischers come. . . .

An enclosed black buggy appeared in the
near distance, and Nellie's heart sank. *Puh*
— no way could it be Caleb. Yet she lingered
in the brush, beginning to shiver. Surely
Caleb would have an explanation as to why
he was this late, if he came at all.

She had heeded his suggestion and worn
two sets of long johns, donning her heaviest sweater and warmest black coat over her
dress and apron. She guessed she was a sight
to see, surely having expanded a few inches
in girth.

She observed the horse and carriage as it

slowed. Lo and behold, it came to a complete halt. Suddenly there he was — Caleb, leaping off the buggy! He paused momentarily, evidently searching the area.

She stepped out into the clearing. *Goodness, he is here.* She placed her hand over her heart as it fluttered with joy. "Caleb," she whispered.

He let out a stifled whoop and began running through the snow, straight to her. "Nellie Mae!"

Ach, Caleb . . . She struggled to keep her composure at the sight of her beau, her love.

His arms opened for her and she fell into him, welcoming his crushing embrace. "Oh, I missed you so," she whispered into his long woolen coat.

He pressed his cheek against hers. "Oh, Nellie, honey . . . your face is like ice." He leaned back to look into her eyes; then he happily hugged her again. He seemed reluctant to release her, but he reached for her hand and led her toward the buggy. "Come, let's get you warmed up."

As they walked, he explained that he'd taken the extra time to go to a cousin's and plead to borrow his new carriage. "I figured we'd be frozen sticks otherwise. There should be enough heavy lap robes to keep you cozy, love."

Love . . .

Oh, the sound of his voice.

The thought of warmth, after having been so very cold, as well as of having this private time with him, made Nellie hurry to match Caleb's stride.

"We've got ourselves a family buggy." He chuckled.

"Jah, I see that."

"It's not for courtin', but it'll keep us much warmer."

She laughed as he literally lifted her into his cousin's carriage.

Oh joy!

CHAPTER 11

Once settled in the buggy, Nellie realized just how chilled she was, especially her fingers and toes. As soon as the horse pulled forward onto the road, Caleb let go of the reins and began to warm her hands by rubbing each finger, one at a time, between his own hands, next kissing the tips of them.

She laughed softly as he did so rather comically. "Oh, you silly," she whispered, leaning against his arm.

"No sillier than you." He had taken great care to wrap her in the woolen lap robes. "My cousin'll be glad we put these to good use."

"He's got himself quite a nice buggy." She eyed the dashboard.

"Nice is right. Cousin Aaron purchased a dilapidated family buggy back when he first got married, so he's needed a new one for a while. He wasn't too keen on partin' with this fine one, even for one night. I had to beg, which is why I took so long."

"Maybe he suspects what you wanted it for."

He smiled and picked up the reins. "Well, he had his share of forbidden loves, too."

"Ach, really?"

Caleb explained that Aaron had never been of the Old Order Amish but rather one of the "team Mennonites," who drove black buggies — close cousins to their way of life. "But Aaron dated some progressive Amish girls, I'm told, and sneaked around doin' so."

Like us tonight.

The carriage moved down the road with a gentle jostle, and Nellie wondered if Cousin Aaron might be one to betray Caleb, though she didn't want to mention it.

"How've you been, Nellie Mae?"

"Oh, all right."

"No . . . really," he urged. "Catch me up on what I've missed."

They'd never sat together so privately like this, sheltered from both the elements and observers. The carriage was a marked change from Caleb's open courting buggy. The dimness of its interior felt strangely intimate, and Nellie felt self-conscious, although she would have welcomed Caleb's presence in any circumstance.

"Well, let's see. I'll start with Christmas. My brothers and their families all spent the day, and my nieces and nephews took turns stringing popcorn near the cookstove. Emma, Mamma's favorite — no secret, I daresay — was awful cute, reciting a poem she'd learned from my brother Ephram's oldest boy. I clapped when Emma finished, and Rhoda said I should quit teachin' her to be vain." As soon as Nellie uttered the words, she felt ashamed.

"Rhoda's got a lip on her, then?"

She wanted to make quick amends, for she was not one to speak against her family. "Well, she was prob'ly right," Nellie added.

"Aw, honey . . . it's okay to say what you feel."

His response made her wonder if there were things he, too, would like to share about a family member, namely his father. But she wouldn't bring up that sore topic. "How was Christmas at your house?" she asked.

He leaned back, nestling her in the bend of his arm before answering. "Worst ever . . . without you." He leaned closer. "Next year, just think, we'll be man and wife."

Nellie blushed, glad for the darkness, but she wondered how on earth he would ever get his father's blessing. *If he's sure it will happen, I should simply relax and quit worrying.*

"I'll convince Daed that we belong together, you'll see." He paused. "I say we tie the knot right away in November, all right?"

Happily she nodded, surprised he was suddenly so open with her when things had seemed quite bleak before. Had something changed? "When the time is closer, I'll talk it over with Mamma. She'll want two weeks to get things ready, I'm thinkin'."

He agreed, lingering near. "I think often of you bein' close like this, Nellie Mae. Think of it all the time."

She sighed, letting herself rest in his arms. Just knowing he had found a way for them to be married was mighty encouraging.

He kissed her cheek. "I love you."

She kissed him back, a mite closer to his lips than she'd intended — a daring thing, but she wasn't one bit sorry. "I love you, too."

He reached around her and drew her startlingly close, and the lap robe slipped off. "Oh, goodness, look what we've done."

"We? *You* did that!" She could hardly stop giggling.

Leaning over, he pulled the thick blankets back onto her lap, letting her tuck the edges in once again, keeping both of his hands on the reins now.

They rode for some minutes in total silence, although Nellie was stifling another laugh. She might have let it free if Caleb hadn't spoken. "My father and I talked about my future this week — went over every detail of the land transfer." He was quiet for a moment before adding, "Honestly, I believe Daed will relent where you're concerned . . . in due time."

"Such good news, Caleb." She found his demeanor surprising. Something had radically changed between David Yoder and his son — something Caleb wasn't telling her.

"We might not see each other much, or at all, in the meantime. Do you understand?"

Having experienced how delightful it was to be with him again tonight after being apart just over a month, Nellie would gladly wait for him. She would make the days pass by keeping busy with chores and all the baking required of her. The busy life of running a bakery shop would certainly be a comfort.

Yet even as she looked ahead to a life with Caleb, Nellie worried that, despite her beloved's reassurances, his father would be the one to have the last word. She hoped with all her heart that Caleb was not sadly mistaken.

Betsy had a sinking feeling as she lay in bed, wide awake. She couldn't shake the notion that something was amiss. Her eldest daughter had not returned home from work yet — if, indeed, Rhoda had been there at all. It was close to ten o'clock already, as she could tell by the position of the nearly three-quarters moon that shone beneath the window shade.

She'd noticed a fifth necklace today on Rhoda's side of the dresser she shared with Nan. The growing collection doubtless marked a growing interest in the world, as well.

Nellie Mae, on the other hand, was as Plain as Betsy was and always would be — or so it appeared. Since one was not privy to another's heart, how was it possible to fully know, even about her own daughters?

She'd heard from Esther and Fannie — who, like her, both attended the New Order church — that Jonathan and Linda Fisher had joined the Beachys, just as her own son James and daughter-in-law Martha had. Would the fancier, more progressive group divide yet again? *Everyone's splitting away, it seems.*

And what might Bishop Joseph think of all this? His doing away with any shunning for a full three months might have backfired in some ways, causing this air of leniency.

Betsy slipped out of bed, aware of Reuben's deep breathing, his arm flung over his head. The dear man worked the bulk of each day outdoors, from before dawn to as late as after supper, feeding, grooming, and exercising his horses, training them over time to become accustomed to reins and bridles and harnesses.

She did not begrudge Reuben these moments of needed rest. Going to the window, Betsy moved the shade slightly to peer out at the moon-whitened snow and trees.

Dear Lord, please look after Rhoda this night. I fear she is far from you. And please put your arms of love around my hurting Nan. Send her a kind and loving man to wed. As for Nellie Mae, I trust you'll watch over her wherever she may be. Cover each of my children and grandchildren with your grace, goodness, and your love. I ask this in Jesus' name. Amen.

Rhoda guessed her clothes surely reeked of cigarette smoke. She had been sitting at a booth in the Honey Brook Restaurant since well past the supper hour, having gotten a ride to town with Mr. Kraybill, who'd run an errand. She'd felt she might simply burst if she didn't get away and do something completely different — even daring — for a change. Impulsive as this outing seemed, Rhoda wanted a quiet place to browse the latest car ads in the newspaper, somewhere far from the prying eyes of her family.

Suddenly, though, she had no idea how she would be getting herself back home.

Silly of me not to plan ahead, she decided now that the place looked to be emptying.

She'd met the nicest folk here tonight, some more talkative than others. Yet her mind had remained fixed on her task, and she had pored over the ad section of the newspaper Mrs. Kraybill had kindly allowed her to take from the house. Presently Rhoda circled the ads that piqued her interest, though was disappointed to see most were well over two thousand dollars — at least the most recent models were. She couldn't imagine spending even that.

Rhoda regretted having saved only four hundred fifty dollars in the past three months. *Too many frivolous purchases.* Still, she thought she could handle payments, assuming she had enough to put down on a car loan.

A brown "fully loaded" 1963 Rambler caught her eye, as did a red 1965 Rambler convertible, impractical as it was, and a blue 1960 Falcon. The thought of a black 1964 Imperial sedan inexplicably brought to mind her brother Benjamin's courting buggy, long since traded in for a family carriage.

Rhoda sighed. Truth was, she hadn't the slightest idea how to go about purchasing a car, unless she got some credit. But who would lend her the money?

Will the Kraybills continue to hire me to keep house? A big consideration. Dat had always said never to count your chickens before they're hatched. She wondered how far into the future she could hope to be employed within walking distance of her father's house.

Returning her attention to the paper, she spread out the several pages. She reveled in trying to decode the ad for each car.

Eventually she felt someone's gaze and glanced up to see a nice-looking man, his deep blue eyes seeming to inquire of her.

"Excuse me, miss. I happened to notice you sitting here alone."

She nodded, feeling terribly awkward. What a sight she must be — the only young woman in the whole place wearing a cape dress and a head covering. He must be wondering what she was doing circling car ads so eagerly.

"I'm lookin' for a nice, well, a used car," she explained. *The perfect car . . .*

He was not a waiter, she realized when he asked hesitantly if he might help. "May I join you?"

She looked around. "Are ya askin' to sit with me?"

"Only if I can be of help, miss."

"Rhoda," she was quick to say. "And do sit, if you'd like."

He introduced himself as Glenn Miller, named after some band that had made a debut in New York City the year he was born. He was surprisingly friendly and chatty — polite, too. Possibly he was curious about her Plain attire just as others had seemed to be, yet everyone she'd visited with this evening had been exceedingly gracious.

Rhoda realized it was her turn to say more about herself, so she mentioned that her father bred and raised horses. "We've got a bakery shop on the premises, too. Seems an ad's even been runnin' in the Lancaster paper 'bout it."

Glenn repeatedly blinked his blue eyes. "I'm sorry, Miss Rhoda . . . I guess I don't follow."

She felt ever so silly. "No, maybe it's me that should be sorry. I'm surely speakin' out of turn, jah?"

"I wouldn't say that." He winked at her and she blushed immediately. "You go ahead and speak however you wish." He flashed another smile. "Now, which cars have your interest?"

She didn't think she ought to say — suddenly she felt all ferhoodled, sitting in an English restaurant with such a fine-looking man. Was it a good or bad sign that he kept smiling at her? In truth she had no idea who this Glenn fellow was.

"Well, I oughta be gettin' home," she said softly, wondering why she had announced that. By implication, she'd pretended to know how she was getting home, when she certainly had no idea.

"You got your horse and buggy out back?" Glenn glanced out the window. Rhoda could see by the streetlights that it was beginning to snow again.

"Not this time," she admitted, lowering her head.

"You need a lift, don't you, little lady?"

Little? This was the first she'd heard that since she was maybe ten or so. From then on she'd grown to become pleasingly plump, although perhaps chubbier than most fellows cared for. Most, except for Glenn here, who was now reaching across the table for her hand with the most endearing look. "I'd be honored to take you wherever you want to go, Miss Rhoda."

She hesitated. Should she let this strange man touch her hand?

Rhoda had never been told she was or

wasn't a good judge of character, so when Mr. Glenn Miller, with his appealing smile and crisply ironed white shirt and handsome knit sweater vest, asked her yet again if she wanted a ride, Rhoda actually considered saying yes. She felt sure that if she looked hard enough into his clear eyes — the windows to his soul, as Mamma said — she would know whether it was prudent to accept his kind offer.

CHAPTER 12

Rhoda was not so much alarmed as she was tired when Glenn pulled his car over onto the shoulder and slowed to a stop. She'd done the selfsame thing with the horse and buggy when she'd lost her way. She and her newfound friend — an Englischer, of all things — were apparently lost somewhere in Chester County, well beyond Beaver Dam Road. She wished for a map to guide them back to Route 340, but she didn't dare mention it. Glenn had talked nearly nonstop since they'd left the restaurant, describing a number of bossy women in his life, as he put it. Several at work . . . two younger sisters and suchlike . . . but not a word about a girlfriend.

She was determined to show him by sitting demurely in the front seat that she was not the bossy type. No, Rhoda was satisfied to wait for him to decide what to do about their having gone astray. At least they hadn't run out of gasoline, like she'd heard happened occasionally to others. On such a clear and brilliant moonlit night, surely they would find Dat's house in due time.

A thin cloud passed over the moon, and Rhoda gazed at the vastness of the dark sky, filled with jewel-like stars. They reminded her of the several necklaces she'd purchased so spontaneously. *My weakness,* she thought, realizing she'd have to curb that impulse if she was to have enough to make car payments.

She turned her attention to the man behind the steering wheel. Glenn seemed to be in no hurry to discover where they'd gone off the beaten path. More eager to get home now, she asked, "Are you thinking we should retrace our steps?"

"Not just yet."

She felt tense suddenly . . . and irritated.

"We'll turn back soon enough," he said.

Trying not to sigh too loudly, Rhoda guessed Glenn merely needed to sit there and talk awhile longer.

Nellie felt fully contented while riding over the back roads in Caleb's borrowed carriage. She relaxed as he rambled, talking now of his Yoder relatives who'd left the Old Ways decades ago. "I scarcely know them, but they're close with my cousin Aaron and his family."

"Oh?"

"Their grandparents made the mistake Preacher Manny and so many are makin' even now."

He means my parents, too.

"Turning away from the Ordnung?" she asked.

"Well, more than that. Not only did they leave the church, but they skipped over a few of the more conservative churches, makin' a beeline for the Mennonites."

"Who do ya mean?"

He paused.

Had her question caused him distress, asking about this branch of his family tree, no longer in the fold? "It's all right, Caleb. I don't have to know, really."

"Well, I daresay you oughta . . ." He reached for her hand. "I 'spect their leavin' the People influenced your Suzy away from the church . . . which led to her death."

"What?" Startled, she looked at him.

"I recently heard that several of my own cousins were with Suzy the day she drowned. Dreadful news."

Nellie wouldn't admit already knowing as much from Suzy herself. "She was with a whole group of young people that day," she pointed out.

"Oh, there were plenty there, all right. But my own kin would never have been present had their grandparents remained in the old church. Don't ya see, Nellie, everything has its consequence? You choose where you'll go, what you'll do. Everything affects everything else."

His words seemed important, even insightful. "This troubles you, ain't so?" she said.

"I can see the future. Ours." His words were barely audible. "If we don't exercise our will —"

"Over your father's?" she interrupted. "Oh, Caleb . . . this seems very hard."

"I'll find a way for Daed to accept you." He kissed her hand. "I must."

He leaned his head against hers as though they were molded in thought. Deeply upset, he was, and no wonder. Their future, their love, was entwined with strife.

She choked back tears. "Sometimes I see a boat in my mind . . . like the rowboat Suzy fell out of," she began. "Dat, Mamma, my family — all of them — are in it, leavin' me behind for a distant shore. I feel that if I don't catch that boat somehow, I'll be stuck on the other side forever. It worries me somethin' awful, to tell you the truth."

He squeezed her hand. "Your heart's tender toward your family, is all."

Hearing his care, the gentleness in his voice, Nellie began to sob. "Don't you see? If I keep refusin' to go to church with Mamma and Dat, I'll miss out on knowing more 'bout Suzy's faith. Yet if I join the new church and you remain in the old, we'll never have a chance to wed." She wept into her hands.

"Oh, Nellie. Don't cry . . . don't."

Caleb fell silent. More than anything, Nellie hated the thought of being divided from either him or her family. Yet she could not help but notice the excitement her parents and Nan now had for Sunday Preaching and evening Scripture reading.

Caleb's voice broke into her thoughts. "Nellie, we mustn't lose each other. Not for anyone or anything."

She wished she could clearly see his dear countenance . . . his hazel eyes. "I must sound all mixed-up to you, and believe me, I am sometimes."

"Well, you don't need to be confused. Just remain in the Old Ways, where you belong."

She breathed in the icy air. "I hope you understand why I worry so." She stopped for a moment, hesitating. "God's Word — that's what Dat calls the Bible — changed everything for the better for Suzy. And now for Dat and Mamma, too. So many of my family." She wiped her tears.

"Aw, Nellie Mae . . ." But his voice trailed off as he lifted the reins and held them firmly.

"The tabernacle over at the Tel Hai campground played a big part in Suzy's life last spring."

Caleb let out a low groan. "She had no business there."

"But she went all the same."

"You've never told me this, love." He slipped his arm around her. "You'll get all this salvation talk out of your system, sooner or later."

Nellie was still. Bewildered as Caleb no doubt was at her admission, she believed that if he loved her, he would understand.

A fleeting thought nagged at her, and she shuddered to think she might lose her beau forever. Pushing her fear aside, Nellie yielded to his loving embrace.

Rhoda leaned against the car door as Glenn Miller continued to talk a blue streak. Several times now he'd reached beneath his seat to bring a small bottle up to his lips. This being her first experience with anything like a real date, she wondered how Nan and Nellie Mae managed to stay out all hours.

She was in no way accustomed to being up so late, and she was second-guessing her decision to allow this stranger to drive her home.

"I'll take you car shopping if you'd like," Glenn offered, reaching for her hand. "How about it? Tomorrow?"

She pondered her response, not sure she wanted him holding her hand right now. "I have chores with my mamma after work."

A frown crossed his brow and he squeezed her hand. "Now, honey-bunch, you've surely got yourself a host of sisters. One of them can cover for you this once."

He slid across the front seat toward her, and she became aware of his dreadful breath. Why, it smelled like the moonshine some of the wilder church boys brewed and brought along to Singings, unbeknownst to the brethren.

What'll I do?

Her free hand fidgeted near the door. Why should she have such conflicting feelings when she'd yearned so long for a man to give her the time of day?

Glenn's arm was around her shoulder now as he inched closer. His reeking breath annoyed her.

But even as Rhoda leaned away, he asked if he could see her again. "Why not tomorrow evening? I'll pick you up wherever you say." He stroked her cheek slowly with the back of his hand.

She clenched her jaw. *What if he tries to kiss me?* She had always assumed her first kiss would be ever so special, saved for her husband after the preacher said they were joined as man and wife, "under God."

"I have chores after work," she repeated, hoping her words wouldn't provoke an angry reaction.

Glancing at the door, she noted the handle. She didn't think the door was locked, but she was already leaning so hard against it she doubted she could get it open. Even if she did, wasn't it a terrible idea to leave the car's warmth on a night like this?

I could freeze to death.

"Let me take you to look for cars tomorrow. I know the best used-car lot. You'll have your pick of the place." He raised her hand to his mouth, his lips brushing her knuckles. "Aw, honey, you know you want to."

"I . . . I'd rather you didn't do that."

He ignored her request. "I can help you, Rhoda. Take time with you . . . teach you . . . things."

"You mean hunt for a car?" She pulled her hand away.

"That, too."

The slur of his words put the fear of the Lord God in her. "Glenn, please —"

"Oh, you're *asking* me now, are you? Well, sure, honey. You say *please* mighty nice, don't you?" He leaned in and kissed her cheek before she could stop him.

Tilting her head against the ice-cold window, she said, "No!" She spoke the single word loudly — louder than she'd ever raised her voice to anyone.

"Rhoda, my little girl . . . you can't mean it. You're so pretty, honey. You're just the sweetest thing I've —"

"Let me go!"

Scrambling quickly, Rhoda managed to get out of the way as she yanked on the handle. The door flew open and she leapt out. Glenn toppled partway out, too. She didn't stop to look back to see if he pulled himself back into the car or was now making chase.

Rhoda ran as hard as the coyotes in the nearby woods. Soon her lungs burned from the fierce cold, but she struggled to keep up the pace, certain from the position of the moon that she was heading west.

Surely I'll reach a crossroads somewhere.

She heard no sound of pursuit behind her, but her noisy panting and the crunch of her own feet on the snow-packed road could easily block out all else. To think that what had for a while seemed so exciting and enjoyable now had her running for her life. A few unwelcome kisses might not kill her, but they would certainly spoil everything she hoped for . . . and put a blight on her, for sure.

Ahead a light flickered. With new energy, she forced her legs still faster and ran toward a distant farmhouse, her heart pounding hard against her rib cage.

Suddenly she heard the sound of a car motor coming up alongside her on the road. She dared not look over her shoulder lest she accidentally plunge off into the uneven snow. Terrified, Rhoda willed herself to press forward as the car drew ever closer, slowing as it came.

CHAPTER 13

Rhoda spied an open gate at the end of the long lane leading to the farmhouse. Quickly she dashed up the drive. The car had stopped out by the road. Was it Glenn's?

Oh, she wished she'd never darkened the door of that restaurant. What had she been thinking, asking Mr. Kraybill to drop her off there?

She ran up the porch steps, rapping hard on the front door, glancing over her shoulder to see if Glenn was indeed in pursuit of her.

A tall young man wearing a navy blue bathrobe appeared in the doorway, eyes squinting against the light. He peered at her sleepily. "Hello?"

"S-someone's . . . followin' me," she sputtered.

The man looked past her and she froze with fear. What if he didn't let her inside?

"Teresa, come quick!" he called over his

shoulder. A woman, presumably his wife, rushed into the front room as he opened the door to Rhoda, who swiftly stepped inside. "Call the police," he instructed Teresa.

"*Nee* — no! Just let me stay here . . . till it's safe." Rhoda turned to look out the window, and her heart dropped at the sight of Glenn but a few yards from the porch. "Ach! Don't let him in, whatever ya do. Oh, please don't."

"Come!" Teresa reached for her hand and led her back into the kitchen. "You'll be safe here, I assure you."

The blond, soft-spoken woman couldn't have been more than twenty-five or so, Rhoda guessed, but her lack of terror was remarkable. Her eyes radiated a calm strength that reminded Rhoda of Mamma.

A loud exchange commenced at the front door, and Rhoda trembled as she covered her ears to block out the angry, slurred words of the man she'd thought was a newfound friend.

You'll be safe here, the young woman sitting next to her at the table had promised. This same woman was folding her hands in prayer.

Say your prayer aloud, Rhoda thought suddenly, removing her hands from her ears, curious to hear what this unruffled woman

130

might be asking the Lord God.

In a few minutes the front door closed and she heard the husband set the lock. Then he made his way to the kitchen, where he stood next to his seated wife. Teresa looked up from her praying.

"I'm going to take this intoxicated man to his house. He has no business driving." He looked kindly at Rhoda. "Are you all right, miss?"

"Now I am."

"If you'd like a ride someplace, I'll be glad to drive you when I return."

She nodded. "Denki ever so much."

His gaze indicated his bewilderment — why had she, an Amish girl, been chased down by such a man?

Rhoda felt obliged to explain why she'd found herself in a predicament that justified interrupting the couple's sleep. She gave a quick summary, stopping short of admitting her interest in the stranger. "It was a rather stupid thing to do, I realize now. Thank goodness you were home."

"We're glad to help," Teresa said when Rhoda stopped to catch her breath. "By the way, we're Timothy and Teresa Eisenberger."

"And I'm Rhoda . . . Rhoda Fisher."

Teresa rose to boil water for tea as Timothy

excused himself to drive Glenn home. "The Lord sent you to us, I believe," Teresa said softly to Rhoda as she removed two teacups and saucers from the nearby cupboard.

Rhoda had heard of divine guidance at Preacher Manny's meetings, but she'd never thought of it as a reality.

"God leads us in our distress." Teresa took out a box of chamomile tea. "I've experienced it firsthand."

Jah, distress it was, Rhoda silently agreed as she offered to help with the tea. She couldn't believe her foolishness in having needlessly put herself in harm's way. The thought crossed her mind that if God had truly directed her here, then she ought to pay closer attention to Preacher Manny's sermons from now on.

It's the least I can do.

Betsy heard Nellie Mae's bed creak and was relieved her daughter was home at last. Breathing a prayer, she was determined to set aside her frustration over Caleb Yoder's pursuit of her youngest. She had overheard his mother say in passing at a work frolic that her husband planned to have Caleb take over the family land as soon as he was wed. Betsy was smart enough to know the Yoder farmland was tied to Caleb's staying in the

Old Ways. A stern man like David Yoder would have it no other way.

Tomorrow being the Lord's Day, Nellie and the rest of the family would undoubtedly go their separate ways, as had sadly become the norm. Nellie had made it plain she was not interested in joining them for worship.

Sighing, Betsy rolled over. She looked at Reuben, sound asleep. It was highly unusual for him not to be already awake and nuzzling her neck. Had he awakened in the night, walking the hallway to pray over the family as he often did?

She sat up and pushed a bed pillow behind her, leaning against the headboard to await the sunrise. Her thoughts wandered from Nellie to Rhoda, who'd only recently returned home in a stranger's car, of all dreadful things. Had her eldest daughter fallen in with a fast crowd, like Suzy? She'd seen the driver who had dropped Rhoda off, definitely an Englischer. The young man had accompanied Rhoda all the way to the back door.

She must trust in the Lord's care more fully. With that in mind, she turned her thoughts to Reuben's parents, Noah and Hannah, wishing she and Reuben might make a trip to Bird-in-Hand. Perhaps tomorrow, after the common meal? It was high time they visited, or they might appear to be distancing themselves.

Betsy leaned forward, lifting her long, heavy hair and letting it fall behind her. No need for their family to slip out of reach just because they no longer saw eye to eye. They were kin, after all, and she missed seeing her mother-in-law and hearing her stories at quilting bees. How was Hannah feeling since her minor stroke?

Glancing again at the sleeping Reuben, she wondered how he, too, was dealing with the painful rift. He and Noah had always been close.

She rose to turn on the gas lamp and then picked up the Bible from the small table next to the bed, opening to the book of Proverbs. Preacher Manny had said it was a good idea to make a point of reading a proverb each day. *It'll change your life.*

So much to absorb, really. Betsy had been largely unacquainted with the knowledge in God's Word for so long, she wanted to glean as much as possible from every reading. She was glad for this quiet moment while Reuben lingered in his slumber.

Even as she began to write, there was a stirring within Rosanna. She had stayed up instead of returning to bed after the twins' early morning feeding. Now was as good a time as any to jot down instructions for making blessed thistle tea. One of her aunts had claimed it worked miracles for her own struggle with baby blues.

Pour 1 cup boiling water over 1 1/2 to 2 grams of crushed blessed thistle. Steep for twelve minutes. Drink one cup 2 to 3 times per day, before meals.

"Maybe Kate'll try this," she muttered to herself, sitting in the kitchen as the day began. She hoped it would settle her cousin.

She folded the small paper with the tea-making directions on it and set it squarely beneath the cookie jar. Pleased with herself, she prepared to bake bread for the noon meal. In no time now Elias would be up and dressed, looking forward to having a quiet breakfast before he headed outside for another day of helping the next farmer over with repair work on some bridles. Later he planned to go to a farm auction near Smoketown.

"If I'm quick, maybe I can make sticky buns, too," she said, liking the idea of filling up the kitchen with the delicious cinnamon scent.

Maybe I can even offer some to Cousin Kate this morning . . . along with her tea, of course!

Elias would find that amusing. He would lean his head back and laugh heartily before taking her in his arms to kiss her.

Rosanna smiled. Elias would have every right to chuckle. *Anything to cure peculiar Kate!*

Rhoda breathed deeply, stretching as she opened her eyes. *Thank goodness I'm home . . . and safe.* She glanced over at Nan, who was still sleeping, despite a thin ray of sunshine peeking beneath the green shade. She considered what might have been, but she did not allow herself to linger on that; the memory of last night still caused her turmoil.

Hadn't she wanted a peek into the world of fancy men and cars? Cars she could take, but fellows like Glenn Miller she could do without.

Even so, how did a girl tell a good apple from a rotten one? Fact was, Glenn had fooled her but good.

She got up and tiptoed to the window and lifted the shade a bit, careful not to awaken Nan. What had happened last night seemed like a bad dream now that she was secure in Dat's house, having shared the comfort of the bed with her younger sister. Why had she placed herself in such jeopardy?

Nan must never know about Glenn, she resolved.

Rhoda looked out at the sky, clearing to the east as the dawn penetrated the dreary gray. A ray of hope, perhaps?

Turning, she stared at the pretty necklaces she'd collected and strung along her side of the dresser mirror. Was it wrong to feed her fancy desires in this manner?

Brushing aside her musing, Rhoda went to the row of wooden wall pegs and reached for her bathrobe. She slipped it on and headed downstairs to the washroom, where her father had gone to the trouble of putting indoor plumbing in their house. Even so, the small bathroom was nothing compared to the thoroughly modern, even glamorous *two* at the Kraybills' house.

She closed the door and ran the water for her second bath in less than twenty-four hours, preparing to wash away the memory of Glenn — his offensive breath on her neck and face, his arms around her. . . .

Rhoda shuddered. Had he planned to lose his way all along, tricking her by saying they were lost? Was he like some of the church boys who whispered sweet nothings, hoping to get a girl to let her hair down before her wedding night? She'd heard some terrible stories from Nan, especially, about a handful of young men in their church district — well, their former one. She honestly didn't know much about the new church's youth, because she'd refused thus far to attend any gatherings. She was tired of being overlooked by Amish fellows, even though her sisters and Mamma all had told her she was plenty pretty.

As had Curly Sam Zook, five long years ago. But though that was an eternity past now, she couldn't forget how he'd held her hand and said the nicest things out behind the barn one cold night, only to break her heart a month later. Like Nan's beau had done not so long ago.

She shivered anew, thinking what a *Dummkopp* she'd been with both Sam and Glenn. No way would she let such a thing happen again. *I won't be anybody's fool!*

"One day I'll have me a fine automobile and a nice young man, too," Rhoda promised herself while staring into the small mirror over the sink. She slid her glasses up the bridge of her nose and then opened the mirrored medicine cabinet, looking for an aspirin to alleviate her headache. But the aspirin bottle was empty.

Frustrated, she was determined to get a bottle of her own and put it in one of the drawers in the room she shared with Nan.

Stepping into the warm bath, Rhoda wondered why it was suddenly so important that her things belong solely to her, just like her future.

CHAPTER 14

Before Saturday breakfast, while Reuben was pulling on his work trousers, Betsy brought up the daily ad for Nellie's Simple Sweets. "I've seen it with my own eyes — just ain't befitting us at all." She stood near the loveseat at the window, holding the very paper.

"Why do ya say that, love?"

"Because it isn't. Honestly, I see no reason why Rhoda would do such a thing."

He stopped dressing, suspenders pulled midway up. "You know for sure she did?"

"Nan assumes it, and since they're ever so close, I guess she should know."

He found Betsy's conclusion flimsy. Just because Nan said Rhoda placed the ad, why should Betsy blindly believe it? Nan had been known to misinterpret things in the past. But he refused to point that out. If more customers came to Nellie's bakery shop because of the ads, then the tables and chairs he'd made might come in real handy.

"Why not simply ask Rhoda?" he suggested.

"Jah, I will."

"Well, *gut*." Reuben had more on his mind than Betsy's notions. For one, he was still put out with Ephram — Bishop Joseph, too. Not only had he butted heads with his son, but his frustration over his conversation with his older brother — revered as the man of God — continued to escalate in his mind.

He combed his oily hair, wishing it were closer to bathing time tonight, when he would wash for the Preaching service over at Cousin Manny's place. Presently Bishop Joseph was overseeing both Manny's New Order church and the Old Order group, as well as trying to persuade those who were still inclined toward the Beachys to say no to cars and telephones.

As for himself, Reuben had no inclination toward the Beachys, though he relished the idea of bathing more often. *A right pleasant thing.*

"What do ya say we go 'n' visit your parents after church tomorrow?" Betsy suggested as he put away the comb.

He missed chewing the fat with his father. "Jah, a good idea, indeed."

Heading downstairs, he wished that whoever was tying up the washroom would hurry so he could get in there and shave his upper lip. He chuckled to himself as he waited near the door. Sure seemed you could never have enough of most anything, no matter how much of it you already had. But if cleanliness was next to godliness . . . he was ready to take a dip in the bathtub each and every day.

He heard what sounded like Rhoda in there muttering to herself. Abandoning the idea of waiting, Reuben headed for the kitchen and wondered what was keeping Betsy, impatient now for his first cup of coffee and a cinnamon bun or two.

From the moment they arrived at Marsh Creek State Park on Saturday, Chris Yoder knew it was a mistake. Yet Zach insisted they stay, getting out of the car nearly before Chris set the brake. Zach stood stiffly near the front fender, eyes fixed on the enormous lake.

It was late morning and the sky was as dismal as any January day Chris could recall. Everything from the lake to the boat launch was gray and solidly blanketed with ice and snow.

"If you don't want to stay —" Chris suggested, not sure of his own voice.

"No, we're here now," Zach interrupted,

heading for the lake without inviting Chris to tag along.

Yeah, we're here, all right. Chris clumped through the deep snow, eyeing the lake — more than five hundred acres fed by a nearby watershed.

Today was a bleak contrast to the clear and balmy June afternoon the last time they'd come. He would never have imagined Zach would want to take him up on driving out here. Winter had stolen what little remained of its summer allure.

Turning, he saw Zach walking gingerly on the ice. Chris hoped it was good and thick. After months of frigid weather, he assumed so. He watched Zach make the labored trek toward the middle of the lake.

Where Suzy died.

But as Zach trudged onward, Chris breathed a prayer that it might be a healing time. *Somehow.*

Zach folded his hands momentarily as he went, either praying or talking to himself, his lips moving. Occasionally he looked toward the sky, then back at the frozen surface.

Shifting his muffler to cover more of his face, Chris headed toward the area where Suzy had fallen overboard and drowned. He recalled how perfect the day had been when the whole bunch of them had piled into several rowboats, bringing Suzy along for the first time. One of their older brothers had pointed out how the sunlight looked like diamonds bobbing on the water's surface that afternoon. Some of the guys began to row harder, showing off a bit for Suzy and several other girls from church who were with their three older brothers in two more boats. Once they were well toward the center of the lake, Zach suggested they drift awhile, having in mind a quiet moment to present a gold bracelet to Suzy.

Chris hadn't intended to stare, but it had been hard not to watch their infectious smiles as Zach had placed the delicate bracelet on her small wrist.

Moved by the memory, Chris shook his head. He forced air through his pursed lips, looking again at Zach in the distance. *Why does God spare some and not others?* Sure, God was sovereign. To seek to understand the whys was not as important as putting one's complete trust in God's will. He'd learned this from his parents, observing the way they chose not to fret over the challenges that came their way. They believed Suzy's death would prove to be part of the "all things" found in Romans chapter eight, verse twenty-eight — that some good might ultimately come from her death.

All the same, Chris's private questions plagued him, especially because he saw such a discrepancy between prayers that were obviously answered and those that were not. He'd heard a sermon after Suzy died about letting waiting times be trusting times as one sorted out the complications of life. Difficult as it was, especially for Zach, they both attempted to be patient, waiting for God's timing in helping them — as well as Suzy's family, who were often in their prayers — through this tragedy.

Pushing forward, he managed to catch up with Zach, who had clipped across the lake at a surprising pace. Chris stood next to him as they absorbed the silence, interrupted only by the calls of a few hardy winter birds. Chris could almost guess what Zach's thoughts might be, for his own weighed heavily.

"I promised myself I'd never come back," Zach admitted.

Chris understood. This was new ground for them. Besides losing Suzy, nothing truly dreadful had ever happened to them or their family.

Zach continued. "Just thinking . . . this is the last place Suzy was before . . ." He stared at the spot, and his shoulders heaved.

Chris clapped a hand on Zach's shoulder.

"It's tough, I know." He sighed, fighting the lump in his throat.

"All of us should've worn life jackets." Zach's words were a desperate whisper.

What were we thinking?

After a time, Zach motioned to leave. "Let's get out of here."

Chris was ready, too.

They crossed the lake, heading back toward the parking area, where some rowboats were stacked near the shore. "I can't remember which boat we took," Zach said. "When Suzy fell . . ."

He squatted beside the upturned boats, their bows held off the ground by a metal rack. Reaching over, he fingered the state-park identification numbers. "I doubt the office would have a record of which boats we rented that day."

"Probably not."

Zach shook his head. "Man, they all look the same." He started to get up, then dropped back to his knees. "Wait a minute. What's this?"

Chris wouldn't have bothered to look, except Zach was staring hard. *Surely he doesn't think . . .*

"Could it be?" Zach said, brushing away the excess snow.

Chris peered closer. He saw what appeared

to be a glint of gold in a clump of frozen leaves and other debris.

"See it? Right there." Zach pointed.

"Could be anything."

"I think it's her bracelet."

Chris wasn't convinced. Suzy's bracelet was most likely at the bottom of the lake.

"It must've slipped off her wrist when she fell."

Highly unlikely. Chris hoped his brother wasn't setting himself up for disappointment.

"We need something to pry this loose." Zach looked around. "Anything in the trunk we can use?"

"Not that I know of."

"We'll have to come back with a hatchet or something to cut it free."

Come back? That was more than Chris had bargained for. "Come on, let's go."

On the drive home, Zach reminded Chris of the Scripture verse he'd had inscribed on the bracelet. "Her favorite. Remember?"

Chris nodded.

"Just think, her whole family probably knows what she believed," he said unexpectedly. "Suzy wrote in a diary every day, you know."

"No kidding?"

Zach nodded, breaking into a faint smile.

"She didn't want to forget a single thing. It was all so new and wonderful to her."

Although it was good to see the sparkle in Zach's eyes again, Chris was alarmed at his brother's new obsession. And by the time they reached home, Zach was convinced he had indeed discovered the bracelet. "I have to know for sure," he muttered, determined to get back to the park before anything could happen to it.

Chris knew Zach well enough to realize there was no stopping him once he fixed his mind on something. His zeal for God was rivaled only by his feelings for Suzy Fisher, and evidently his passion to connect with anything related to her wasn't about to let up. No, the trip to the lake hadn't helped to heal Zach at all. If anything, his brother was more troubled than ever.

CHAPTER 15

Nellie was thrilled about the prospect of a visit to *Dawdi* and Mammi Fisher's, as Dat announced at breakfast Sunday. They would leave the minute they all returned from Preaching. "We'll see how Mammi Hannah's doin'," Mamma added with a smile.

Nellie hoped, if time permitted, she might also have the chance to slip away and see Cousin Treva. Perhaps she could finally persuade Treva and her sisters to come visit sometime and have a look around the bakery shop.

Her father eyed Nellie conspicuously as she ate her cold cereal and fruit. The way he looked at her evidenced his growing concern over her, living under his roof and holding firm to the Old Ways.

As soon as the dishes were dried and put away, she hurried to the washroom to scrub her face carefully, knowing Caleb would surely be looking her way this Lord's Day.

Not that he didn't every other Preaching service, but since their recent reunion, she felt even closer to him, longing for their wedding day.

Will Caleb succeed with his father? Nellie intended to do all she could to make sure David Yoder saw no reason to find further fault with her.

Closing the door behind her, she reached for a fresh washcloth. No need to stew. She drew the water and applied the homemade soap, pushing away thoughts of church baptism. Dat undoubtedly had that in mind. Choosing Caleb and the Old Ways over her parents' faith was the hardest choice of all.

When it came time for the womenfolk to form a line outside Ephram's farmhouse, Nellie was happy to see Rebekah Yoder waving to her. Caleb's sister, her fair hair shiny and clean, slipped in beside her.

"How're you?" Nellie wondered if Rebekah had any inkling of Caleb's disobedience — or their secret meeting.

"Oh, fine. Did ya walk clear over?"

"Jah, but I should've hitched up the sleigh, I s'pose. Bein' it's just me . . . ." She didn't explain further, but surely Rebekah understood.

"Been wishin' I could get away to visit Nan again," Rebekah whispered. "Doesn't seem right, not seein' her."

"Same with missin' nearly half the People, jah? So many have jumped the fence."

Rebekah agreed. "Must be they're afraid to wait too long. I've heard some say they might as well get it over with before the Bann's a threat — just go ahead and make the leap." She frowned, glancing over her shoulder. "'Tween you and me, I'm awful curious 'bout the new church, Nellie Mae." Her hand was on Nellie's arm now. "Don't breathe a word, all right?"

"You're thinkin' of visiting Preacher Manny's?"

Rebekah leaned close. "If I can find a way, I'd like to go next week," she whispered behind her hand.

Taking care not to react, Nellie was curious what Caleb's sister had in mind, but she'd have to wait till after the common meal — if Rebekah was willing to talk further. Meanwhile, she quieted herself, preparing to be most reverent as the line moved forward toward the temporary house of worship. As she did, she reached into her coat pocket and felt the strings from Suzy's Kapp, a constant reminder of her dear sister. The strings seemed oddly out of place here.

Seeing sweet Nellie made Caleb miss her already, not knowing when he might make another escape from Daed's house. He didn't want Nellie to become impatient or to lose heart because he was staying home from Singings and such.

He placed his black felt hat on the long wooden bench near the stairs and took his seat next to his father and older married brothers. He bowed his head when his father did and folded his hands. The three-hour meeting stretched before him in his mind, and he struggled to keep his thoughts on the Lord God and heavenly Father. Truth was, his recent date with Nellie Mae was continually before him. When could he possibly arrange to see her again? Each time they shared made him yearn even more for the next meeting, and the next. *The way of love,* he thought. When you met the girl you wanted for your bride, you pursued her . . . moved heaven and earth to be with her.

Opening his eyes, he turned his attention to the front of the large room, where he noticed Ephram Fisher, Nellie's older brother, standing there in his black frock coat. He and his wife, Maryann, had themselves another little one, although Caleb hadn't laid eyes on the baby yet. Some women stayed home longer with their infants than others.

One thing seemed definite: Ephram had not budged one inch since the church split late last fall. Ephram's four brothers were nowhere in sight, however, and Caleb assumed they'd followed their father, as had Rhoda and Nan. Mighty enticing, the newfangled ways. He himself fought against the desire for a tractor, knowing how much easier it would make farming.

There were times when Caleb worried that if something didn't happen soon, Nellie also might succumb to the urgings of her parents and the New Order. He could lose her forever.

I won't let that happen.

Rosanna settled onto a bench at the back of the room, close to the kitchen. She'd tiptoed inside with Essie, her sister-in-law, who sat next to her, helping with the babies. Rosanna had purposely chosen to hold Eli during the Preaching service. He nestled against her during the first long hymn from the *Ausbund* while Rosie slept soundly in Essie's ample arms.

Other than to Elias, Rosanna had not breathed a word of Cousin Kate's obvious preference for Eli, nor her insistence on continuing to act as a wet nurse. Wondering what Essie might think if she knew, Rosanna joined in the singing of the second hymn, the *Loblied*, as the People awaited the bishop and two preachers. It would be several more minutes before Bishop Joseph returned with the other ministers from upstairs, where they were deciding which of them should have the first sermon and who would preach the lengthier main sermon. She secretly hoped their bishop might be the one to offer the second sermon today, since at times she sensed something deeper in his messages. Perhaps that was merely because he was the eldest man of God in their midst.

Kate Beiler glanced back at Rosanna. *Oh no, is she thinking of changing seats?* Very soon the introductory sermon — the *Anfang* — would begin and there'd be no moving about. Rosanna held her breath, suddenly realizing she'd forgotten to bring along the herbal tea brewing instructions for Kate.

Eli made a soft little sound in his sleep. Oh, the sweet way his wee hands fell across his rising chest . . . the long, long eyelashes. *Such a beautiful child.*

Looking up, she half expected to see Kate staring back, jealous as all get out — certainly she seemed that. But Kate sat straight now, face forward, as she should be. Still, it was painfully obvious Kate was behaving strangely toward her and the babies. Even Elias had privately voiced his concerns to Rosanna. After all, they had only the bishop's blessing on their raising Eli and Rosie, not a fancy judge's decree. Was it enough?

After the common meal, Caleb slipped outdoors in hopes of seeing Nellie, who'd left for the outhouse a few minutes before. His mind was alive with ideas and he wanted to reassure her not to give up hope. He was convinced that if she was still on this side of the fence after the practice of the Bann was resumed, it would definitely sway his father.

If he was quick, he might catch her on the way back to the house. *Even a few stolen moments would be worth the risk.*

The cold was brutal as the sun splayed blinding light across the snow-laden field. He shielded his eyes, looking for Nellie, not daring to call out for her with several other foolhardy folk milling about, braving the chill.

He shivered. He hated feeling as if he were doing something wrong by tailing Nellie Mae on the Lord's Day. Was it so terrible to want to be with the girl you loved . . . even though in his case, doing so meant willful defiance?

Waiting near the barn door, he was caught off guard when Daed called to him from near the corncrib, waving in a high arc. "Caleb! Over here, son!"

Looking toward the path that led to the outhouse, he glimpsed Nellie walking his way. *Puh, such ill timing!* His heart sank.

Did Cousin Aaron snitch on me?

Caleb scuffed his boots against the barn's threshold and then strode out into the snow, his neck tingling as he crossed paths with his sweetheart. He dared not so much as glance Nellie's way, however, keeping his eyes trained on the father whose will seemed fixed on bending his own.

CHAPTER 16

Nellie stood in the shadow of her brother's barn, observing Caleb and his father talking up yonder. She couldn't help but wonder what David Yoder was saying so dramatically, but lest her presence add fuel to the fire, she waited where she couldn't be seen if either Caleb or his father happened to look her way.

How could his father continue to treat Caleb's feelings with such disregard? She watched them, David Yoder's breath rising in a straight line from his black winter hat. Caleb, however, was strangely silent.

Nellie would have worked her way around the side of the barn to continue watching, but right then, Rebekah emerged from inside. "Ach, you scared me half to death," she said when Rebekah reached for her mittened hands and pulled her back into the barn.

"I *have* to talk to you." Rebekah's eyes were watering. Was she crying, or was it from the fierce cold?

"You all right?"

Rebekah nodded, leading her toward the milking stanchions, the smell of livestock thick in the closed-up space. "I've already told ya what I want to do." She looked over her shoulder.

"Won't you be in terrible trouble with your father?" Nellie asked.

"I won't wait any longer to see Manny's church for myself," Rebekah whispered.

"Do you think you can really get away next Sunday?" Nellie recalled what Rebekah had told her before Preaching.

"I'm goin' to try."

"Does Nan know? Do my parents?"

"You're the first I've told."

Nellie was stunned. "Are ya ever so sure, Rebekah?" There was no telling what consequences might befall Caleb's sister if she was found out.

Rebekah nodded. "So will you tell Nan . . . hush-hush?" At Nellie's nod, she sighed as though a great burden was lifting. "I'll wait along the road, if your parents won't mind pickin' me up."

What'll David Yoder say when she's not at home next Sunday?

"I must do this . . ." Looking down, Rebekah blinked. "Even if I'm . . . disowned, or worse."

Ach, what could be worse?

"Be prayin' for me, all right?" Rebekah gripped Nellie's hands again.

Nellie was startled by this turn in their conversation. She hadn't the slightest inkling what to say, nor did she know how to go about sharing any of this with Nan.

Just then they heard the sound of heavy boots on the cement beneath the strewn hay.

Ephram, maybe?

The girls ducked down, and Nellie Mae held her breath for a long time before she exhaled slowly, too aware of her own heart's pounding. "Who was that?" she whispered after a time.

"Sounded like Caleb. His walk — I'd know it most anywhere."

Nellie had seen him outside earlier, looking as if he'd spotted her but didn't want to let on — not with his father calling to him.

"Ach, Nellie, my brother's head over heels for you," Rebekah said softly, "in case you don't already know."

Nellie's heart fluttered at Rebekah's admission, but with Caleb going behind his father's back in order to see her, she wasn't about to let on that she felt the same about him. If he was working on a way for them to be together without jeopardizing his birthright, then woe unto her to mess things up.

"We best be goin'." She glanced around them at the dozens of milk cows waving their tails above the manure ditch.

"I'll go first." Rebekah smiled sweetly before slipping away.

When Nellie rose, she spied the top of a man's black hat. Was it her beau, hoping for an opportunity to talk secretly?

Not at all sure of herself, she walked slowly, assuming that if Caleb was there waiting, he would call to her to tell her not to leave.

She was pushing the barn door open when a man's voice rang out.

"Nellie Mae Fisher!"

She froze in her tracks.

Caleb's father? She turned and there he stood, his face glowering and red. His black felt hat was tipped forward, nearly concealing his eyes.

"You stay far away from my son, do ya hear?" David Yoder demanded.

Has someone spied on me and Caleb? Who?

Without thinking, Nellie bolted directly out the barn door and ran all the way to the shelter of Ephram's house.

Caleb was downright furious. To think he'd been caught merely darting outside to see Nellie Mae. His hands shook with frustration as he hitched his courting carriage to his horse. He was in the mood to do something crazy — like have a wild buggy race. If only this were any other day but Sunday. He had to blow his stack somehow . . . somewhere.

Worse yet, Daed had threatened to go find Nellie. First, though, his father had raised his voice to Caleb, saying he suspected him of sneaking around with Nellie Mae all along — something Caleb had done only once.

Now his father was threatening to cut him off if he did it again . . . and he was requiring Caleb to promptly make amends or be disinherited immediately. His father's way of having him do this — his demand — struck Caleb as utterly ridiculous.

Caleb rubbed his hand across his face. He could hardly believe he was considering doing his father's bidding. Yet what choice did he have?

It wasn't such a difficult demand to fulfill, really. And it would buy him more time. Susannah Lapp was, after all, a treat for the eyes. Why not satisfy his father's unreasonable order and spend a little time with her?

Nellie wouldn't have to know. Now that they were no longer able to regularly see each other, she appeared less interested in going to the old church's Singings. And if she did find out, he could simply explain himself. After all, he'd be doing it for Nellie Mae . . . to preserve any hope of a future together.

He'd do *anything* to be with his beloved, and now his father's blessing was tied to Caleb's agreeing to see Susannah — just once.

Clucking his tongue, he hastened the horse, glad for the openness of his courting buggy. He wished Nellie were there, just the two of them. *Later . . .*

For now, he must prove to his father that neither Susannah nor any other girl held any interest for him. Maddening as it was, there was no getting around the fact Daed held the reins of his life. His father's land was everything . . . he must have it; otherwise he could offer nothing to his bride. Nellie deserved everything he had to bring to their marriage and much more.

Unnerved, Nellie stayed around to help with the kitchen cleanup, prickles of uneasiness plaguing her. She stopped drying dishes to talk with Maryann, who asked her to hold the new baby — a darling girl named Sadie — while Maryann hurried upstairs to tend to young Becky and Katie, putting them down for a nap. So convenient since Preaching service had been held there at her own home.

Never had Nellie enjoyed gazing into a baby's tiny face so much. *Will Caleb's and my babies be as pretty?* she wondered, then silently chastised herself, wishing also for inner beauty for each of her children . . . some sweet day.

Even after her sister-in-law returned to the kitchen, Nellie continued holding Sadie, fondly admiring her newest niece's soft hands and face. Oh, she could just hold this little one all day and never get a speck of work done. Sadie's company was a balm after the alarming run-in with David Yoder.

Cousin Kate and her family followed Rosanna and Elias all the way home, never bothering to ask if it was a convenient time for her to visit. She hopped out of the Beilers' family buggy when Elias pulled up to the back door, leaving her six young children and husband, John, as she scurried up the snowy walkway on Rosanna's heels.

The gentle shifting of the buggy had lulled both babies to sleep in Rosanna's arms. She couldn't think of anything more pleasant than a nice long nap, but Cousin Kate's unwelcome presence made that impossible for her now. Kate stepped in close, face glowing as she eyed Eli, still in Rosanna's arms. Rosanna longed for Elias to come and rescue her, but he was unhitching the horse and buggy in the barn . . . obviously keeping his distance.

Without a word, Kate took Eli from Rosanna the moment she'd shed her coat. She carried him into the front room, cooing into his ear, acting for all the world as if this were her home rather than Rosanna's. Suddenly Kate began to cry. No, it sounded like she was out and out sobbing.

"Well, for goodness' sake," whispered Rosanna, handing Rosie to Elias when he stepped into the kitchen. What could be done to soothe her cousin's wounded heart?

Elias shrugged and marched toward the back door, peering out as if wondering whether he should go solicit John's help.

He muttered something under his breath before coming over to whisper, "If things get out of hand, come get me." Then he lifted Rosie to his shoulder, taking her upstairs and leaving Rosanna to console Kate.

She supposed it was a good idea to simply let her cousin cry it out. Kate was bawling now, and Eli's irritated wails blended with her keening.

This just ain't right. Rosanna paced the kitchen, stewing up a storm. Was it possible to hold her tongue any longer on this Lord's Day?

She went to the window and looked out. Kate's husband was also pacing out there in the snow, talking occasionally to the children, who were piled into the back of the buggy as they waited. No doubt they were all wondering how much longer Kate would be, and why Elias would let them sit in the cold like this.

"What a knotty problem," she said right out, gripping the shade at the window and firmly pulling it down.

By now, Elias was surely resting upstairs, like she wanted to be.

The cries from the front room continued, and Rosanna knew she must speak up. Heading through the sitting area and into the front room, she stood over her cousin — this woman who'd done the unthinkable for her and Elias. "What is it you want?" she asked softly. "What will make you happy again?"

"I don't know," Kate said as Eli continued to howl, his arms and fists shaking. "Here, you take him."

Rosanna pulled all of her will together and took her son calmly. "Your husband's weary of waitin', I daresay."

"Jah, I s'pose I best be goin'." Kate wiped her eyes and rose.

"Before you leave, I have something for you." Rosanna headed to the kitchen, swaying as she went to soothe poor Eli. She took the instructions for the blessed thistle tea from beneath the cookie jar.

Kate accepted the card without ever looking at it. She kissed Eli's hand before heading for the back door, and Rosanna did not feel obliged to see her out.

By the time Nellie Mae arrived home, she discovered an empty house. She'd completely forgotten about Dat's plans to visit Dawdi and Mammi Fisher.

Going to the kitchen table, she spied an apologetic note in Mamma's quick scrawl, declaring they'd "waited and waited" for her, but Dat had urged them on so that they could return before dark.

"Phooey!" She poured some milk and took a chocolate chip cookie out of the jar to soothe herself. "How'd I forget?" Yet even as she voiced it, she knew the answer: The events at Preaching, first with Rebekah and then David Yoder, had been most distracting.

Heading upstairs, she passed Rhoda and Nan's bedroom. Immediately she backtracked and went to sit on their bed, pondering what all of them might be doing right now in Bird-in-Hand. Were they laughing and listening to Mammi Hannah's tellin's? Enjoying her famous apple pie with gobs of real whipped cream?

Nellie wished Dat might have been content to wait a bit longer before leaving. Was this his way of making a point to her? Was this how life would be once the whole family joined the New Order?

Feeling truly left out, she stood to inspect Rhoda's necklaces. Curiously she reached up to touch the only long golden pendant, which she'd never seen before. Running her fingers lightly over the chain, she wondered if the gold was real. If so, where had Rhoda gotten it? Surely not as a gift from a beau. Or was an Englischer interested in her out there in the world of the fancy Kraybills? Was that why she had come in late this past Friday night?

"Oh, to return to simpler days." Nellie placed the necklace back on the mirror and went to stand at the window, staring at oodles of snow in all directions. Soon, very soon, the bishop would reinstate the Bann, and where would that leave them? Which side of the fence would Rhoda be on by that time? And Nan? Was she leaning toward joining up with the tractor and car folk?

According to Dat, giving up one's will for the sake of God's was the key to salvation. The prospect sounded very hard, if not impossible, yet could she be truly content otherwise?

Without a doubt, Nellie knew she wanted to marry Caleb. How could she possibly be happy without her beloved? She didn't want Preacher Manny's church to dictate the future to her differently, or to force her to choose between her dearest love and Suzy's Savior.

CHAPTER 17

The silo behind Dawdi and Mammi Fisher's glittered like highly polished silver, but sunbeams lacked warmth on this harshly cold Lord's Day afternoon. Even so Rhoda stood outside, watching Nan fling dried bread crumbs on the snow for the birds, chirping quite like a winter bird herself.

They'd both bundled up to wait while Dat and Mamma talked privately with their grandparents indoors. Rhoda figured what was up; it was obvious Dawdi wasn't so keen on living clear over here in Bird-in-Hand when most of his immediate family was back in Honey Brook. Dat likely saw this as another opportunity to discuss the new church with his parents — it seemed to Rhoda that anymore he was always seeking to recruit folk into Manny's fold.

The minute they arrived home, she would talk to Mamma about having her own space in the house. She craved more privacy and freedom, even though her first real attempt to satisfy the latter had backfired. Of course, she hadn't given Glenn Miller a second thought in a romantic sense since running away from his clutches. What a hard lesson indeed, and one she would not repeat.

She and Nan were nearly as frozen as icicles when Dat finally began to hitch up the family carriage to the horse. Rhoda realized again how tired she was of traveling so pitifully slow. *Twenty-five minutes by car,* she thought. There were plenty of things she had become weary of — a wood-warmed house, the same dull evening chores, endless Bible reading, and an early bedtime. She'd seen the way Mr. and Mrs. Kraybill lived, with their toasty warm central heating, a fine compact radio in the kitchen . . . and a nice-sized color television in what they called their living room, where they actually spent most of their leisure time. Nothing like the front room where her family went only to shiver the evening away, far from the woodstove and the warmth of Mamma's big kitchen, the place they usually gathered. No, their *front room* was not the family's gathering place at all, but merely the room located at the front of the house. As such, it was used primarily for setting up large quilting frames and — when it was their turn — to

170

hold the congregation for Preaching.

Lately word had it that the tractor and car folk had already located a meetinghouse in which to worship, splitting the original splinter group down the middle. But the New Order, as Preacher Manny called his group, would continue to turn their front rooms and kitchens into temporary houses of worship.

She heard Mamma saying her good-byes to Mammi, the two of them hugging as Dat and Dawdi shook hands amicably. *Good. Maybe Dawdi will return to Honey Brook.*

She found out differently on the ride home. Fact was, Dawdi and Mammi had no intention of moving in with them on Beaver Dam Road, not as long as their family was "cluttering up" their minds with the "wrongful message" being spread far and wide by Preacher Manny — no matter that he was Dat's first cousin.

Rhoda gathered all of this from the things Dat and Mamma said in snippets to each other, as if they'd managed to forget Rhoda and Nan were sitting in the seat behind them, fully able to read between the lines. It was quite clear what had transpired while Nan was out feeding the birds and Rhoda was bored silly.

The painfully slow *clip-clop* of the horse

made Rhoda more determined than ever to buy a faster means of transportation — and escape — even if doing so meant plunging herself into great debt.

Elias turned to face her as Rosanna lay down to rest, and he began to discuss Kate. "What do ya think your cousin was doin' coming here right after she saw the babies at Preaching? Didn't ya say she'd nursed Eli there?"

"Well, you didn't make matters any better," Rosanna replied softly. "You could've gone outside to talk to John."

"What good would that've done?"

She wanted to cry. Ferhoodled Kate had messed everything up, and Rosanna could scarcely bear it.

Elias fell silent, and she had the thorny sense she'd overstepped her bounds. Immediately she was sorry.

She knew him well . . . he was undoubtedly rehearsing what had occurred earlier. *Why hadn't he intervened with Cousin Kate, sending her home?*

He closed his eyes and sighed. "Ach, Rosanna . . ." Then he rolled over, away from her.

"Doesn't matter, really. Kate's gone now," she whispered. "Just rest, love."

He lay still, hardly breathing, and she assumed he'd fallen back to sleep. She ought to do the same if she was to be wide awake enough for suppertime and tending to the babies' needs, as well as being good company for Elias later.

Rhoda stood in the doorway of James's former bedroom first thing Monday morning. Oh, the things she could do with a spot like this!

Stepping boldly inside, she eyed the double bed, with its pretty oak head and footboard, pieces made by her father when James was only a boy. Mamma would be suspicious of her when she asked — *if* she had the courage. Yesterday had not presented an opportunity, but today, this very day, she would request the move.

Touching the lovely bed quilt, she noted the striking purple, red, and navy blue Bars pattern, delicately double stitched by Mammi Hannah long before James was even born — before Mamma was married, too. Mammi Fisher, along with Mamma and her sisters, had kept this family warm for many years with many layers of quilts.

Smiling, Rhoda hoped against hope Mamma would agree. Making this empty room — presently kept for overnight guests — her own was but the first of two things she wanted, and wanted badly. She'd take steps toward the second today, when she went with Mrs. Kraybill to look at used cars after work.

Mamma startled her, mop in hand, and Rhoda stepped aside. "Oh, sorry."

"No . . . no, that's all right." Mamma glowered. "How would you like to dry mop and dust this room?" She squinted. "Seems you've got some time on your hands."

"Honestly, I best be goin'."

Mamma pressed the mop to the wide-plank floor. "Guess you'd rather clean an Englischer's house."

There was a surprising sting in Mamma's words, but Rhoda refused to react. She headed down the hallway to her room with Nan. So much for talking to Mamma about James's room.

Later, she poked her head into Nellie's bedroom and said, "We missed you yesterday at Mammi's."

Nellie nodded. "I lost track of time, is all."

"Well, it's too bad, 'cause it would've been nice to have you along." Pausing, she sighed. "How long before we get over there again, ya know?"

"I know, and I feel just awful 'bout it — not seein' our grandparents and all." Nellie put down her brush, her rich brown hair flung over her shoulder and draped like a thick curtain down to her waist.

Rhoda hesitated for a moment, then said, "Seems you and I have something in common."

"Oh?"

Slowly she nodded. "Jah, you're far removed from this family, so to speak, just as I am."

Nellie Mae looked befuddled. She resumed her hair brushing and turned to face the window. "The church split's caused plenty of problems, I'll say that."

Rhoda saw the flicker of pain on Nellie's face. "I don't suppose you'd let me see Suzy's diary."

Nellie frowned. "What for?"

"She was *my* sister, too."

"Why now?"

"I'd just like to read it, that's all." Rhoda wouldn't stoop to pleading.

Nellie set down her hairbrush. "Best not."

Rhoda had figured as much and left the room. Sometime when Nellie was sleeping, she would simply borrow it. . . .

At breakfast, when Rosanna passed the basket of muffins to Elias, he surprised her by saying, "I heard you prayin' this morning, love."

She started. "Oh. Didn't realize —"

"And you've been studyin' Scripture, too."

Had he seen the Bible lying open, or the list of verses Linda Fisher had written down?

She held her breath while he paused, looking at his callused hands.

"I've been thinkin'," he began. "We ought to at least look into Preacher Manny's group. See what it's all about."

Hope filled her. "Really?"

"I've talked to a few of the tractor folk, too."

She heard the excitement in his voice and feared he might want to bypass the New Order flock, the group most interesting to her. Biting her lip, she wanted to word her question carefully, so as not to sound critical. "Is it the farm equipment that has your interest?"

"I won't deny it would be a great help, what with so many years before little Eli can work alongside me," he replied. "But it's more than that. I've been talkin' to Reuben Fisher. Ach, the things he's shown me in Scripture — wonderful-gut things, Rosanna . . . things I've never heard before. Well, I want to learn more, too." He looked at her. "I hope this doesn't scare you."

Oh, how she loved him. "I've been more

than curious, too . . . wanting to know more — wanting to know the Lord God truly as Linda Fisher does. I've felt this way for some time, Elias."

He reached for her hand. "I thought as much."

"You aren't angry with me, then?"

He rose and kissed her cheek. "I'm hopeful, love. I want Eli and Rosie to study God's Word — not just follow the ordinance. To hear Reuben talk of Suzy, the comfort of knowing she's with her Savior, that they'll see her again someday . . . I want that for all of us. For our family."

"We are a family now, ain't so?" She glanced over at the playpen, where the twins slept side by side.

Nodding, he smiled. "We always were, but now all the more, with God's gift of these two little ones."

Nellie smiled, unable to suppress her glee as a whole group of customers left the bakery shop for their cars. "Oh, Mamma, what's happenin' to bring in so many folk? And scarcely anyone Plain."

Her mother leaned on the display counter, looking ever so pretty in her green cape dress, her hair somewhat looser than usual around the sides of her round face. "Must be that ad someone put in the paper, is my guess." Mamma stifled a chuckle. "I asked Rhoda 'bout it, but it wasn't her."

Nellie shook her head. " 'Tis a mystery."

"I should say."

Looking over the remaining cookies, bread, rolls, and coffee cake, Nellie worried they might actually run out of baked goods. "Well, if the ad brought those Englischers, then prob'ly there'll be more, jah?" She hoped so, since they had much catching up to do in the way of income.

"No question in my mind why they came." Mamma threw away the pieces of paper where she'd totaled up the sales amounts for each of the last twenty-five or more patrons. "I've never laid eyes on any of those ladies before, have you?"

"They're new to me, jah." Nellie noticed another car pulling into their lane. "Looks like more, too . . . a right steady flow."

"Dat will be prancin' with joy." Mamma pressed her hands to her face. "Ach, I don't know when I've had such a fine time."

Pleased as she was about the increase in business, Nellie was glad for the slight lull in customers, so they could catch their breath. She expected she'd have only a short time to talk with Mamma about the things on her heart. Perhaps while they cleaned up the noontime dishes there would be additional time . . . if Nan was off somewhere else, maybe. Otherwise, she'd have to wait till afternoon. By then surely they'd have run out of the day's offerings and have to post the Closed sign on the door.

Such a good problem to have, Nellie thought, wondering again just who'd placed the newspaper ad.

CHAPTER 18

Betsy glanced through the bakery shop window, delighted to see daughter-in-law Martha arrive for yet another visit with her three littlest ones in tow. The unexpected sight of her beloved granddaughter running through the snow toward the bakery shop took her by surprise. Dear Emma looked so like a young Suzy. Betsy's heart tugged ever so hard, and here just when she'd begun to feel some better.

"Oh, Nellie — Emma's come to visit!" she announced over her shoulder and rushed to the shop door.

Nellie Mae dutifully remained behind the counter, helping customers while Betsy ran out into the cold, arms flung wide. Emma fairly flew to her, wrapping her little arms around Betsy's neck and squeezing ever so tight.

"Mammi Betsy, I missed ya!" Emma said, her plentiful kisses raining on Betsy's face.

"Emma, darling, let your brothers have a hug now, too, please," said Martha, who was carrying a very bright-eyed and smiling two-year-old Matty.

Jimmy, three and a half, clumped forward in black boots too big for his feet, squealing, "Mammi, Mammi!"

Betsy released Emma and received Jimmy's hug, then kissed him on his chubby red cheeks. She was quite aware of Emma, who stood beside her all the while. "Go and get warmed up in the house." She shooed Martha along. "I'll be down later. Nellie Mae and I've got our hands full today."

"Business is pickin' up?" Martha patted Matty's head as he giggled, now reaching his arms out to Betsy, who gladly took him and gave him a sound kiss.

She nodded. "Never busier. Nan's making a nice big pot of chili for the noon meal . . . so yous can stay and eat with us, maybe?" She nearly held her breath, waiting for Martha's head to bob in agreement. Then she waved and leaned down to give Emma another kiss on her sweet cheek before hurrying back into the bakery shop, where Nellie Mae looked red in the face.

Betsy hurried around to the other side of the counter to help the next two women in line, with the more outspoken woman paying for both orders. She watched Emma run to catch up with her mamma outside, trying not to smile too broadly when Emma turned and looked back toward the bakery shop before she reached the walkway leading to the back door.

Bless her heart!

Oh, but it was hard to keep her mind on the work. Thankfully, they'd all be eating dinner soon, enjoying some of Nellie Mae's moist corn bread, and Emma would plant herself right next to Betsy at the table.

Sighing, she counted change for the two women, grateful they and all the others had come on such a nippy day.

When the bakery shop cleared out a bit, she touched Nellie's hand. "You doin' all right?"

"Why, Mamma?"

"Well, ya looked tuckered out earlier."

Nellie nodded. "Don't know when I've ever had so much goin' at once." She glanced toward the windows and took a deep breath. "Mamma, I've been wanting to talk to you. . . ."

Betsy's heart fluttered. *What about?*

"You're just so happy since, well . . . since you and Dat started goin' to the new church." Nellie fidgeted with the keys on the cash register. "No, I guess it's more than that — it's your joy. Honestly, Mamma." Her lower lip quivered.

"Oh, honey-girl." She slipped her arm around Nellie's slender waist. "Come, now."

"No, you *are* happy, Mamma. Your eyes are a-shinin' all the time."

"Ain't my doin,' dear one." She measured her words. "The change came right in here, thanks to the Lord." Patting her heart, she hoped that maybe Nellie was hungering after the things that had brought light and life to her and Reuben.

Nellie Mae's eyes filled with tears. "You prayed for me . . . when I was ever so sick. Remember?"

Oh, she remembered, all right.

Eyes pleading, Nellie asked, "Will ya keep prayin', Mamma?"

Her heart nearly broke at this from her girl who'd seesawed about the New Order. It appeared Nellie was more curious again. Could it be Nan's doing? She'd noticed that daughter had devoted much more attention to Nellie this past week. "Why, sure I will."

A car pulled into the lane, inched up to the bakery shop, and parked. Four more English customers got out, heading toward them.

"Remember, you're always welcome to attend Preachin' with us," Betsy said, frustrated that this important conversation must come to a premature end. When might she and Nellie Mae ever again talk so freely?

More than a dozen crows flew over the road directly in her line of vision as Rosanna drove the enclosed family buggy with baby Eli snuggled in one arm. The birds looked exceptionally large and black against the starkness of the white snow, and their *caw*-ing sounded menacing. Rosanna held the reins with her free hand, glad to have left Rosie at the neighbors', not wanting to risk taking both babies in the carriage by herself for even this short drive.

She had begun to suffer a bad case of cabin fever. Hopefully the ten-minute trip to see Linda Fisher would suffice for getting some fresh air on this most beautiful, yet cold, Monday morning. She'd hung the wash-ing right early while the twins conveniently slept. She smiled at the memory of rushing back and forth to check on them, not want-ing to leave them alone for more than a few minutes, even though they were snug in the cradles Elias had brought down to the warm kitchen first thing in the morning. What's more, he had helped by giving Eli his early morning bottle before heading off to a nearby farm sale.

She began to hum a church song, hoping Eli would continue to sleep till they arrived at Linda's. Church songs and church itself were less interesting these days; it was Elias's curiosity in the newly formed New Order group that had her most excited. Preacher Manny's flock attended services every Sunday — the "off" Sundays were for Sunday school — setting the People all abuzz.

How strange it would seem to go each and every Lord's Day. Rosanna supposed they could get used to going so often. *Especially if the sermon and Scripture readings are understandable.*

Not wanting to hurry the horse, she embraced the thrill of their future — so many possibilities. Surely the winds of change had begun to blow already, with Elias on the verge of jumping the fence . . . or at least seriously thinking about it. And even though it seemed like a wonderful-good thing to do, she feared how her father and her extended family might take such news. At least making the leap before the bishop declared the return of the Bann meant they could continue to enjoy fellowship with their family and friends in the old church.

Looking into the tiny face of her son, she whispered, "Your pop wants you to know all the good things found in God's holy Word.

You and your sister both." She kissed his peachy cheek. Rosanna would leave it to Elias to decide if such things as tractors, electricity, and telephones were for them.

No matter which new path her love might choose, the future seemed ever so bright to Rosanna as she pulled up to the Fisher home.

Linda greeted her at the back door. "Come in, come in!"

Rosanna moved into the warm kitchen with Eli, who'd mercifully slept during the buggy ride.

"Well, this is a welcome surprise!" Linda began to flutter about to put some cookies on the table.

"Can't stay long . . . must be gettin' back to Rosie." Rosanna explained why she hadn't attempted to bring both babies.

"I can imagine it would be difficult to travel alone with them both, at least till they're old enough to sit up." Linda stopped her preparations to make over Eli, who was peeking at her with one open eye as he slowly roused. "He's a handsome boy, that one."

Rosanna lifted him onto her shoulder. "He'll be hungry here 'fore too long."

"You should sit down and have something for your sweet tooth while you have the chance." Linda put a pot of water on to boil and returned to the table, sitting across from Rosanna.

They talked of the cold weather and all the snow, of the farm auctions, and how many folk had already scattered churchwise.

"Jonathan's downright pleased 'bout seeing so many converts." Linda's big brown eyes sparkled. "I daresay you've heard as much."

It was interesting to hear Linda talk like this — about grace and electricity mixed into one convenient package. "Jah, we've heard, and between you and me, Elias said at breakfast just this morning that he'd like to visit Manny's church. 'Course, he also talked about tractors, so he might be leaning toward the Beachys. He could surely use a tractor's help in the fields."

"A tractor?" Linda was smiling. "Well, wait'll ya see Jonathan's new car. It's a beauty."

It was so odd hearing this from Linda, although the grapevine had already heralded the news. "Where's it now?"

Getting up, Linda looked out the window. "He's out taking his driving test — hired a man to teach him, can ya believe it?"

"I declare." Rosanna laughed softly, repositioning Eli on her lap. "This one might like helping his daddy on a tractor when he's a little bigger. Ain't so, darlin'?"

Linda looked her way, smiling at Eli. "Some of the farmers up the road plan to take their boys along, come spring. One farmer even paid extra for air-conditioning in the cab. Now, what do ya think of that?"

"Ach, really?"

Suddenly there was a commotion in the lane, and when Rosanna looked, she saw Linda's husband sliding up toward the barn door in his automobile, narrowly missing it as the brakes caught at the last minute.

"Such a time to be out driving, jah?" Linda rushed to the back door and outside, leaving Rosanna to sit with Eli in her arms.

"What's the world comin' to?" she whispered. "Cars and all the newfangled whatnot."

Even so, she was mighty curious.

"Dat's lookin' to buy a car, Mammi Betsy," confided Emma in whispered tones before they sat down to the noon meal.

Nan glanced over at them from the stove, where she was stirring the chili, and Nellie Mae's eyebrows shot up. Betsy was thankful Reuben hadn't come inside yet for dinner.

"Now, Emma," Martha said quickly, eyeing Betsy. "Your Dat's only talking 'bout it — nothin's for sure."

188

Oh, but it won't be long, thought Betsy sadly. Wanting to change the subject, she asked Emma, "What new sewing project have you started since Christmas?"

But the child was not to be dissuaded. "We'll be able to go ever so fast then, ain't so, Mammi?" Her big blue eyes fairly danced.

Jimmy started to frolic about the kitchen like a very fast horse, and Martha, quite flummoxed, turned her attention to Matty, on her lap.

Nellie Mae made a suggestion. "Here, Emma, put this basket on the table for me."

Emma nodded and carefully carried the large wicker basket of corn bread over to the table. "There," she said, gently setting it down. "What else can I do?"

Apparently glad she'd succeeded in getting Emma's attention, Nellie looked over at Betsy, smiling. "Put all the napkins around, too." She showed Emma how to fold them in half, placing the first one under the fork on the left side of the plate. "Do this for each fork, jah?"

Emma set about doing as Nellie asked, any further talk of automobiles evidently forgotten.

Later, when Reuben was washed up and sitting at the head of the table, he bowed his head and prayed longer than usual.

Betsy wondered if the content of the audible prayer was for Martha's benefit, as Reuben undoubtedly had already heard of James's plan to purchase a car. Maybe that was why he ended the prayer with "And, Lord, keep us — all of us — ever mindful of the narrow way that leads to life everlasting. Amen."

The light filtered through the side window of the enclosed family carriage as Rosanna headed home. Ever so glad she'd made time in her busy day to see Linda, she shifted Eli in her arms. He had been perfectly placid and sweet all during both the carriage ride there and during the visit.

She stopped to pick up Rosie at the next farm over and decided it was safe to let the horse lead them home, the reins draped loosely across her lap blanket as she held both babies near.

Upon her arrival, she got Eli and Rosie settled inside the house in their playpen. She was glad to see Elias coming for dinner, willing and ready to help with unhitching the horse for her and leading it to the barn.

One less thing to do, she thought, rushing to reheat the chicken corn chowder she'd made on Saturday. Now all she needed was to put some dinner rolls on the table with several kinds of jams, and Elias would be smiling.

Fast as a wink, she took off her coat and went to wash her hands at the sink, where she spotted a note with her name printed on it in bold letters.

Dear Cousin Rosanna,

I stopped by to nurse Eli today and you were gone! How can you possibly think it's safe to take Eli and Rosie in the carriage by yourself? Or did you have help, maybe? I certainly hope you had that much sense!

Well, I'll see you later today, if I can get away. This is such an inconvenience to me, I daresay, your being away from the house and all.

Till later,
Your cousin,
Kate Beiler

It was Martha who took charge of stacking the dirty dishes and gathering up the silverware with a little help from Emma. Nellie was pleased to see her sister-in-law again, happy she'd come by to have a meal with them now that Nellie was well enough to join in the visit. Meanwhile, Mamma was in a hurry to get back to the bakery shop, rushing off to wash her hands and face in the washroom "right quick."

The more she pondered it, the more fascinated Nellie was by the recent change in her mother. Initially worried sick about Mamma's grief-stricken state in the weeks and months after Suzy died, Nellie could see how near-jubilant she was now. Momentarily, perhaps all of them had lost their way, but truly for Mamma, *her* life had changed, apparently for the better. She'd begun to refer to this life journey as a "gift of grace" even while living in the midst of great grief, and Nellie doubted the change had come because she'd pulled herself up by her own bootstraps. No, Mamma's joy came from an intangible source beyond anything Nellie had known.

"Nellie Mae," Dat said before leaving to return to his woodshop. "The new tables and chairs will be ready later this afternoon. Maybe I could bring them over after you close?"

"That'd be ever so nice."

"Just in time, too." He said it with a twinkle in his eye.

"Ain't that the truth!"

Nellie stepped outdoors as Martha got the children bundled up and settled into the carriage with some help from Dat. Emma carried on with extra kisses for her Mammi and a wave for Nellie Mae.

Turning her attention back to the bakery shop as they drove away, Nellie was anxious to see how many customers might come yet today.

Did I bake enough?

She wasn't sure, really, though they'd soon know. She looked forward to seeing first-hand how inviting her father's tables and chairs made their corner of the shop. She hoped the women who frequented Nellie's Simple Sweets — both the new customers and the regulars — might stay longer to visit . . . and open their pocketbooks and spend more while doing so.

Pleased as pie, she waited for Mamma to return from her good-byes, thinking they might resume their previous discussion, if time allowed.

She considered Mamma's words and her invitation to church. She knew what her parents longed for. Except for Ephram and Maryann, she was supposedly the last to come to her senses. But all the confusion of folk splitting off from the old church and becoming even more broad-minded, getting cars — like James and Martha were talking of doing — made Nellie even more sure that the Old Ways were best . . . at least for her and Caleb.

Yet she couldn't dismiss her curiosity

about the transformation in Mamma's life, especially. *Much like Suzy herself changed,* she thought suddenly.

One thing she would never understand, however, was the desire to own or drive a car. What was James thinking? Nellie shook her head. She'd ridden in automobiles enough to know she preferred to leave the driving to the Mennonite folk her father occasionally hired. Besides, Nellie saw no need to go so fast or so far. Life wasn't meant to be lived that way, was it?

CHAPTER 19

Nellie made a complete circle in the bakery shop, admiring the way the small alcove and window across from the display counter made for a cheery spot on a sunny day, thanks to Dat's beautifully made tables and chairs. With twelve places for customers to sit and nibble, the shop was the perfect spot to visit with friends.

For now, Nellie Mae was the only one who sat there, grateful her father had taken the time and care to do this thoughtful thing for her and her customers. On a slow day, Nellie and Mamma could even sit down themselves to relax, enjoying a cup of cocoa and a bite of cookie, perhaps. Of course, a day like today kept both of them on their feet.

Nellie daydreamed of Caleb during the short lulls in business. She envisioned him coming up the lane on foot or in his fine black open buggy, just to see her. On different terms . . . in a different time, he might have done so. What a lovely thing it would be if the schism had never happened, if the People had continued in the Old Ways as they had for more than three hundred years. She could scarcely imagine what it might be like for Caleb to court her as he wished, even though that, too, would have been in secret, as was their custom.

But now theirs was a desperate sort of secrecy, their courtship completely forbidden. Was that what made them all the more determined to be together? She hoped that wasn't the case, for if true, it seemed to diminish their love.

Nellie dismissed the idea. They loved each other deeply. Sometimes, if she were to admit it, she even loved Caleb fiercely. She would do almost anything to be with him. She knew her own heart, which beat with Caleb's name. Surely his did the same for her.

Just then, the small bell on the door jingled loudly. She jumped, startled. Turning, she was surprised to see Nan jostling inside, all wrapped up in one of Mamma's heavy woolen shawls, her own black outer bonnet on her head.

"Hullo, Nellie . . . I hope I'm not intruding." Nan looked around. "You alone?"

"Jah."

"Well, do ya mind?" She sat down. "I . . . wanted to see the chairs. Dat said they were all set in place." Nan ran her hands over the backs of the finely sanded oak chairs, her face solemn as could be.

"Sit for a while."

Nan looked somewhat relieved.

They were quiet for a time, relishing the silence. Then Nan said, "I'm takin' a big step come midsummer. I wanted you to know directly from me."

"What's that?" She couldn't imagine what her sister wanted to say.

"I'm goin' to take baptism instruction — to join the new church."

"Preacher Manny's?"

Nan nodded and smiled. "Jah, the Lord God's helping me set aside any longing for modern conveniences. I've been thinking 'bout it for a while now and I believe He's calling me to do this."

Nellie felt surprise at the earnest tone in Nan's voice; she'd never known her to be so serious about such matters.

"Won't ya think on it, too, sister?"

For so long she'd yearned for this sort of sharing . . . this special closeness with another sister — the way she and Suzy had always been together. "Does anyone else know?"

197

Nan blinked back tears as she slowly shook her head. "I thought of tellin' Rhoda first, but 'tween you and me, I fear we're losing her to the world. I can only pray that our oldest sister does not fall prey to the fancy."

"She must find her own way —"

Nan looked pained. "No, I don't believe that. Not at all."

"What do you mean?"

"Just that Rhoda *is* following her own will, desiring her own way. Left to her plans, she could fall into sin. I'm ever so worried." Moving her hand over the tabletop, Nan sighed. "I won't be joinin' church to go through the motions, Nellie Mae."

Did Nan have more to tell? Had she perhaps found herself a new beau already? Joining church usually signaled a wedding.

"I've found what Mamma has . . . and Dat . . . in the Lord Jesus."

Nan reached for her hand across the table, palm up. "Ach, I haven't been a very caring sister, Nellie Mae. I'll be changin' all of that, believe me. You'll not be grieving alone anymore."

"Oh, but . . ." Now it was she who could not keep back the tears.

"I love you, Nellie."

Nellie nodded, accepting her dear sister's hand. "And I love you, too." She looked at their clasped hands. "There is something I promised to tell you. Something your closest friend asked me yesterday to share with you."

"Rebekah?"

"She has made an equally difficult decision. Well . . ." She paused. "Possibly more so."

Nan frowned, her radiant expression suddenly clouded. "Is Rebekah all right?"

"I'm thinking so. She asked if she could ride along with you, Dat, Mamma . . . and Rhoda to church next Sunday."

Nan clapped her hands, leaned back, and made a little whooping sound before quickly composing herself. "Ach, what news! Did ya tell her she could?"

"Well, there wasn't much to say, really. She seemed to have pondered it at length and said she'd be out on the road on foot, and if Dat wouldn't mind, he could stop and pick her up."

Nan covered her mouth. "Oh . . . she'll be in such straits with her father, jah?"

"I brought that up, but Rebekah was unwavering." She paused. Such a good time she was having here with Nan as dusk settled in around them. "You can be proud, even *thankful,* to have such a strong-willed friend, I daresay."

"And you're not equally strong willed, Nellie?" Nan's comment threw her off guard. "Surely you're still seein' Caleb, despite his father's —"

"Nan . . . you silly, we're talking 'bout Rebekah — of her interest in your church, nothin' more."

Nan giggled, and with that Nellie rose, torn between what she wanted to revel in and knowing what she must do to protect her beloved.

A single glance at Nan, still sitting, led Nellie to wonder if she ought to have shared openly with this sister who seemingly desired to make amends. *Jah, I should have.* But the moment had passed, so she slipped into her coat and bid Nan good-bye, pulling the door shut behind her.

The lights strung high over the car lot nearly blinded Rhoda as she stepped out of Mrs. Kraybill's gray-and-white Buick Electra, with its white sidewall tires. She'd seen the term "loaded" and wondered if Mrs. Kraybill's comfortable car would be considered that.

She'd fantasized about what she wanted in a car, and this evening she might just lay eyes on it. Mrs. Kraybill, looking pert in her rimless glasses and woolen hat and tweed coat, had asked on the drive there what price range she'd had in mind. Rhoda told her precisely what she could afford. "No higher, and I'd rather spend less."

Glancing around now, she admired the neat rows of cars, looking for all the world like some kind of fancy crop. The lot was light and bright and thankfully quite devoid of customers. Someone had plowed the area so people could easily walk without slipping in the snow.

Soon, a man dressed in a long gray overcoat and matching hat walked across the lot to them and politely extended his hand. "Good evening, ladies. I'm Guy Hagel," he greeted them. "Any chance I can help you find the car of your dreams? I'd like to make tonight worth your trip."

Rhoda immediately liked him. Mr. Hagel was both well-mannered and considerate, walking clear around the lot with them, pointing out the features of each car and offering to let them take first one and then another "for a spin," in spite of the snowy streets.

"Now, here's something really special — a sixty-one Chrysler New Yorker in a striking dubonnet red color. Took it as a trade-in just last week." He waved his hand toward a bright wine-colored two-door with rear fins

— a mite too flashy for Rhoda's tastes.

Rhoda spoke up. "Thanks for your help, but we're just seein' what's here." At this Mr. Hagel looked dubious, and with a bit of embarrassment she realized she did not appear to be someone who would be in the market for a car.

"If you don't mind, my friend and I will keep looking for a while," Mrs. Kraybill added, relieving the awkward moment. "We'll certainly let you know if we need any assistance."

They continued to wander rows of Buicks of all kinds — convertibles, Rivieras, LeSabres . . . and even several Electras like Mrs. Kraybill's. Black and white seemed to be quite popular, as were a soft gray, a pale blue, a tan, and a sort of turquoise green. But it was not so much the color that appealed to Rhoda as the entire package.

They took their time, with Mr. Hagel allowing them to sit in the cold interiors of three different cars, all as nice as could be. So nice, in fact, the cars were beginning to run together in Rhoda's memory. How would she ever narrow it down to one?

"We'd best be headin' home," she said quietly while Mrs. Kraybill sat in the driver's seat of an especially eye-catching coupe, admiring its plush upholstery and chrome-accented dashboard.

By then Mr. Hagel had excused himself to meet another customer, and Rhoda could hear him repeating much the same words he'd said to them earlier.

"Well, what do you think?" asked Mrs. Kraybill, her black-gloved hands still on the steering wheel. "Do you have your eye on one in particular?"

"They're all so perty, ain't?"

Mrs. Kraybill smiled. "They truly are . . . especially *those* fetching machines." She laughed heartily, pointing to the convertibles next to them.

"Jah."

"It's getting too cold to be out, dear. Shall we call it a night?"

Rhoda agreed, torn between wanting a car right away and wanting to be able to actually drive it. "Could we come back tomorrow in the daylight?"

Mrs. Kraybill agreed that was a good idea, and she offered to teach Rhoda how to drive. "However, you'll need a learner's permit first."

"Oh?"

"I'll take you to get one soon, if you like. First you'll need to study for the written test. I can pick up a copy of the *Pennsylvania*

Driver's Manual the next time I'm in town."

Though her mind was now reeling with the decision ahead and all she had to learn, Rhoda was determined to do whatever it took to get what she wanted. *To think of being forever finished with horses and buggies!*

More than an hour later, Rhoda bowed her head while Dat offered a tedious prayer, followed by an equally lengthy Scripture reading. Tonight the passage was from the first chapter of 1 Peter. Dat read a verse about souls being purified by obedience several times . . . and something about a pure heart, too. She didn't feel he was singling anyone out in doing so, but he *was* clearly urging their attention on that particular verse.

He'd be furious if he knew where I went tonight.

She wanted to make sure her father — both of her parents, really — was unaware of her car purchase till it was too late for him to intervene. Not like some of her older brothers who actually sought out Dat's advice beforehand. Nan had reported that their own brother James was interested in buying a car, too. She assumed it wouldn't be long before the oldest boys — Thomas and Jeremiah — would also have one each. Or maybe they'd share one between them. They seemed to like to do that sort of thing, living as they did in a large farmhouse, split in half by a center hallway. One side for Thomas and his wife and children, the other side for Jeremiah and his.

After evening Bible reading and prayers were finished, Rhoda waited around, hoping to talk to Mamma. When the time came, she said, "I'd like to move into James's old bedroom."

Immediately it was apparent Mamma wasn't keen on the idea, shaking her head right quick. "Nee." She frowned. "There's no need, Rhoda. You and Nan are just fine together in your present room."

Well, that was that. No one in her right mind would think of arguing with Mamma. Rhoda knew she was stuck, exactly as she feared she might be if she didn't hurry and set her plan in motion to purchase a car — and net a fine husband.

More than anything, Nellie longed to write a letter to Caleb, but that was out of the question. She sat on her bed, several pillows supporting her back, and tapped her pen on the stationery, frustrated that Caleb could send *her* a letter, but she could never reply. Their situation felt as lopsided as all getout, and she pushed away her resentment toward David Yoder.

Puh, my future father-in-law!

Wondering if Caleb might also be thinking of her now, she leaned against the headboard, considering their love. Could it survive the expected separation?

The Lord willing, Nellie surprisingly found herself thinking. Suzy had often written that in her diary, following her conversion.

Would it take God's intervention for them to marry? She really didn't want to think that way. Such thoughts of divine miracles and interventions were appealing, but they went against the teachings of the Old Ways she and Caleb believed.

Writing the date, *Monday, January 21,* Nellie sighed. If she couldn't write her thoughts to Caleb, then what about a nice long letter to Cousin Treva? They'd become good pen pals over the past year, occasionally enjoying personal letters while still sending much of their news in circle letters. Tonight, though, Nellie sought a more personal way to express herself.

Dear Cousin Treva,

Hello from Honey Brook on a very chilly day. Is it equally cold there, I wonder?

Well, my family traveled to your neck of the woods yesterday afternoon and — can you believe it — I missed the trip! I got to holding Ephram and Maryann's pretty new baby, Sadie, and it was like time just stopped. Honestly, have you ever experienced such a thing? I did not want to give that baby back, nohow.

I felt like such a silly, not getting home in time to go with my family to Bird-in-Hand, especially when I might've been able to visit you, as well as Dawdi and Mammi Fisher. Such a Dummkopp I am!

I'm telling on myself, jah? Anyway, I'm hoping you'll come for a visit when things warm up a bit — maybe the next Sister's Day, if you're able. If you want to, you and one or more of your sisters could spend the night in the spare bedroom next to mine. We have two more guest bedrooms downstairs, off the front room . . . and, of course, the Dawdi Haus. That remains empty, even though I know Dat would like to persuade Dawdi and Mammi Fisher to reconsider moving here.

Thinking of that, lots of changes have happened in our district. Nearly half of the Old Order folk have now gone to the New Order or the Beachys. How many are still in the old church there? Do you see Dawdi and Mammi Fisher at Preaching service?

Well, write when you can. I always enjoy

hearing from you.
Hope the new year is off to a good start.
Your cousin and friend,
Nellie Mae Fisher

Personal letter though it was, she didn't think of writing even a hint about her brother James's fascination with cars — no need to hand that off to the rumor mill. Such embarrassing news flew through the community mighty fast.

Much like the never-ending guessing about who's pairing up.

Despite couples' attempts at secrecy, parents and grandparents whispered amongst themselves. It was a known fact that most mothers of the bride had more than an inkling about the groom's identity prior to the couple's intention to marry being announced at church each fall.

Folding the letter, Nellie thought again of Caleb, wondering how to get word to him from time to time. Maybe that was not what the Lord God intended for them. Maybe she was supposed to bide her time — *their* time, since Caleb, too, had his hands tied. Thing was, she had no idea what was going on between him and his father, no idea what good thing was being accomplished, if any, by their painful separation. She felt totally in the dark. Still, she clung to the hope that if she stayed true to the Old Order long enough — proving herself faithful — David Yoder would eventually change his mind about her and allow Caleb's and her marriage.

I must trust that all will be well. . . .

When the house was still and everyone was deep in slumber, Rhoda found the flashlight she kept under her side of the bed for emergencies. She slipped out from under the quilts and into the cold hall, shining the light on the floor. Going to Nellie's room, she tilted the light inside, reluctant to shine it on the bed lest she awaken her younger sister.

Once she'd determined that Nellie Mae was indeed asleep, she turned off the light and knelt on the floor, keeping her head low so as not to be seen if Nellie should awaken. Opening the drawer to the bedside table, she reached inside.

Empty.

She moved her hand all the way to the back of the drawer, wondering if it had slid over to the left side, perhaps. But still she found nothing, even though Rhoda had once seen Nellie stash the diary in there when Rhoda had walked in on her reading it.

Where'd she hide it?

Picking up the flashlight, she managed to crawl out of the room, not wanting to take unnecessary risks by searching further. It was mighty clear Nellie had moved the diary, suspecting Rhoda or someone else would try to snatch it away.

Must be some big secrets in there.

Heading back to bed, Rhoda felt rather defeated. First by Mamma's resounding denial, and now by Nellie's silent rebuff.

CHAPTER 20

It was hard at times to remember just how close she had been to Suzy, although it had not even been a year since her sister's death. Nellie's dreams of her sister only added to the confusion as the dreams and the memories joined together like the pieces of a quilt. Except what remained was not something whole at all, but rather wispy fragments.

Snuggling now beneath several layers of Double Nine-Patch quilts, she wished she had the nerve to ask the Lord God to keep her from dreaming. She needed a reprieve. A good solid night of sleep would be much appreciated.

As she lay there, knowing it was nearly time to begin Tuesday's baking, she wondered if she ought to let Nan in on her secret. She felt bad about shutting her out yesterday, when they'd shared such a sweet moment together alone in the bakery shop. And then if she hadn't gone and spoiled things!

She must seek out Nan and open her heart to her, trusting that her sister would keep this confirmation of Caleb's and her forbidden relationship in strict confidence.

Nellie pushed back the quilt and sat up, yawning and hoping she would be doing the right thing by her beau.

Today is the day! Rhoda thought as she left the house that morning, bundled up with so many layers she could scarcely move, heading to work at the Kraybills'. If she and her father were on better footing, she might've asked to borrow the buggy, but that would have tied up his transportation all day long. Besides, she had no business asking — not considering what she looked forward to doing this very day.

Over the noon hour, Mrs. Kraybill planned to drive her to the nearby bank preferred by the Plain, where she'd fill out the necessary loan paperwork. The thought gave her the willies. If all went well, they would head back to the car lot and make her purchase. Rhoda could hardly wait.

She realized it was premature to purchase a car, but she wanted what she wanted and was tired of being denied. Now was the time to make the leap into the world. Then, once all this snow was gone from the ground, she'd have herself some driving lessons.

Meanwhile, Rhoda would hide her secret out behind the Kraybills' house, where Dat could not be privy to her deed.

Betsy knew one thing for sure — January held the power to signal the first hints of springtime. Most people would look at her with surprise if she dared say it, but she knew it was true firsthand.

So busy was she in the bakery shop with Nellie Mae there was scarcely time to say three words to her daughter. But she was breathing silent prayers for her dear girl in response to Nellie's request. Once things settled down a bit and there was even the slightest letup in the continuous stream of customers, she would tell her what she'd discovered in the cold cellar.

Meanwhile, she was taken aback by Nellie's bold question to a customer, a middle-aged woman wearing a loud red woolen coat and white knit scarf and gloves to match. "If you don't mind . . . did ya happen to see a newspaper ad 'bout the bakery, ma'am?"

The woman smiled and shook her head. "No, I actually heard about this place from my neighbor here." She turned to the younger brunette standing nearby. "But *she* saw the ad in yesterday's paper."

The ad's still running? Who on earth would spend that kind of money?

Betsy was quite surprised at the revelation but said nothing, simply glancing at her Nellie-girl. She knew better than to ask, "What on earth?" That never worked with this daughter. Come to think of it, it didn't work with Rhoda, either. And that one, well, she was up to something for sure. Betsy had seen it in her steady, determined gaze that morning at breakfast. *Jah, Rhoda has her secrets, no doubt about that.*

Nan, bless her heart, had resumed the work of cleaning house and cooking nearly all the meals, now that Betsy was helping Nellie Mae in the bakery shop once again. Nan much preferred the quiet of the house, or so it seemed. Was it a way to mourn the loss of her beau?

Opening the display case and removing two pies, Betsy personally was glad to be working alongside Nellie Mae. *So good of Reuben to allow it,* she thought, grateful he, too, was past the very worst grief. Sometimes Betsy awakened with tears on her face, not remembering ever weeping. Silent tears of loss and of deep joy, as well. Their youngest was with the Lord.

For that reason, September, the season of great salvation for this house, would always be for Betsy the most wonderful-good month of all.

To think it began with my dear Reuben.

Glancing out the window, she noted the low-lying clouds. Winter days were too short, and even this early in the day, sunshine fought to get through the gray haze. *Like the light trying to shine forth in the heart of a rebellious soul.*

She sensed such in Rhoda and could only pray, because confronting her had never worked in the past. Now she wished she had listened to Reuben from the outset; they'd made a serious error in allowing their eldest daughter to work away from home.

"Mamma . . . look, we're runnin' out of pies." Nellie disrupted her reverie. "Yesterday it was cookies, today it's pies."

Betsy smiled, motioning for Nellie to come and sit with her, since it looked as though there might be time to catch their breath.

Nellie commented how thankful she was for her father's contribution of these sturdy, even pretty, oak tables and chairs. Betsy, too, enjoyed having a place to sit and rest a bit, and they could easily see from this vantage point if customers were driving up the lane.

"I've been prayin' for you." She looked right at Nellie Mae, who inhaled slowly and nodded.

"I want to do the right thing, Mamma. Truly, I do."

"And you will . . . the Lord will lead ya." Betsy folded her hands.

Nellie was silent. Then she said, "I sometimes wonder what might've happened if Suzy'd lived a full life. Would she have stayed Amish, do ya think?"

"She may not have been as conservative as Dat and I are . . . but once Plain, always Plain." Betsy smiled. Folks said it was ever so hard to get the Old Ways out of the soul if you were raised in them.

They sat quietly for a time. Then, eager to share what was mighty close to bursting forth, Betsy began. "Yesterday I happened to go to the cold cellar to fetch two jars of peach jam for supper. Guess what I found in the potato storage rack? Sprouting potatoes. Both the red and white potatoes are just a-springin' to life already."

Nellie listened, glassy-eyed, obviously daydreaming.

"Beyond a doubt, the buds have begun to rise . . . and all this in the cool darkness." She sighed. "Of course, we don't count on using *those* potatoes to see us through the winter, but for cuttin' apart, an eye for each section, to plant when the ground is thawed."

"All this is happenin' in the dark," Nellie said flatly. "When everything else seems dead . . . or is."

Betsy smiled. "Jah. On one of the darkest of days comes the first hint of life. 'Tis that way for everything . . . even potatoes." She wanted to reach over and pat Nellie's hand, because all of a sudden her daughter looked to be quite taken with the comparison. But Betsy remained still, letting her remarks sift into her daughter's mind.

Nan surprised Nellie by coming to help carry the few leftover baked goods back down to the house so they wouldn't freeze overnight. Actually, Nan urged Mamma to go ahead of them and leave the work to her. While alone with her sister now, Nellie took the opportunity to apologize. "I was snooty yesterday afternoon, and I'm sorry." She added, "I'd like you to come to my room tonight, after evening prayers. Will ya?"

A flicker crossed Nan's eyes and then she offered a warm smile. "Oh, Nellie Mae . . . I wondered if you'd ever ask."

"I want to tell you something very dear to me."

Now I have to keep my word.

Nan looked both surprised and pleased. "I can't wait. Oh, sister, you have no idea!" With this, Nan kissed her face.

"Well, if you feel as lonely as I do some-times, then I *do* know." Nellie set about gathering up the last pie and a few assorted cookies, unable to squelch her own smile.

Am I wise to tell her my secret? she won-dered, but she pressed on with the chore at hand, refusing to second-guess her resolve.

During supper, Dat talked of the cold hav-ing turned a corner and become dangerously severe. He glanced outside now and then at the heaviness of the snow as it fell silently, covering the earth with yet another layer of white.

Then, during a dessert of pie and cookies, the focus of his comments took a marked turn, and he leaned forward, looking di-rectly at Rhoda. Nellie flinched, wondering what now.

"Rhoda, it's come to my ears that you've committed a most disobedient deed."

At the accusation, Rhoda's eyes turned a stony gray. She pushed away her plate of pumpkin pie, her frown as deep and as harsh as the cold beyond the kitchen walls.

Dat did not beat around the bush about the reliability of his source. "Your brother James spilled the beans 'bout your car." His eyes tapered into stern slits. "He saw you at the car lot this afternoon."

Like-minded souls those two — James and Rhoda, Nellie thought. *Dat must have gone over to try to talk sense to James today, only to find this out!*

"So, then, under God, I ask you, Rhoda, where is your heart in all this?"

Rhoda raised her eyes, her expression moving quickly from embarrassment to anger and suddenly to bitterness. "Am I not of age, *Daed*?"

Nellie was struck by Rhoda's use of the more formal address of their father. *Daed* was the word Caleb used to refer to *his* father.

"Are you not living under my roof, under my authority, daughter? And don't you eat my food? Enjoy the warmth of this house . . . the fellowship of this family?"

Squirming, Nellie held her breath. Rhoda was treading on dangerous ground, and everyone at the table, including Mamma, awaited her respectful response.

"My heart just ain't here." Rhoda rose from the table. "I'm leavin' — tomorrow, first thing."

Mamma gasped. "Rhoda . . . no!"

"Let her be." Dat touched Mamma's arm.

Rhoda left the table and the room, her feet pounding fast on the stairs. It was all Nellie could do not to run after her and beg her to think hard before carrying out what she'd so daringly declared.

Nellie's original plan to tell Nan about Caleb took a backseat to their worries about Rhoda later that night. Mamma's lip had quivered all through Bible reading, and Nellie wished something could be done to smooth things over with their oldest sister. "What'll she do out there in the world, anyway?" Nellie sat on the bed, leaning against the headboard, while Nan sat facing her, her back against the footboard.

"Well, 'tween you and me, I don't see Dat backin' down," Nan said. "I'm worried she'll do what she says and leave tomorrow."

"And then what?"

Nan shook her head sadly. "She may never darken the door of this house again."

"Why do you thing that?"

"'Cause she's so headstrong."

"You oughta be spendin' time with her." Nellie felt bad saying this on the first night Nan had come to talk. *So ill-timed, really . . . like most things these days.*

"I'll go over there in a minute, but you had something you wanted to share with me, jah?"

"It best be waitin'," she said, thinking only of Rhoda.

Nan studied her. "You sure?"

"If Rhoda goes ahead with what she's threatened, we'll be losin' another sister."

Nan agreed. "I'll see what I can do." With that, she climbed off the bed, saying good night and leaving Nellie to wonder what Nan might say to take the stinger out of Rhoda. And if she did convince Rhoda to change her mind, would Dat change his, too?

By sheer coincidence, Caleb had seen Susannah Lapp at a farm sale that morning, though not for more than a few seconds. She'd arrived with her mother, bringing a hamper of food to her deacon father for the noon meal.

He had offered a tentative smile when their eyes met. In all truth, he'd felt deceitful doing so, but he'd hoped a smile might be enough to set up the possibility of a longer encounter at the upcoming Singing. *No sense putting it off.*

Now, ready for bed, he leaned on the windowsill, looking at the inky black sky, recalling the way the dense atmosphere had added to the depth of color, making the sky appear flaming red at sundown, hours ago. He had been on his way out to the barn to check the livestock — his responsibility — when he'd noticed it. He was glad to do whatever he could to prove to his father and grandfather that he was up to the task of taking on this large operation. Willing and ready, minus one small piece of the future — a bride.

Well, he was on his way to fixing that. Once he could honorably report back, man to man, that the deacon's daughter was of no romantic interest whatsoever, Caleb understood he'd be at liberty to pursue the young woman he truly loved. All it would take to finally obtain his farmland was doing things his father's way.

Sunday's the day. . . .

Putting out the gas lamp, he climbed under the bedcovers, leaning his head back on his crossed arms. He felt a peculiar rush of excitement at the thought of seeing Susannah again — excitement that quickly turned to mortification, even though she had been as pretty as ever today when he'd bumped into her. He knew his heart belonged to Nellie Mae and to her alone.

Susannah is the only path to Nellie Mae, he reminded himself.

CHAPTER 21

Rosanna King was up and pacing the floor in the wee hours Wednesday morning, but not with a babe in arms. She simply could not rest, let alone fall asleep. Not with what Cousin Kate had pulled last night before supper. She'd arrived with three of her youngest ones to see "their baby brother and sister," as she put it, propping Rosie in her blanket on the lap of her two-year-old.

Elias had frowned all the while, evidently expecting Rosanna to put her foot down. They'd had words again after she'd fed and tucked in the twins, who continued to sleep soundly now.

The growing tension between herself and Elias gnawed at her. How she resented Kate's coming to visit for more than the agreed-upon midmorning feeding — and she'd worn out her welcome with even that. It was time someone put a stop to it and mighty fast, lest next time Rosanna stoop to sinning and spew fiery words at Kate.

Fuming now as she relived the intrusive visit, Rosanna went to look in on her sweet babies. *Kate's undermining my mothering. Slowly but surely.*

She felt nearly desperate, wishing she could confide in the bishop's wife, Anna, or in one of the preacher's wives, since her own dear mamma was long deceased. Perhaps Nellie's mother would have some wisdom to offer. Sighing, she knew she and Elias needed help with this mess. The empathy she had repeatedly attempted to show her cousin was dwindling fast.

Oh, how Rosanna had longed for a child, and now she loved these babies to pieces. Her family was at Kate's mercy, and things had gone awry faster than either Elias or she could ever have imagined. Truth was, Kate's visits were starting to feel like something completely different from how they had started out.

Something frighteningly different.

Tossing on his robe, Chris Yoder slipped quietly down the stairs and slumped into a chair at the kitchen table. He couldn't sleep — not with Zach in bed on the other side of the room, talking on and on about Suzy's bracelet. His brother had even tried to convince Chris to drive him back to the state park after school instead of waiting for the weekend. He wanted that frozen bit of gold from the ice near the lake, and he wanted it now. Chris had firmly refused; he didn't have time on school nights. Besides, that shiny gold object encased in ice wasn't going anywhere, and it was most likely not the bracelet, anyway.

But not a single line of reasoning seemed to faze Zach — he was single-minded. He must have Suzy's bracelet.

Chris ran his hands through his hair, making it stand up. He worried that Zach seemed in danger of losing his sense of reason. His brother's grief was spiraling off into something weird.

Struck with how helpless he felt, he began to pray. "Father in heaven, I ask for divine comfort for Zach, in Jesus' name. Let your light spring to life in his heart and mind. Soothe his pain, and help me be the brother and friend he needs to walk along this hard path. Guide me and let me know when to silently support him and when to offer words of comfort. I'll thank you for it. Amen."

Leaning his head into his hands, he remembered an evangelist at the Tel Hai campground who said that when you extend yourself to those who are suffering, you find out who you truly are. You discover yourself . . . what you're made of.

He decided he needed to be more patient and understanding with his brother. Here he was complaining to himself, wishing Zach would snap out of it. But he hadn't ever experienced firsthand what Zach was dealing with. He'd never loved a girl that way. Nor had he called upon the Lord for his life mate, fasting and praying for days like Zach had. How quickly the answer had appeared to come . . . only to be taken away!

God's ways are always higher than ours. Knowing full well that his parents had prayed since his birth for the young woman who would someday become his wife, just as they had for each of their sons, Chris realized he'd never once prayed that way.

What am I waiting for?

He felt convicted suddenly. Compelled by it, he bowed his head again, this time with deep gratitude for God's ongoing providence. He didn't ask for his future bride to be outwardly pretty, as Suzy Fisher had been, but he did ask that she be a partner in whatever ministry he would eventually be called to. "Protect her from sin and harm . . . and may she not be discouraged in seeking your will for her life, Lord . . .

wherever she may be. These things I pray in the name of Jesus. Amen."

"I never thought my own brother would tell my secret!" Rhoda bemoaned her state to Mrs. Kraybill that morning. She told how she'd bundled up earlier to trudge through knee-deep snow to the very same brother's house before dawn. "I startled James and Martha but good."

"And why was that, may I ask?"

Rhoda fought the urge to weep. "I asked to move in over there — they've got two spare rooms off the sunroom downstairs."

Mrs. Kraybill frowned and tapped her well-manicured fingernails on the table. "I assume you've given this some thought, Rhoda?"

"All night long I pondered it."

To think Mamma, Nan, and Nellie Mae were all witnesses to Dat's words . . . and mine, she thought ruefully, reliving the suppertime feud.

"Mamma made a noble attempt at breakfast . . . asked me to apologize to my father." She stirred sugar into her black coffee. "But I haven't changed my mind. Honestly, I'm more than ready to start over somewhere new."

"Well, I do hope you'll continue working here — for us." Mrs. Kraybill searched Rhoda's eyes. "You have a car payment now, remember."

She remembered, all right. It was the main reason she hadn't asked to stay with the Kraybills, even for a short time. She needed pay, not free room and board. "I'm rather strapped now, ain't so?"

Nevertheless, she was fond of her beautiful car — a black-and-white four-door Buick LeSabre with under thirty thousand miles on it. It was fully loaded with whitewall tires, a 335 Wildcat engine — whatever that was — power steering and power brakes, and a radio. "The works," Guy Hagel had told her.

Mrs. Kraybill smiled kindly. "You're a determined young woman, Rhoda. I believe you'll do well in your new life."

It was time to spread her wings, anyway, regardless of Dat's probing words. Maybe the car purchase was exactly what she'd needed to propel her away.

"Would you mind ever so much helping me move my things to James and Martha's?" she asked. "I'd be very grateful."

"I'm happy to help." Mrs. Kraybill rose to pour herself more coffee. "I do have to ask you — are you still thinking of keeping your car here?"

Rhoda nodded. Was Mrs. Kraybill concerned she could encounter trouble with Dat somehow? "Don't worry 'bout my father comin' over here and giving you a tongue-lashing. That won't happen, I promise you."

Mrs. Kraybill appeared relieved.

I'm old enough to make up my mind, Rhoda thought, rising to clear the cups and saucers off the table. *No matter how hard Nan tried to talk me out of leaving last night. And no matter how sad Mamma and Nellie Mae looked at the breakfast table!*

The snow had stopped altogether by mid-afternoon, and Rhoda was pleased Mrs. Kraybill consented to go home with her, having left her two preschool-aged children with the neighbors. The eldest was headed to a friend's house after school. They were picking up two suitcases full of Rhoda's clothing and personal belongings, including her necklaces, which left the bureau mirror looking mighty bare.

She was relieved that Nellie Mae and Mamma remained out in the bakery shop, not coming inside for a last-ditch effort to keep her home. Even so, Nan came running upstairs, tears glistening in her eyes. She stood out in the hallway with her hands clasped, staring in at their room.

"If you find more of my things, just box 'em up, Nan," Rhoda said, hating to be so pointed. Nan didn't deserve to be treated this way, but if Rhoda appeared any other way but deceptively strong, she would surely break down and start crying herself.

Mrs. Kraybill carried down the first suitcase, leaving her alone with Nan, who leaned forlornly against the doorjamb. "Listen, I just don't fit here anymore, and I'm tired of hiding the real me. I'm going to the new church now — with the tractor folks, I've decided." Rhoda exhaled forcefully. "Nellie Mae doesn't see eye to eye with our parents, either, but they are a lot more patient with her. . . ."

"Oh, I think Nellie will come around in time."

"Well, I won't. Give up my perty car for a horse and buggy? Not on your life!"

"Rhoda, please." Nan touched her arm.

"No. I've had it with livin' like this. I'm not cut out for the Plain life. I have to get out or suffocate!"

Nan sniffled, her sobs coming in little gulps. But that didn't keep Rhoda from reaching for the remaining suitcase and marching past her dearest sister, right down the stairs.

Nellie comforted Mamma as they stood at the bakery shop window, observing Rhoda and their English neighbor load the last suitcase. "She's really leaving. I'd hoped she'd change her mind." Nellie's throat ached.

"Me too." Mamma reached for her hand. "I should have let her move into James's old room like she wanted."

"This isn't your fault, Mamma."

"Still, I'm takin' this much too hard, I fear."

"Oh, Mamma, no. You love Rhoda — we all do. She's making a mistake, that's certain. Of course you feel ever so bad." She led Mamma away from the window.

All Nellie and Mamma could do was pretend not to wince at the sounds of Mrs. Kraybill closing the trunk of her car and the slamming of two car doors — shutting them out.

Reuben stood near the window in the haymow, leaning forward to watch his eldest daughter making the worst mistake of her life. He wished he might retract last night's statements, yet he felt strong in his stance. Rhoda needed to find where she fit into the

231

family of God, certainly, but she also needed to be less bullheaded.

Will she learn anything worthwhile out there with Englischers?

Betsy had made a point earlier this morning before they'd ever gotten out of bed. *"You're doin' to Rhoda just what your parents did to you . . . and all over a difference of opinion."*

So his wife was put out with him, too.

Betsy's right. He removed his black hat and held it over his chest — over his heart — as Mrs. Kraybill pulled her car forward and turned around, heading down toward the road.

God be with you, little girl. . . . Flee to anner Satt Leit — *the other kind of people* — *if you must.*

He prayed it might prove to be beneficial in the long run. After all, the apostle Paul had relinquished the degenerate man over to the devil for the salvation of his soul.

Reuben moved away from the window and pulled himself together. It wouldn't do for the feed salesman, expected any minute now, to see him all broken up like this.

At half past nine Friday, the twins were back in their playpen for their morning nap. Rosanna was well occupied with bread baking and dinner making, thinking of Elias as she worked. Her husband had been extra kind this morning at breakfast, holding his son and going out of his way to make over both babies, which had started the day on a sweet note.

Seeing his gentle way with the twins made her long to be in his arms again. Instead, she'd made his favorite breakfast of German sausage, three fried eggs, and blueberry pancakes. He always took his coffee strong, with only a spot of cream, but oodles of sugar.

They'd talked congenially, all forgiven. The only thing Elias had to say with any connection to Cousin Kate was that he'd noticed she had cut back on her multiple visits, giving them a reprieve of sorts. Here it was already Friday morning and she'd dropped down to one daily visit since Tuesday. "What the world?" Elias had asked, chuckling.

She'd told him about giving Kate the instructions for making blessed thistle tea — *"just the thing for Kate's baby blues."* Again, he had laughed heartily, and they'd both assumed the herbal tea was doing its job.

"Hopefully," she muttered to herself, rolling out whole-wheat dough for a large beef potpie. She best be getting it in the oven before long or Elias would be twiddling his thumbs when the time came to sit down to eat the main meal of the day.

Carefully she lifted the dough from the counter, pressing the top crust over the beef and home-canned vegetables before poking holes in the top with a table fork.

Glad the snow had ceased falling yesterday, Rosanna yearned for a long, brisk walk, though that was not possible just yet. Still, she thought ahead to the day when Eli and Rosie would be able to walk along and keep up with her on a mild winter's day. *And come summers, too.*

She imagined all the fun the twins would have growing up here — little Eli helping Elias tend to the animals and working the land together as father and son. Such a wonderful-good team they'd be. She would have herself a grand time teaching Rosie to bake breads and pies, passing along everything she knew about quilting and sewing and tatting and cross-stitching to her darling little girl.

Oh, such fun!

Stooping to open the oven, she slid the potpie inside, wishing dear Mamma could see her now. Was she looking down from on high? *Safe and sound in the arms of the Lord God . . .*

Thinking on this, all of a sudden she missed holding her wee babies and went to the next room to look in on them. She cherished watching them sleep or drink from their bottles. Fortunately, they had become quite attached to the latter, especially Rosie, since Cousin Kate had ceased nursing her.

Hearing a muffled noise outside, her heart sank. Cousin Kate had arrived . . . right on time.

She put on a smile and hurried to the back door to greet her cousin, who had little blond, blue-eyed Rachel with her again, seemingly as happy as ever to see Rosanna. Kate gave her a quick hug. "I'm feelin' ever so good today. How 'bout you, Rosanna?"

Kate chattered on about her morning — the baking she'd already done, with some help from niece Lizzy, who was old enough to act as a regular mother's helper and who baby-sat the younger children each morning when Kate came to nurse Eli. Rosanna had been wondering how Kate was keeping up at home.

Sitting down with two-year-old Rachel on her lap, Kate seemed calmer than on previous visits. Curious, Rosanna asked, "Did you happen to try that tea recipe?"

Kate said she had, offering a smile. "I've been drinkin' it several times a day, as a matter of fact . . . awful nice of you."

They talked about various kinds of herbal

teas and how they were reported to help what ailed you. Rosanna actually found herself enjoying this visit, mostly because Kate hadn't rushed into the other room and focused her attention on the babies, or purposely awakened them. It was ever so nice to sit and talk together, like they had long before the twins were born.

Soon they were all three sipping hot cocoa, little Rachel blowing softly on hers while sitting up close to the table on Kate's lap.

So far, it was almost as if Eli and Rosie were of no interest to Kate today, for she said not a word about them. Surprised, Rosanna wondered if she was going to simply ignore the fact that the twin babies were napping in the next room.

It was Rachel who asked in her tiny voice, after the hot cocoa was finished, "See *Bobblin,* Mamma?" Rosanna's imagination flew to Eli and Rosie's second birthday. She assumed Rosie might look a lot like little Rachel, who was now wriggling to get off Kate's lap, wanting to have a "look-see" at the babies.

Kate rose with her daughter and carried her to the doorway. Then she turned and asked, "Is it all right, Rosanna?"

Before Rosanna could think to say not to awaken the babies *this time,* she agreed.

"Why sure . . . show her the twins." But she needn't have worried, for Kate merely held Rachel up to look at them.

"Babies sleepin'," Rachel whispered, holding her pointer finger up to her mouth. "Shh," she said in such a darling way, Rosanna nearly forgot the previously upsetting visits.

Kate straightened and headed back to the kitchen with Rachel still in her arms. "When do ya plan to go to a quilting bee next?"

Rosanna wanted to go soon if the weather cooperated. Her neighbor to the east had offered to baby-sit at least one of the twins so she could handle the reins on the buggy whenever she wanted to get out of the house. "Where's the next one to be?"

"At Esther Fisher's."

"That'd be right nice."

Kate eyed her for a moment. Then, looking away, she added, "Might be best if you don't go a-quiltin' with the New Order womenfolk, though."

"Oh?"

Kate put her daughter down to toddle about. "Bishop Joseph ain't exactly putting his foot down about it, askin' for separate work frolics just yet. But even so . . ."

"Jah, once the ninety days is past . . . what then?" Rosanna sighed. "Hard to know what'll happen."

"Well, one of two things, I daresay. Folk will either be in or out." Kate's gaze was scrutinizing.

"In" meaning the old church, thought Rosanna wryly.

Long after Cousin Kate and Rachel left, she pondered the peculiar change in Kate's demeanor, especially toward the babies. More than anything, she'd wanted to urge Kate to keep drinking more of the blessed thistle tea before she left, but thought better of it.

CHAPTER 22

On Saturday Chris Yoder reluctantly drove his brother to Marsh Creek State Park as promised. With their dad's camping hatchet on the floorboard, Zach was determined to dig up whatever had frozen into the ice and debris under the rowboats.

All week Zach had talked of little else other than cutting the shiny thing loose, obsessed with the idea of retrieving it.

Chris was sorry he'd ever suggested going to the lake in the first place. If Chris had *his* way, they would simply wait for Mother Nature to do her work in a few short months during the spring thaw.

But Zach was not at all interested in waiting.

"Do you ever wonder where heaven is?" Zach asked suddenly. He was staring out the car window. "Up from our planet . . . or out from the solar system on the other side of the sun or something?"

He'd never even considered it.

Chris didn't answer, but Zach continued anyway. "Heaven's closer now. . . ."

Because of Suzy, thought Chris.

"She went too soon — I feel cheated, you know?"

He figured Zach would feel this way, and most likely for a long time, too. Chris didn't say what he was thinking — that there would come a day when his brother would love again. "Yeah. I'm not surprised."

Chris pulled the car into a parking spot near the rowboats. He turned and put his arm on the back of the seat, leaning toward his brother. "Listen, I can't possibly know what you're feeling, Zach. And I can't imagine the pain you live with, either." He glanced at the lake. "I wish we'd insisted on safety that day. . . ."

Zach nodded. "Yeah. Pure stupidity."

"Well, I bear the responsibility. I know that."

"No, we're all guilty . . . we should've known Suzy couldn't swim. She never had a chance." Zach pushed his door open and climbed out.

Chris got out on his side and quickened his pace to catch up.

Armed with the hatchet, Zach strode to

the boats and knelt on the ground. "Hey, it's still here!"

He chopped away at a small cube of ice-encrusted snow and debris, the glint of gold at its center. "Let's get this home and thaw it out."

Zach was more intense than Chris had ever seen him, cradling the chunk of ice and snow like a trophy. He carefully set it in an old cooler in the trunk, and they drove back home.

Together they entered the house quietly, hoping not to run into their mother. Zach carried the cooler upstairs. Chris followed behind him, unwinding his scarf as he trudged up the stairs.

He found Zach in the bathroom, running water over the block of ice.

"You could just wait — it would melt on its own."

Zach paid him no mind, intent on his mission.

Chris hung around, hoping Zach wouldn't be devastated to find an earring or coin or something of even lesser value stuck in there.

Someone turned on a radio downstairs. "Close the door," Zach whispered tersely. "Lock it!" He looked pale now, desperate.

Chris frowned momentarily, worried. What

if he *was* right and this whole thing turned out to be nothing?

He shuddered at the memory — Suzy Fisher sitting in the rowboat, her white prayer cap strings floating in the breeze as she and Zach rowed to the middle of the lake. . . .

"Look!" Zach said now, gently extracting something from the small remaining hunk of ice. "Here it is." He turned off the water and held up the gold bracelet.

Chris leaned closer to inspect it. He could hardly believe it — the very bracelet Zach had purchased for Suzy, the etched Scripture verse still visible.

"See? I told you!" Zach dangled it triumphantly.

"Better keep it down. Mom'll wonder what's going on."

Zach slipped the bracelet into his pants pocket and told Chris to go and keep Mom occupied while he cleaned the dirt and leaves from the sink. Chris didn't like being his brother's conspirator in this weird project but reluctantly complied.

Downstairs, he found Mom in the kitchen, taking a rare coffee break with her latest issue of *Good Housekeeping*. She offered to make him a sandwich, but he told her he was glad to make his own. While he leaned into the refrigerator and pulled out ingredients, she asked, "How's Zach doing, do you think?"

Chris hesitated. Part of him wanted to unload everything, all his worries about Zach's obsessions with Suzy, her photograph, and now the bracelet. But he didn't want to worry their mother, who had enough to be concerned about with three older sons away at college.

"Zach's a little better, I think."

"I offered to buy him a scrapbook for all his mementos of Suzy — the photo, the revival meeting flyer you were handing out when you met her, the newspaper clippings. But he's really defensive about that bulletin board of his."

"I know." Chris stacked roast beef, Swiss cheese, and lettuce between two pieces of bread.

"How long has it been now?" Mom asked.

Chris sighed, his appetite suddenly gone. "Seven months." *Seven long months.* How long would it be until Zach was himself again?

In the backseat of Jonathan Fisher's Rambler Marlin, Rhoda began to doubt her resolve. Her brother James was behind the wheel and Cousin Jonathan sat in the passenger seat beside him, issuing nonstop instructions and advice as if he'd had a license all his life. Feeling the wheels slide across the icy road once more — and her stomach slide, too — Rhoda wished she had waited to ride with a more experienced driver.

It was James who'd egged her on, saying it would be good for her to ride along while Jonathan gave him driving instruction. James had applied for his permit even before purchasing a car, so he was one step ahead of her — legally able to practice with a licensed driver. All Rhoda could do in the backseat was grab the door handle and hang on for dear life.

"That's right. Now tap the brakes gradually. Never slam them on a slick road, or —"

Too late. Seeing the T-intersection ahead, James had already hit the brakes, and the car spun around. Rhoda cried out and gripped the seat in front of her, sure they were about to crash. Instead, the car straightened and rammed nose first into the pile of plowed snow at the edge of the road, cushioning their stop. Rhoda felt queasy and wondered if this was how it felt to spin around in one of those carnival rides she'd seen at the Lancaster County fair.

James tried to back the car out of the snow,

but the wheels squealed and spun.

Jonathan put on his hat. "I'll get out and push." He let himself out and positioned himself on one side of the car, leaning down with hands against the hood. He pushed and James gave it gas, but still the wheels spun. Giving up, Jonathan motioned to James. "Come and push on the other side. We'll need to get 'er rocking. Rhoda, you'll have to take the wheel."

Rhoda was startled. "What? No. I don't —"

"You won't be driving. Just hold the wheel and push on the gas pedal when I tell you."

Rhoda couldn't believe it. This was not at all how she had imagined her first time "driving" a car. Feeling shaky, she climbed out of the back and slid into the driver's seat. She checked the rearview mirror. The Kraybills' yard was behind her across the intersection. She could see the snowman and small fort the children had built earlier in the week. She was relieved the family was not home to witness this scene and that no other cars — or carriages — were approaching.

She rolled down the window to better hear Jonathan as James took up his position on the other side of the vehicle. Both men began pushing in rhythm.

"When I tell you, give it a little gas, Rhoda,"

245

Jonathan called. "Not too hard."

"Jah . . ." Rhoda answered. But she had never pushed a gas pedal before. How would she know how hard to press it?

"Okay, push!"

Rhoda did, but the car stuttered to a halt. She'd hit the brake pedal instead.

"Sorry!"

She saw Jonathan shake his head and James roll his eyes. *Hey, I wasn't the one who got us stuck in the snowbank!* This time, she'd be ready. She checked the rearview mirror again and then glanced down, lifting her hems slightly and poising her right boot directly over the gas pedal. Again, the men pushed.

"All right . . . now!"

Rhoda pressed — hard. The car lurched away from the men and flew backward across the road. She heard James grunt. Saw a blur as James fell face first into the snow. She whipped her head up to look in the rearview mirror . . . just as the car plowed into the Kraybills' yard. She had only a second to glimpse the snowman — jaunty hat, carrot nose, and coal smile — before she flattened him.

The car shuddered to a stop as Rhoda found the brake. She squeezed her eyes shut, humiliated. Her first time behind the wheel, and she already had her first fatality. She shook her head. She would definitely wait until spring to learn to drive.

Reuben felt a certain weariness on this Lord's Day morning, which was accompanied by more than a few aches and pains, the result of fighting an exceptionally spirited horse that had protested yesterday's first-time hitching. His knees ached when he pulled himself out of bed. Later, when hailed by Nan's best friend, Rebekah Yoder, his back pained him so much he nearly lost his balance while stepping down from the buggy.

Nan had only just mentioned that Rebekah was to meet them along the road, "for church." Sure enough if David's daughter wasn't standing along the roadside, wearing snow boots, her black winter bonnet, and all wrapped up in layers, waiting.

Now, here's an enthusiastic soul, he marveled.

Rebekah quickly got settled into the carriage amidst joyful greetings from Nan, who seemed especially glad to see her friend, with Rhoda living at James and Martha's — or so the grapevine had it.

All of them yearning for the world . . .

Picking up the reins, he considered what

an upheaval Rebekah's going to church with them would cause for David Yoder's household. He considered his own family's present disruption — Rhoda's having left in a huff — which had more than added to Betsy's pain of loss. *Dear wife of mine . . .*

The two girls chattered happily in the second seat, talking in low tones. He leaned toward Betsy and whispered, "David Yoder might come a-callin'."

"I was thinkin' the selfsame thing."

"Nothing to fear, love." He reached for her gloved hand. "God is at work."

She smiled sweetly, flashing her pretty blue eyes.

When they arrived at the host family's farm and the *hostler* boys had unhitched the horse and led it to the stable, Reuben got himself situated in the house meeting, mighty pleased to see Elias King sitting in his frock coat a few rows away. He'd thought Elias was leaning toward the tractor folk, but so far, apparently not.

Curious, he gave a discreet glance toward the kitchen area, where the nursing mothers congregated, and there was Rosanna sitting with Nan and Rebekah, who each held an infant. *Rosanna and Elias's twins,* he thought. Fatherhood was a heavy responsibility, Reuben knew, one that made a man more aware of his need for divine guidance. Reuben prayed that even today the Lord would call Elias to repent and open his heart to the Lord and Savior.

Betsy sat near the front of the large room, where the wall partitions had been removed, making a spacious enough area to accommodate the growing number of members.

Already, a good many of the youth had indicated they planned to join church come fall, after baptism instruction next summer, as she knew Nan would. And now it looked as though Rebekah Yoder, of all people, had an interest, as well.

Betsy was happy to see both Rosanna and Elias King in attendance. Rosanna especially appeared to be listening intently to all Preacher Manny was saying, her eyes fixed on his face. And later, when Elias went forward to surrender his life to God, tears streamed down Rosanna's cheeks. Tears filled Betsy's eyes, as well. How she wished she might see her own Nellie Mae heed the call one day.

Soon . . . very soon, they'll all have to make up their minds.

Betsy bowed her head and prayed silently. Along with Nellie Mae, Rhoda topped her mental list for prayer — poor, mixed-up girl.

Surely she would tire quickly of the world.

She thought again of Nellie Mae's heartfelt request for prayer. *May Nellie find you as her Lord and Savior in your way and in your time. In Jesus' name. Amen.*

A new snowstorm began to squall around noon, blotting out the edges of the barren cornfield and nearly obliterating Nellie's view of the barn and woodshed from her spot at the kitchen window. Sighing, she hoped Dat, Mamma, and Nan would arrive safely home from the New Order Preaching service. She fixed herself a light meal using cold cuts and some pickled beets and hard-boiled eggs, because it was the Lord's Day. She had never questioned the unspoken rule of no cooking or baking on Sunday, simply taking it in her stride. As an avid baker, she believed the first day of the week was something of a fast day for her, since she was giving up that domestic task most dear to her.

Sitting alone at the table, she looked over at Suzy's vacant spot, left so even when the whole family came together to eat, out of respect for her sister's life . . . and her death.

"It's hard to believe you're gone sometimes," she whispered. "The truth of it is slowly dawning on me, though."

Considering her losses, Nellie contemplated Caleb and the evening's Singing. If she chose to attend, she faced the prospect of going alone and having to drive herself back home. Caleb wouldn't ask her out tonight — nor any night for ever so long, she realized anew.

She fidgeted, thinking about going through the whole winter long, and possibly the springtime, too, without Caleb near. How she missed him!

No sense even bothering to go to any of the youth gatherings, Nellie decided. She would simply stay home and keep Mamma good company.

Rhoda was thankful to ride home from the Beachy church with James and Martha and the children instead of having to walk, what with the blowing snow already creating near-blizzard conditions. Balancing Jimmy on her knee in the front seat, next to Martha, who held Matty, she stared out the window. The wind was so fierce it seemed to lash the color right out of the sky. The stone walls along the roadside were nearly impossible to make out.

She thought again of her Buick, getting snowed on over at the Kraybills'. *So good of them to let me keep it there.*

Had she been less impulsive, she wouldn't

have made the jump to getting the car before the license, somewhat equivalent to getting the cart before the horse. Even so, she had what she wanted now. Come summer, she could drive a whole carload of folk to the Beachy meetinghouse.

Rhoda liked the idea of a separate church building, as opposed to the same old approach to things — turning the first level of a house into one enormous room and cramming in two hundred grown-ups and oodles of babies and children.

To her way of thinking, it made perfect sense to live in your home and attend Preaching in a separate church building. It wasn't that she appreciated the sermon or the prayers and hymns any more — none of that was terribly important to her. Her mind had been on the several good-looking young men sitting over on the right side. She knew which ones were married and which weren't based on whether or not they wore a beard. Courting-age men were clean-shaven and sat with others their age, rather than next to their fathers — not at all different from both the old church and the New Order, come to think of it.

Won't I be something? Rhoda thought, anxious for winter to roll into spring. Anxious, too, to drop a few more pounds. Then she'd show the fellows what they'd missed!

Nellie watched from the front room window, choking back tears as she kept looking for Dat's buggy. The afternoon snow was so heavy, she could hardly see the road. Strangely, she felt the urge to pray for her family's safety. In silence, she asked the Lord God to guide the horse home if Dat had any difficulty directing with the reins in these white-out conditions.

Recalling Dat sometimes concluded his spoken prayers with a grateful addition, she said right out, "And I'll thank you, Lord. Amen."

She sat on the wide windowsill, reaching into her pocket for Suzy's Kapp strings. Holding them up to the frosty window, she caressed them. "Oh, Suzy . . . you'd prob'ly giggle if you knew I kept these."

Clutching the long, ribbonlike ties, she held them against her heart and wept. It had been quite some time since she'd felt so helpless to stop the flow of tears. Missing Suzy and not finding much solace at all in her prayer, Nellie rose and went to the next-door Dawdi Haus, going from one east-facing window to another, her heart in her throat. She wouldn't let herself think that something dreadful had happened to her family. In due time, Nellie returned to the kitchen of the main house to make some hot tea, hoping to get her mind on other things.

Opening the cupboard where Mamma kept her many herbal teas, Nellie pulled down a package of chamomile leaves. She glanced out the window yet again as the wind shook the house. Then she set about adding logs to the woodstove and brewing some nice hot tea in an attempt to calm herself.

By the time Mamma walked in the back door, Nellie had already drunk three cups of tea, waiting for the herb to take effect. In her relief, Nellie was taken by surprise at the sight of Caleb's sister coming in the door along with Nan, snowflakes dusting her shoulders and black candlesnuffer hat.

Well, for goodness' sake! Given the weather, she had not expected Rebekah to follow through with her plan to attend Manny's church, though Nellie was glad for another opportunity to see her again so soon. Rebekah and Nan sat down at the table for some tea, as well, after removing their coats, scarves, and boots and laying them out near the stove to dry.

Dat stood with his back to it. "The Lord saw fit to spare us out in that storm," he remarked. "I daresay only by His providence did we make it home."

Mamma nodded, going to run water over her cold hands. "Thank the dear Lord."

Nan and Rebekah were talking quietly, and Nellie heard bits and pieces of their conversation without intending to. Rebekah revealed to Nan that she'd slipped out of the house early that morning, not having said a word about her plans.

"You mean your parents don't know where you are?" Nan asked softly, her blue eyes wide.

"I didn't tell them."

"Nee, you don't mean it!"

"Well, I'd never have gotten out of the house today, otherwise."

Nan nodded. "I s'pose."

"No supposing 'bout it — I'd be sittin' at home today."

Nan glanced over at Nellie. "If the snow stops, would ya want to go with us to the Singing?"

She knew better than to ask which one. Undoubtedly Nan was referring to the new church group. Her sister wasn't about to stop inviting Nellie to the various youth functions sanctioned by Preacher Manny. "Well, not this time."

"Oh, Nellie Mae . . . that's what you always say. Won't you give it a chance?" Nan pleaded.

"Jah, come with us to the Singing," Rebekah chimed in. "Please?"

Nellie had no intention of succumbing to their pleading. "I'll drop you two off, how's that?"

"Sure, if the weather improves," Nan reminded.

She'd momentarily forgotten about the storm, so intrigued was she by Rebekah's being there against her father's wishes. *Ever so risky to go out in this.*

Pouring more tea, Nellie was struck by Rebekah's brave stand against her father's position on Preacher Manny's group.

Will Caleb be as tenacious . . . for our love?

CHAPTER 23

Caleb opened his eyes to the coming twilight. He'd fallen asleep in the haymow after going up there to consider his plan for that night's Singing, supposing travel was even possible. The insidious cold had awakened him, and he wriggled through the hay hole, dropping down to the stable area below.

Outside, the wind and snow had ceased, though the impending dusk signaled suppertime — and very soon the Singing. Caleb wanted to make it clear to his father where he was headed, not wanting to put any suspicions into Daed's mind about Nellie Mae this night.

Despite the strange, nearly tangible calm that now prevailed, the temperature was still bitter cold enough to keep some of the youth from showing up. He couldn't help wondering if Nellie might venture out. If not, this certainly would be the best time to seek out Susannah and invite her riding afterward

. . . if she came, that is. *Best be getting on with what I must do — the sooner the better.*

When Mamm called everyone for supper, Caleb hurried to wash up before taking his place at the trestle table. Tomorrow at breakfast, he would be ready to speak up to his father about his intention to marry Reuben Fisher's daughter next November. He hoped Daed wouldn't insist he seek out Susannah Lapp more than one time.

Daed walked to the table and pulled out his chair. He stood there, his hand clenched on the back of the chair. "Rebekah's still among the missin'?"

Mamm nodded. "Haven't seen hide nor hair of her since breakfast."

Daed looked at the rest of them lining both sides of the table. "What 'bout any of yous? Did ya see her leave the house earlier?"

Caleb and his siblings shook their heads.

"Run off, maybe?" Daed's flippant response surprised Caleb.

Mamm grimaced and made a point of folding her hands to wait for the silent prayer. The fact that she uncharacteristically revealed her emotions demonstrated how put out she was at Rebekah, who knew better than not to say where she was heading — especially on the Lord's Day.

"Oh, I wouldn't worry," said Caleb's older

258

sister Leah. "She's prob'ly over at one cousin's or 'nother."

"No doubt," offered Emmie, another sister. "Hopefully she's out of this cold."

Caleb didn't know what to think of Daed's taut expression and furrowed brow. His father clearly suspected something intolerable, and Caleb hoped for Rebekah's sake that she could give an acceptable explanation.

Nellie was more than happy to take her sister and Rebekah Yoder to the barn Singing, two miles away. She delighted in Nan's obvious excitement, knowing how much it meant for her and Rebekah to spend the day together. But there had been no mention as to how the night would end. Would Rebekah simply let a boy from the new church take her out riding and then back to her father's house? If she was somehow caught with a boy from Preacher Manny's group, wouldn't she be met with even further disapproval from her father?

None of that had been discussed within Nellie's earshot, but Nellie knew both girls were sensible enough to have a plan. Still, because of Caleb's father's tendency toward annoyance, she hoped Rebekah knew what she was getting into. *Sure glad it's not me,* she thought.

Rebekah's voice broke the stillness as they slowly made their way through the ice and snow. "I have to thank you both for welcoming me so kindly."

"Any time," said Nan. "Ain't that so, Nellie Mae?"

She glanced at the two of them sitting to her left on the front seat of Dat's enclosed buggy. "Awful nice you could visit Nan's church today."

"Well, you oughta try it sometime, too," Rebekah said. "Honestly, I think you'd like it."

"Oh, Nellie's already been there." Nan gave a little laugh.

Nellie had to smile at their constant efforts to convert her. *Doesn't Rebekah know what would happen to Caleb and me if I went back?*

"My father won't know what to think when he hears I've visited 'that brazen bunch,'" Rebekah announced.

"Brazen?" Nan was aghast.

"Oh jah — and far worse."

Nan covered her ears playfully. "I can't bear to hear more."

Rebekah sighed. "I don't know how I'll make it through what's ahead of me tomorrow mornin'. . . ."

"You'll catch it but good," Nan said sadly.

"I can only imagine. . . ."

"Well, if you ever need a place —"

"If it comes to that," Nellie broke in, thinking what a big to-do it would be if Rebekah ended up staying with them. *One more black mark against the Fishers.*

Nan was the one who sighed now. "Jah, I s'pose. I just wish there wasn't such tension among the People. It's terrible."

"Can't be helped, I daresay," Rebekah said. "I believe I've found what I've been needin' — what I've been looking for."

"You too?" asked Nellie. Out of the corner of her eye, she saw Rebekah nod her head.

"I've never felt such peace," Rebekah admitted. "I want to go again next Sunday."

"Fine with me," Nan said. "And I'm sure Dat and Mamma won't mind one bit, either."

"Well, we'll see if my parents even let me out of the house!" Rebekah sat up straighter. "If I tell them where I've been, that is."

Sounds like poor Caleb!

The golden light from Preacher Manny's farmhouse windows beamed a welcome, and Nellie reined the horse into the driveway, aware of several cars parked along the side.

"Looks like some of the Beachys are here, too," Nan said. "We'll have a good crowd."

"Your father wouldn't hear of you buyin' a

car, now, would he, Nan?" asked Rebekah.

"*Nix kumm raus* — nothing doin'."

"I thought as much." Rebekah turned and thanked Nellie for bringing them, asking her yet again if she wouldn't consider staying. "It'd be fun — something different, for sure."

"Denki, but not this time."

"Well, *another* time, maybe?" Nan piped up.

"Go on, both of you." Nellie laughed and held the reins steadily as they climbed down from the buggy and waved back at her, heading toward the light of the two-story barn.

Have yourselves some fun . . . before the axe falls, she thought, hoping Rebekah's risk would be worth the pain of David Yoder's displeasure.

Tugging the reins, Caleb steered the horse into the lane leading to the barn, glancing at the empty spot next to him where Nellie Mae had sat before tonight. He groaned inwardly.

For a moment, he hoped Susannah Lapp might, indeed, have stayed home on this miserable night. But if that was the case, he would have to wait yet another two weeks to accomplish what his father had demanded.

Jumping down from the open buggy, he

was glad he'd worn boots, since the snow was midcalf where he tied up the horse to the fence post. He glanced at the sky, noting the moon's brightness.

To light the way, he thought, wishing he might have borrowed Cousin Aaron's covered carriage so as not to be readily seen with Susannah. *So as not to be found out by dearest Nellie.*

When the time was right, he would explain everything to Nellie. He hoped that she would be understanding.

Caleb entered the barn, noticing right away that only a few boys had shown up thus far — odd to see far more girls than boys present. Undoubtedly some of the fellows would be taking two or more sisters home instead of pairing up.

The weather was but one factor in the low attendance. Truly, he suspected the Singing at Preacher Manny's had drawn some of the Old Order teens away, though Susannah wouldn't be one of them.

A fleeting thought crossed his mind, and he wondered if his "missing" sister might be over with the New Order youth, looking for new courting options, maybe. Daed would lock her up, and mighty fast, if she were so bold-faced. Besides, he couldn't imagine Rebekah doing such a thing.

Moseying over to stand with the other young men, he was filled with sudden trepidation when he spotted Susannah Lapp in a cluster of girls, laughing and obviously the center of attention. She wore her blond hair looser in front than he'd ever noticed before, although it was still pulled back into a bun. Even so, the look was suggestive for a deacon's daughter.

Nevertheless, he found the style to be quite appealing, although he refused to stare, lest anyone notice and think he was flirting.

Looking around for Nellie Mae, he already viewed himself as a betrayer. Yet he must follow through with his father's bidding. As the Lord commanded Judas — what you must do, do quickly.

Part of him hoped to goodness Nellie might quickly appear in the barn door, arriving with some of her cousins. That would surely save him. But the more the boys stood around joking and laughing, passing the time till they were to sit down and begin the actual singing part of the evening, the less likely it seemed Nellie would brave the weather. Even if she did come, they could do no more than trade smiles because of their necessary parting. *Soon to come to a happy end, after tonight,* he thought.

A band of moonlight shone through the

uppermost barn window, high in the rafters. Caleb managed to make his way to the long table to sit on the boys' side, not wanting to be situated directly across from Susannah. It was best if she didn't catch him looking her way more than, say, once or twice during the course of the songs. It would make things easier in the long run.

During the second hymn a few more girls trickled in, taking their seats among the other young women. Still no sight of Nellie Mae, however.

Recalling the first time he'd ever driven her home, he could scarcely continue singing. She had been so sweet that night . . . so trusting of him, letting him talk a blue streak while listening like a good wife — er, sweetheart — should. She had taken his heart by surprise in every way.

Then, suddenly . . . if Susannah wasn't looking directly at him this minute. He glanced away, nearly embarrassed, before remembering that he should probably look back at her.

She's even more forward than I thought. . . .
The songs carried them through the next hour or so and then the pairing up began. Quite by accident, Caleb literally bumped into Susannah before he was ready, although Susannah, wide-eyed and all smiles, didn't

seem to find it a surprise at all. No, he sensed she'd planned it right down to the second.

All the same, he walked with her toward the side of the barn, where the couples liked to either sit or stand, talking until it was time to go riding.

"How're you doin', Susannah?"

"Ever so nice to see ya here tonight, Caleb Yoder."

He knew she meant it was nice seeing him here *alone,* but he forced himself not to recoil at her flirting. She was, after all, right pretty, and it wasn't a hardship to listen to her talk, her face aglow with his attention.

"Is your . . . well, is Nellie Mae around?"

"You mean is she comin' tonight?"

She nodded ever so sheepishly at first and then her expression changed. "Might be too cold for her, jah?" She batted her pretty blue eyes. Honestly, the girl was flirting up a storm, and Caleb was seized with a desire to run.

She planted herself near him, leaning ever closer as she talked about one frivolous thing after another. All the while he could think only of Nellie Mae and how *she* shaped her words and ideas. The things she enjoyed discussing with him were so much more interesting, and he always felt he was talking with a friend, if not an equal.

He listened politely to Susannah, forcing an occasional smile.

Susannah was babbling about the Fishers now — something about Nellie's bakery shop. "All the fancy folk over there have no doubt put a wedge 'tween the two of you, jah?"

Well, it sure hadn't helped matters any, that was certain. His parents were livid about the whole notion of Nellie catering to Englischers. In fact, he wasn't so keen on it himself.

"No doubt your father is disturbed 'bout Nellie's little bakery shop. But really, Caleb, I don't blame Nellie one bit. She wants to help support her family, jah?"

Caleb's face grew warm.

Susannah touched his arm, walking backward slowly, toward the hay bales, as if she wanted him to follow. For the moment, he did. She stood close enough for him to smell her perfume.

"Of course, I don't blame your father, either. After all, we need to uphold the traditions of our forefathers, ya know, not follow after the world."

He shrugged, ready for this conversation to end. He'd heard enough. Then it struck him hard. Why *was* Susannah so interested in talking about Nellie's bakery shop?

"Aw, Susannah, Nellie's not responsible for

any wrongdoing." He observed her closely. "Nobody knows who placed the newspaper ad."

Her face looked innocent. She was smiling a broad, full smile that stretched clear across her heart-shaped face. But her eyes revealed something else.

"Susannah?"

She folded her delicate hands, her eyes brightening as her eyebrows rose. "Jah, Caleb?"

"Do *you* know who placed that ad?"

In the split second before her face fell, Caleb saw it again. Deception.

"Why . . . Caleb. Why would I?"

Their eyes locked, and she gave him a knowing wink.

Caleb grabbed her arm. "You did it, didn't you, Susannah? You took out the ad for Nellie's Simple Sweets!"

She opened her mouth to protest but stopped. Glancing down at his grip, she smiled. "You have such strong hands, Caleb. And I do like strong men."

Immediately he released her. "So you admit it, then?"

Her eyelashes fluttered again. "Ask yourself why Nellie Mae didn't simply close up the shop when all those Englischers started linin' up. In her heart, she's leanin' toward the fancy, Caleb, and you know it." She touched his arm lightly. "Might as well face it: Nellie Mae Fisher will never, *ever* be able to please your father."

Caleb was stunned at what lengths this girl was willing to go to stir up trouble for Nellie and her family. "Nellie and me — that's none of your concern!" With that, he turned away, intending to leave Susannah standing alone.

Just that quick, he raised his gaze and spied Nellie Mae standing near the door, her brown eyes piercing his.

His brain was scrambled; his beloved had arrived late. What had she observed? How long had she been there? He groaned, wanting to talk to her, to set her mind at ease.

Oh, Nellie, it's not what you think. . . .

Fast as a flicker, she turned her back, as if to shun him. Then, making a beeline for the barn door, she hurried into the night.

Walking toward the other side of the barn, he wanted to run after her but hesitated, his father's battle cry ringing in his ears. The hay bales seemed to taunt him as young couples blurred alongside them in his vision.

No!

With all that was in him, he had to right this wrong with Nellie . . . not caring what the grapevine might trumpet back to his father's ears. In the whole world, there was only one girl for him, and Nellie had to believe that. *Now,* lest she trust what her eyes had witnessed and not what was truth.

Images of what Nellie might have seen raced through his mind — Susannah and himself over in the corner so privately. The brazen girl had touched him more than once, and as if in a dance of sorts, she'd followed each time he'd stepped away.

Caleb winced.

Even though it would mean disobeying his father once again, he knew he could not break Nellie's heart. He must pursue her.

Not caring what Susannah or anyone else thought, he jogged across the wide-plank boards. He dashed out the barn door into the bitter night, looking to the right and left. But he had waited too long. There went the Fisher carriage, moving rapidly away on the snowy roads.

Himmel . . . He was disgusted with himself. *You are a fool, Caleb Yoder.*

CHAPTER 24

The white spray of moonlight on newfallen snow could not have been more untimely. Nellie longed for the concealment of darkness as she rushed home with the horse and carriage.

Caleb's flirting with Susannah? What on earth?

She'd deliberated coming to the Singing at all after taking Nan and Rebekah clear to the other side of Lilly Road. But then, not wanting to spend the evening at home, with Rhoda gone to James and Martha's, she'd decided in favor of the Old Order Singing. Slipping in ever so late, her eyes had searched for Caleb. Oh, the pain in her heart when she had finally seen him over in the corner with Susannah, all privatelike.

She wanted to cry; she wanted to holler, too. She didn't know which feeling to express, because she simply could not understand what she'd witnessed. For sure and for certain, Caleb and Susannah had looked like a courting couple!

She tried to remember precisely what she'd observed — the interplay of flirtatious glances, not just Susannah's, but Caleb's, too. She hadn't known for sure how to interpret the dreadful scene, but Caleb had looked mighty guilty when his eyes had met hers.

She'd never before had any reason to distrust him. Yet there he'd been with Susannah . . . why? Had he thought this a good night to cozy up to the deacon's daughter, since it must have appeared that Nellie wasn't coming? Had he been seeing Susannah all along?

No, surely not. How could she think such a thing of her darling?

Then she realized it must have been Susannah's doing; the girl had always made her interest in Caleb perfectly plain. Yet as Nellie fretted and fumed, she didn't want to think that way about it, either, presuming Caleb to be vulnerable to Susannah's wiles.

Like Samson and Delilah . . .

Nellie tried to shrug off the comparison, only to begin to weep so hard she could hardly see her way home.

Caleb rode all over creation, alone in his

courting buggy, wishing there was a way to smooth things over with Nellie immediately. Even so, he knew he deserved to feel the way he did. Nellie had fled from the barn, surely believing he'd been caught red-handed. She probably thought little of him now . . . and rightly so.

He drove aimlessly, his mind on Nellie and her sweetness, wondering what it would be like to kiss her soft lips someday . . . if he'd ever have the chance.

Caleb finally arrived home. He eyed the tobacco shed, his worry-sick mind wandering. Although he'd never mentioned it to his father, he thought it wise to tear down the dilapidated outbuilding and build a new one. Daed's approach to it — or at least what he'd done in the past — was to buttress the whole thing, basically propping it up so it wouldn't fall down.

His father and grandfather before him had always raised tobacco. There had been some talk against growing the crop lately, though. Tongues wagged and word got around mighty fast when it was a preacher who was declaring it a sin to raise tobacco. Surprisingly enough, a good number of farmers were in agreement with the outspoken Preacher Manny.

He heard some commotion behind him as

a courting buggy pulled up to the front of the house, over near the mailbox. He was far enough into the lane to be somewhat disguised, he knew, and a quick glance over his shoulder told him it was his long-lost sister, saying good-bye to a beau. Had she been with him all day?

She was obviously interested in the fellow, for she stood near the buggy, looking up at him as they talked. Then he jumped down and walked her partway to the house.

After Rebekah had gone inside, Caleb let the harness slide down his horse and then heaved it off. Taking his time unhitching the buggy, he pondered his sister's desertion for the day, so unlike her.

Where *had* Rebekah gone? It was none of his business, really, yet he wondered how she had managed to stay safe and warm on this brutally cold day. Now that he was stabling his horse, he realized how near frozen he was himself. Rebekah could not have spent the day out in this.

He made his way through the stable area and pushed the barn door open. Heading across the way, he heard the crunch of snow beneath his boots, glad he'd worn an extra pair of woolen socks. As he entered the back door, he heard voices — Daed's and Rebekah's. This was no time to emerge from the utility room.

"I know where you've been!"

Caleb was stunned at the sting in his father's voice.

Total silence from Rebekah.

"You never think before you act, do you, daughter?"

Caleb cowered, concealing his presence.

"If you were out where I think you were, you ain't welcome in this house!"

Wisely Rebekah remained silent. *As a lamb brought to slaughter . . .*

"Did you attend the New Order church today?" came the angry inquiry.

"I will not lie, Daed."

Caleb slumped.

A crack — the sound of his father's fist slamming against the table, the one he'd made decades before. Surely this blow had split the wood.

Caleb could see there was no talking to Daed tonight about his own decision. No, he would bow out, and quickly, hoping for a reasonable discussion at a later time.

"Get out!" Daed shouted. "I do not want to see the likes of you."

No! Caleb wanted to defend his sister, but once again he felt trapped beneath his father's dominion . . . and his desire to protect any future with Nellie Mae.

What will Rebekah do?

"Jah, I was disobedient," his sister said meekly. "But I choose to follow my Lord Jesus Christ."

"Then begone from my sight!"

Caleb heard sniffling, then sobs, as Rebekah dashed up the stairs to pack a bag in submission to their father's unreasonable punishment.

I won't let her flee alone into the night, he decided, slipping out the door to hitch up his poor tired horse yet again.

Nellie's tears were nearly dry by the time she arrived home. She unhitched the carriage from the horse and left the enclosed buggy near the barn for Dat to tend to in the morning. Refusing to give Caleb another thought, she led their best driving horse into the stable.

Once inside, she hurried to her room, where she sat for the longest time, unable to move.

She heard a creak in the rafters and finally removed her heavy bonnet. Then she reverently removed her Kapp and slowly prepared for bed, slipping into a fresh nightgown. Oh, how she wished the sights of this evening could be shed as easily as her clothes. Now that she was home, she wondered if Nan was back from the New Order gathering. She longed to share her heartache with someone, and Nan was the most natural choice.

Moving silently down the hall, she stopped at what had always been Rhoda and Nan's bedroom. *So many changes lately,* she thought, poking her head in the door.

Seeing her sister already tucked into bed and thinking what a comfort it would be to simply slip in next to her, Nellie did just that. She was careful not to lean too hard into the mattress on Rhoda's former side so as not to awaken her sister. The warmth from Nan's slumbering body soothed her as she settled herself beneath the heavy layer of blankets and quilts.

Then, lying as still as could be, she realized she could not sleep. The image of Caleb's handsome face rose up in the darkness — the light in his eyes as he'd talked to Susannah . . . the set of his lips, his whole body in alignment with hers, or so it seemed. Would she ever be able to erase the vision of her beloved talking so intently with Susannah? Standing so close . . .

Every breath she took was filled with missing him. Yet he'd deceived her so. She groaned inwardly, struggling to hold herself together in the bed where her older sisters had often talked late into the night, before

Rhoda got the ridiculous urge to chase after the fancy.

Nellie recalled the fervent hope in Rebekah's face — and the upturn of her determined mouth — as she departed for the Singing tonight. What would come of Rebekah's departure from the Old Order for a full day was yet to be known.

She's fortunate to have such a faithful friend in Nan.

Nellie slid her hand toward her sleeping sister, stopping when her fingertips touched the edge of Nan's gown, spread out against the flannel bed sheet.

The hope of sharing her heartbreak with Nan faded with each of her sister's rhythmic breaths, and Nellie missed Suzy more than ever.

Rebekah's sadness resonated with Caleb's own this night. He sensed it in his sister's slumped posture as she sat next to him in the carriage, even though she showed no other outward sign of grief. As far as he could tell, her resolve was remarkably intact as they made their way to the Fishers'. "You sure Nellie's . . . er, Nan's house is where you want to stay tonight?"

She was quick to nod. "Ever so sure." Her teeth chattered.

He endured the frigid temperature as best he could, dreading the return ride, chilled as he was to the bone. But Caleb felt he deserved whatever punishment the elements meted out. Hadn't he broken Nellie's heart tonight?

That he hadn't done so intentionally offered no consolation. To think he was heading right now to her father's house, to shine his flashlight on her window as he had done once before, this time to get her attention for his outcast sister's sake.

He gripped the reins and tried to will away what had transpired earlier at the Singing — the searing pain in Nellie's pretty eyes.

"You feelin' awkward 'bout this? Taking me to the enemy, so to speak?" Rebekah glanced his way.

"No." He wouldn't let on precisely how awkward the whole situation was.

"Seems kinda odd, really. And Nan's goin' to be surprised, I daresay."

He considered that. "Well, maybe not."

"S'pose you're right." After all, Rebekah had spent the entire day with the Fishers. Surely Nan could guess what Daed's response to that might be.

"Did the whole Fisher family attend the new church?" he asked, not wanting to come right out and inquire after Nellie

Mae's whereabouts.

"All but Nellie."

So there it was. His sweetheart was being true to the Old Ways . . . and to him.

But now? What would happen between them? Would she accept his explanation, once given?

He couldn't allow himself to ponder that now. Truth be told, he must first see to it that Rebekah was safely settled for the night — take on the responsibility of a good brother, something Daed had unknowingly handed off to him. He shook his head at the memory of their father's permitting things to escalate out of hand. As far as Caleb was concerned, it was Daed's fault that Rebekah was out on her ear tonight.

Rebekah was still in her running-around years, not having joined the church yet, so why should she be punished for visiting Preacher Manny's church?

None of this made a lick of sense.

At last they reached the end of the Fishers' drive, where he left the horse and buggy, his sister still perched inside. Caleb crept up the lane and shone his flashlight high onto Nellie's window. He waited, holding the light there, wondering how long it would be before he might attract her attention.

He waited with no response. He thought of

knocking, but he didn't want to wake Nellie's parents, who had no doubt been asleep for hours.

Again he shined the light, leaving it poised there. Then, when Nellie did not appear, he moved the flashlight around in circles, still shining its white beam on the glass. When even that failed to bring her to the window, he rotated the light back and forth between the two west-facing windows.

Perhaps she was ignoring him. He certainly couldn't blame her for that. Fact was, she had not so much as peeked out from behind the shade to see who was standing down in the snow, shivering beneath his long johns and heaviest wool coat.

"Caleb!" called his sister from the road. "I'm terribly cold."

I'll try one more thing before I wake the whole house. Quickly, he turned off the flashlight and leaned down to scoop up a small bit of snow. Then, rolling it even smaller, he tossed it lightly so as not to make a loud thud.

He waited, growing more concerned for his sister as the seconds ticked past. Twice more he threw a snowball.

Could it be that Nellie had decided to give him a taste of his own medicine and ridden home with someone else? Caleb dismissed the niggling thought. Not his Nellie. Even so, where was she, if not sound asleep in her bed?

Nan started and rolled over, apparently surprised to encounter Nellie lying there next to her, wide awake. "I didn't mean to scare you. I simply couldn't be alone." Nellie sighed, wanting to open her heart to her sister. Yet she hesitated, wondering if she should unburden her woes when Nan was still smarting from her recent breakup.

"I'm glad you're here." Nan inched closer. "What's wrong, Nellie?"

"Caleb's betrayed me," Nellie said softly.

"Oh, dear sister . . ."

Then the misery of her discovery began to pour out of her like a dam breaking apart. She told Nan everything, beginning with the secret meetings at the old mill, walks along the millstream, Caleb's letters, their forbidden love. "We've willfully disobeyed his father, just as you and Rebekah have." She struggled to speak. "And now . . . this . . . with Susannah."

Nan reached over and cupped Nellie's cheek with her hand. "I'm ever so sorry, Nellie. Truly I am."

"After all the planning — for our future together — he ups and does this baffling thing." Nellie could not hold back her tears.

"I never would've believed it if I hadn't seen it with my own eyes. Oh, Nan, it was like he's held a torch for her all this time." She wept so hard, the bed shook. "How could I not have known?"

She thought of the times she'd seen Susannah flirt with Caleb or attempt to during youth gatherings — one hayride in particular, she recalled. And there had been plenty of other times, too. But she had never noted any interest from Caleb toward Susannah — till now.

"Oh . . . it hurts so bad." She clung to Nan, certain her broken heart would never mend.

"Nellie . . . Nellie." Her sister held her as she wept, saying no more, soothing her by stroking her hair.

"Caleb?" Rebekah's voice was laced with worry. It sounded as if she was about to cry.

He hurried back toward the buggy, thankful for the traction of his boots against the hardened snow. "I can't raise anyone. I'm terribly sorry." He leaned against the horse, hugging him for warmth. "Come here, Rebekah." He must not let his sister get so chilled that she became ill. That, on top of being ousted from home, was a trial she should not have to bear.

"This is . . . just awful," she said.

"Don't cry. Your tears will freeze to your face."

She wiped them with her mittened hand.

"I guess we'll just have to knock," he said.

"What if I simply slipped inside?" Rebekah glanced toward the farmhouse. "I know right where Nan's room is. . . . I could go up there . . . try not to startle her."

"Would you be welcome, do ya think?"

She nodded, trembling now as he pressed her against the horse, sandwiching her between himself and the steed. "Nan wouldn't want me to freeze to death."

"Nor would Daed." The words escaped him. Surely their father would not wish for Rebekah to suffer. Why *had* he abandoned her? Had he no concern for his own flesh and blood this bitter night? Caleb could not imagine treating a son or daughter this way.

"Come, sister, I'll walk you to the house."

Rebekah reached for his arm, and he felt the weight of her, though she was ever so slight.

Stepping quietly into Reuben Fisher's enclosed back porch, Caleb felt like an intruder in more ways than one. But getting out of the elements for a few moments was essential now.

"I'll do my best to keep in touch," Caleb whispered. "Somehow we must."

Rebekah only nodded.

Once his sister had stepped into the kitchen and out of sight, he contemplated Nellie's whereabouts once again, hoping she was not still riding around in this cold.

Nellie Mae was a sensible girl. Certainly she was not one to get revenge. She would have headed directly home after their brief encounter at the barn Singing. Doubtless she was here in this house and so deep in slumber — hopefully not weeping — that she hadn't noticed his flashlight on her window.

Caleb consoled himself with that and let himself out of the house as quietly as he'd entered a few minutes before.

A sudden sound in the hallway made Nellie's ears perk up. She strained to listen, and then there was nothing. "Did ya hear that?" she asked Nan.

"It's late . . . could it be Rhoda comin' back?"

"Rhoda's long gone, I daresay," Nellie replied.

More creaking came from outside the bedroom door. Then they heard, "Nan . . . it's me, Rebekah." This brought Nellie and Nan straight up in bed.

"What the world?" Nan leapt onto the cold wooden floor. "Come in. Ach . . . are you all right?"

Caleb's sister sniffled as she entered. "Daed's done kicked me out."

"Oh, you poor girl!" Nan gave her a quick hug.

"My brother Caleb brought me here."

Caleb went home without riding with Susannah?

"I thought I might stay here for —"

"Stay as long as need be," Nan said, still hovering near Rebekah.

Nellie leaned her arms on her knees, astonished at Rebekah's late-night appearance and moved at Nan's loving concern for her friend.

Rebekah sat on the edge of the bed. "I'll try 'n' find somewhere else to stay after tomorrow, though, so you won't be stuck with me."

"Puh, don't be silly. You're welcome here," Nan insisted.

Nellie had an idea and she said it right out, thinking Rebekah might wish for solace from her stressful night and for the comfort of friends, as well. "Nan, let's untuck the bed sheets and lie sideways across this bed . . . you know, like you, Rhoda, Suzy, and I used to."

"When we were just girls?" said Nan.

"Jah, when we were ever so little." She sighed at the thought of the changes the years had brought . . . each broken heart there.

Without another word, they did precisely that, pulling the bedclothes off quickly to remake the bed horizontally. Nellie went to her room to get a third pillow. Then they all crawled into the bed and curled up — Nan and Nellie at the head and foot of the bed, with forlorn Rebekah between them.

CHAPTER 25

"I'm behind on my washing." Rosanna bemoaned the fact as her cousin came in the back door Monday morning.

"Well, here, let me help," Cousin Kate said, reaching for baby Eli.

Grateful, Rosanna hurried downstairs to complete the task of doing the laundry. She'd begun with two loads of the babies' clothes and was now sorting Elias's trousers and long-sleeved colored shirts. She put the clothes into the old wringer washer powered by a small gasoline motor.

Soon she made her way up the stairs and discovered Kate in the front room, swaying slowly as she held Eli, talking quietlike. Rosie, too, was awake now and crying in the playpen, and since it was nearly time for the next feeding, Rosanna went to the kitchen to pick her up. Despite Kate's offer of assistance, Rosanna sensed a real sadness in her cousin — her cheeks drooped and her eyes were swollen. Had she been crying?

Kate didn't return with Eli to the kitchen as Rosanna wished she might. Instead she sat in the rocking chair in the front room and opened her dress to nurse him within view of Rosanna, two rooms away.

Rosanna squelched the lump in her throat. Kate was again willfully ignoring her request that she adhere to the original plan and stop nursing either baby at two months of age, a date that had passed nearly a month ago. She might break down if she didn't keep herself in check — either that or storm in there and tell her cousin what she really thought for once.

Not wanting baby Rosie to sense her frustration, Rosanna breathed deeply and asked the Lord for patience, praying the way Preacher Manny had taught them yesterday at the worship service. Thinking of the wonderful-good gathering, the joyful sermon, and Elias's conversion, she already missed the fellowship of those who'd come to hear the Word of God and were eager to do it. She truly hoped Elias was in favor of returning next Sunday . . . and the next. If so, they'd be joining that church next spring, after council meeting and a day of fasting. Rosanna was so thankful to the Lord for calling her husband as He had her.

Doing her best not to stare at Kate with Eli, she prepared Rosie's bottle, gazing into her darling face all the while. Rosie blinked up innocently at her, her big eyes ever so trusting. "You're hungry, aren't ya, sweetie?" She kissed Rosie's ivory forehead. "Won't be long now, I promise."

All of a sudden the emotions she'd been masking since Kate arrived began to shift from deep in her heart to her throat and now, this minute, to the tip of her tongue. If she didn't hurry and get Rosie's bottle ready, she might not be able to see due to her tears.

Why does Kate torment me so?

She moved to stand in the doorway between the kitchen and the small sitting area, watching Kate rocking and cooing. But Eli was hers now. *Hers.* How dare Kate come here and disrupt things — incite near rage in her?

Returning to the kitchen, she covered her eyes so as to shut out the cozy sight in the front room. But she found herself moving forward, heading toward Kate while Rosie rutsched against her own bosom.

Rosanna marched into the front room, stopping smack-dab in the center of the large braided rug, glaring at Kate with Eli

at her breast. She gasped, then muttered, "I
. . . you . . ."

Kate looked up and smiled. "You all
right?"

"Not one bit!"

Quickly her cousin's smile faded into a
frown. "What's a-matter, cousin? You not
feelin' so well?"

That too.

"Here, pull up a chair." Kate motioned to
the corner and the old cane chair Elias had
recently redone. "Sit with me . . . I want to
talk to you."

Rosanna pulled the chair over, surprised
at herself for being this compliant when all
she really wanted was to snatch her son from
this cruel woman. Even so, she sat and lifted
Rosie onto her shoulder, patting her back
and willing herself to remain calm and listen
to Kate.

"John and I were talkin' this morning,
early . . . before breakfast."

Rosie squirmed.

"We're concerned." Kate paused. "If you
continue goin' to the new church, well, more
than likely, Eli will make his kneeling vow to
that church." Kate looked down at Eli, stroking his hair.

Rosanna was confused. "What're you
sayin'?"

Kate shifted Eli to her shoulder and rubbed his back, waiting for the burps, which came quickly in a series of two . . . then a softer third.

"John wants our children to remain in the Old Order, where they belong . . . where you and Elias ought to stay," Kate said, her voice trembling.

Rosanna held Rosie close, fear rushing through her.

"And . . . 'specially Eli." Kate kissed the top of his head. "We worry what might happen if the lot, the divine ordination, were to fall on him when he's grown."

Rosanna was all befuddled. So the divine appointment was of concern suddenly because of her and Elias's visit to Preacher Manny's church? Was that it?

"I say, if God appoints Eli for His service, then who are we to question?" Rosanna choked back a breath.

"That's why John and I want our son raised up in the Old Ways . . . in case the Lord chooses him to be a man of God."

"You're most worried 'bout Eli, then?"

Kate nodded slowly, deliberately.

"Rosie here doesn't matter?" Rosanna cuddled her daughter near.

"Why, sure . . ." Kate said unconvincingly.

"Well, she could end up a preacher's wife . . . we just don't know." Kate's favoritism angered her, but Rosanna chose to push it aside. "So it seems you know where we went yesterday."

"Ain't a secret, that's for sure."

"Elias and I didn't intend to hide it."

Kate sighed loudly, guiding Eli to latch on to her other breast. "How could we have known this was goin' to happen?"

"The church split?"

"Jah, back when we promised the babies . . ."

Rosanna sucked in her air too quickly and had to cough. "Well, I hope you don't regret it."

Rosie began to whimper, and it was time to get the bottle out of the hot water, lest it be too warm for her tender mouth. Rosanna made her way to the kitchen, unable to think. Kate seemed truly sorry she'd given up Eli and Rosie. On the other hand, was this merely because of the baby blues? Maybe Kate needed more herbal tea. *Blessed thistle . . . do I have any on hand?*

Beset by the smell of scorched baby formula, she placed Rosie in the playpen and rushed to the cookstove. Using a potholder, she plucked the boiling hot bottle out of the pan and placed it in the sink. Clearly the formula was unsalvageable.

"It's my fault for listenin' to that woman babble on," she whispered. She poured it out and went to prepare another bottle for wailing Rosie.

Her daughter's cries pierced the silence that had gripped the house, creating even further agitation in Rosanna as she shushed and gently jostled her. She moved from one window in the kitchen to the next, looking out at the icy coating on the sheep fences running in neat, boxlike patterns across the snowy grazing land, and the silvery garlands on the few evergreens up near the crest of the hill, by the woods.

"It's all right," she repeated, knowing the words were meant not only for Rosie but for herself.

Once the bottle was warm, Rosanna sat with Rosie suckling hard. She rocked in Elias's favorite rocking chair, aware of the relative quiet — the void left by Rosie's wails as she was soothed with warm nourishment.

Yet Rosanna's fury still raged within, increasing when she heard Kate declare to Eli in the front room, "You must grow up in the fear of the Lord God . . . on the right side of the fence."

Rosanna shuddered and steeled herself,

looking into Rosie's contented eyes. She mustn't let her frustration get out of hand.

Surely Kate would settle down as she always did. One thing or another had upset her ever since the twins had come to live here. Perhaps it *had* been a good idea for Kate to continue on as Eli's wet nurse, soothing herself some, as well as baby Eli.

Rosanna prayed silently for wisdom — no need for Kate to confront her about speaking her prayer aloud. Bad enough the grapevine had delivered the news of her and Elias's attendance at Manny's church to the Beilers' ears, although she was not sorry. She couldn't imagine them returning to the old church now, not after Elias's heartfelt repentance.

She caressed Rosie's hair, soft and wispy as corn silk, recalling her first miscarriage . . . the bleeding, then cramping pain, followed by a constant dull ache low in her back. It was not the physical symptoms that had caused the greatest suffering; rather, it was the knowledge of losing what she'd longed for, the wee one growing beneath her heart.

Her bottle finished, Rosie relaxed, but Rosanna knew she must be burped or she'd suffer colic pain later. "Let's get some of that gas up," she whispered, moving her forward to a sitting position and pressing gently on her little tummy while patting Rosie's back. She realized as she did so that her anger had subsided. She did not know how this could be, unless the Spirit of God — as Preacher Manny had referred to the Holy Spirit yesterday in his sermon — had removed her resentment.

Truth be known, she was relieved to be free of it. She got up and held Rosie against her shoulder, going downstairs to check on the laundry. She'd left a wicker basket lined with soft baby blankets there because she always seemed to have one twin or the other in her arms when doing the washing.

Today was no different, so she placed Rosie inside, knowing she'd be only a short time running the clothes through the wringer. She talked to Rosie as she worked, delighting in her gurgles and the cute way she made tight fists of her hands.

"You're a happy little one, jah?" Her heart was so full of love for Rosie and her twin brother. She marveled at how both of them could raise their heads momentarily when she put them on their tummies. They were growing stronger each day.

The wringer got stuck and Rosanna had to open it and start over with a pair of trousers, glad for Rosie's patience.

Finally she finished and, reaching down to bring Rosie up to her face, kissed her. "Now Mamma's ready to get ya to sleep." She nuzzled her and headed for the stairs.

In the kitchen, she went to the cupboard, found some herbal tea to offer Kate, and set the teakettle on the stove. Then, settling down in the rocker, Rosanna sighed and leaned her head back, closing her eyes for a moment and reminiscing about the days when she and Elias were still waiting for a child . . . Kate and John's baby.

Rosie started in her arms, and Rosanna glanced down at her perfect rosebud mouth. A mule brayed in the distance, and the steady ticking of the day clock came from the sitting room. Other than that, peace prevailed.

Then she realized how quiet things seemed. The creaking had ceased in the front room, where Kate was also rocking. Rosanna bit her lip, refusing to ponder further Kate's pointed talk about the old church versus the new.

Sighing, she rose and carried Rosie to the playpen. Once she was tucked in, Rosanna looked into the front room. The rocker was empty.

Must be upstairs in the nursery for a diaper

change, Rosanna thought and decided not to follow Kate, who was adept at such things, having six children of her own. Eight, if you counted — She caught herself, believing that Kate's twins were, indeed, her very own. In every way that was important, Eli and Rosie were her dear ones, connected by both blood and love.

Returning to the kitchen, she started some cookie dough, hungry for chocolate chip oatmeal. She glanced out the window as she worked. "What the world?"

Dashing to the back door, she looked out. Kate's horse and buggy were no longer parked in the driveway. Her gasp caught in her throat.

Swiftly Rosanna ran to the foot of the stairs. "Kate?" Then her voice rose to a shout. "Kate!"

Only silence. That and the beating of her own heart, louder and louder in her ears.

Kate left without sayin' good-bye? "Why . . . why?"

Oh, but she knew. She knew as the wrenching pain hit her soul — the same pain she had known when her babies had died in that special place near to her heart. *Dear Lord, no.*

Rosanna flew up the stairs. Panic rising and tears streaming, she ran frantically from room to room. There was no sign of precious Eli. Even the afghans and quilts and things she'd lovingly made for him . . . gone.

CHAPTER 26

Rosanna raced from the house to the barn, not bothering to put on a coat. "Elias!" she called as she ran. "Elias!" He would know what to do. He would rescue Eli, would rescue them all. . . .

"Elias, come quick!" No answering call. She threw open the barn door and dashed in, but there was no sign of him or the family buggy, either. Glimpsing the hay in the barn, she remembered: Elias had taken the buggy and gone to help a neighbor fork hay. *Himmel . . . no.*

Only then did she feel the icy cold reach her overheated skin. What to do? How to find help? For the first time in her life, Rosanna wished she owned a telephone.

She left the barn and searched the yard, the driveway, and the road beyond — as empty as her arms. The wind gusted and she thought she heard a cry. Had Rosie awakened? A new panic filled her. Kate hadn't come back for Rosie, too, had she? Fear fueled her, and she hurried back across the yard and into the house. Lungs heaving, she found Rosie, still asleep in the playpen. Safe.

Oh, Lord in heaven, keep Eli safe, too. Rosanna prayed no harm would befall him, especially out on these snowy roads, with mad Kate at the reins.

Leaning over the playpen, she laid her trembling hand on Rosie's soft head. She needed to touch her. "I'm sorry, little one," she whispered. "I'm sorry I didn't watch over your brother more closely. I didn't know . . . I never thought . . ." Her tears fell unchecked. "I'm so sorry."

What was Kate thinking, leaving with Eli? Like a kidnapping, really, right out from under her nose.

Trying to keep her mind and body occupied, Rosanna paced the full length of the house, from the front room — eyeing the rocker where Kate had sat with Eli — all the way back to the utility room, where Elias's work boots and their winter things were neatly stored.

When she could bear it no longer, Rosanna returned to the side of the playpen holding Rosie so that she could keep her eye on her wee daughter. As if something dreadful could happen to make her vanish, too.

She reached in again and this time touched Rosie's tiny fist, crying quietly, not wanting to wake her darling girl.

Oh, Kate . . . how could you do such a terrible thing?

She thought of Elias, knowing he was more tender toward Eli, and it made her weep all the more. Why hadn't she suspected what Kate was up to — hadn't she nearly spelled it out there in the front room, with all the grim talk about the New Order?

Holding her middle, she peered out the frosty windows. How could Kate possibly keep Eli warm out there?

Lest she make herself sick worrying, Rosanna straightened her apron and sat in the rocker. She began to pour out her heart to the Lord, beseeching almighty God for protection and care for both Eli and Kate . . . and a double portion of grace for poor Elias, who loved Eli with his whole heart.

Betsy Fisher could no longer quell her yearning to visit Rhoda, to reassure herself that Rhoda was indeed all right. Since Rebekah Yoder was with them today, helping out in the bakery shop, Betsy thought she could be gone for an hour or two without leaving Nellie shorthanded. Knowing it was Rhoda's monthly morning off, Betsy decided to take a chance that she might find her at James and Martha's.

Betsy drove the family carriage along the edge of the road, the old buggy bouncing and jerking over the hardened ruts of packed snow. When Elias and Rosanna's house came into view, she thought of Nellie's friend, suddenly the mother of twins. She remembered her own firstborn sons — twins Thomas and Jeremiah — and felt a pinch of nostalgic longing to hold a baby in her arms again.

Why not stop in and visit Rosanna? she thought. The sudden urge took her by surprise. *No. You're headed for Rhoda's. Don't want to be gone all day . . .*

She decided she'd come another time and clucked her tongue to prod the horse to go faster. But again, she felt she ought to stop. Was the Spirit of the Lord prompting her? Did Rosanna need some advice about caring for two at once? Some help, just maybe?

Betsy pulled on the reins and turned the horse into the Kings' driveway.

She tied up the horse and walked onto the porch, only to hear weeping before she even reached the door. *What's this?*

Knocking, she called, "Rosanna? It's Betsy Fisher. Are you all right?"

The door opened and there Rosanna stood,

her face a startling mixture of red blotches and gray pallor, her eyes wild and teary, her prayer Kapp askew.

"Oh, Mrs. Fisher! I thought you might be Kate come to her senses."

Rosanna sobbed and turned away from the door, leaving it open for Betsy without inviting her in. Betsy followed anyway, a terrible dread balling up inside her.

The kitchen counter was a mess. Mixing bowls, open canisters, and flour were strewn all around.

"You didn't pass Elias on the road, did you?" Rosanna asked desperately.

Betsy shook her head. "Rosanna, what is it? What's happened?"

Rosanna stared bleakly out the kitchen window. "Kate has taken Eli from me. Took him right from the house."

Betsy gasped, moving toward the table, leaning on it. "You mean she snuck him out? Just left with him?"

Rosanna nodded, fresh tears on her cheeks.

Betsy was stunned. *What a wretched thing!*

"I don't know what to do!" Rosanna wailed. "Elias is off somewhere with the buggy."

"Did Kate say anything? Leave a note?"

"No. She walked out with Eli while I was

down in the basement. I should have known. I should have watched over him better. Maybe I'm not a fit mother . . . maybe that's why —"

"Nonsense, Rosanna. You're a perfectly loving mother. This is Kate's fault, not yours. How long ago did she leave?"

"More than an hour ago. Poor Eli! I hope she got him home safely. At least I assume she went home. Where else would she go? You don't think she would do anything crazy, do you?"

As if kidnapping her own flesh and blood isn't crazy? "Shh . . . Kate may be mixed-up, but she would never do anything to harm Eli," said Betsy. *Lord, let it be so!*

"I'm so frightened," Rosanna said.

Betsy remembered how God had nudged her to stop here at this very time. "I'm going to pray for you, Rosanna. For you and Kate and Eli, too. All right?"

"Oh yes! Please . . ."

Betsy took the younger woman's hand right there in the kitchen and beseeched the Lord out loud to watch over every member of the family and bring a peaceful solution to this most hurtful of acts. "Oh, Lord, calm this mother's heart, I pray. Give her your peace. Help us trust you with our lives and the lives of our children. . . ." Betsy thought of

Rhoda, whom she worried over and longed to see. Could she trust the Lord for her children, just as she had prayed for Rosanna?

Betsy sped home, dismissing her plan to see Rhoda. Leaving the horse and carriage in the yard, she jumped down and ran into the barn. There, she found Reuben tending to one of his colts.

"Reuben! The most terrible thing has happened. . . ." She repeated all that Rosanna had told her.

"Rosanna is completely heartbroken," she concluded.

Reuben shook his head. "Kate can't be thinkin' clearly. Does John know what's going on, I wonder?"

"Who's to know? But to do such a thing to Eli and Rosie! The Good Lord makes a strong bond linking twins. I've heard it — seen it, too — many a time. Think of our own Thomas and Jeremiah. Why, they're grown men and still they can't seem to be apart from each other."

Reuben nodded, chewing his lip.

"And think of Rosanna . . . and Elias. They've longed for a child, and now to have this happen." *They even named the babies after each other!* Betsy thought.

Nellie burst into the barn. "Mamm, are

you all right? I saw you leave the horse and run —"

"Oh, Nellie. It's Rosanna. Kate's taken baby Eli back."

Her daughter looked stricken. "Ach no! When?"

"Only a few hours ago. Elias may not even know yet."

"Poor Rosanna!" Nellie turned pleading eyes toward her father. "Dat, isn't there something you can do?"

Reuben pulled on his beard, shaking his head doubtfully. "I don't know. I suppose I can go to John, see if I can talk to him and Kate. Might not be till tomorrow, though — I've got a man arriving from Ohio to look at horses this afternoon."

"Oh, thank you, Reuben!" Betsy said. "I told Rosanna I was sure you would help."

"Don't thank me, Betsy. I fear there's little I can do. We had *all* better pray."

Betsy nodded and breathed a prayer right then and there. *Please, dear Lord. Help Kate come to her senses!*

Rhoda reclined on Mrs. Kraybill's luxurious sofa, reading the entire article on weight loss from start to finish, glad to be alone a while. Mrs. Kraybill had come to pick her up for a half day of work, then promised to go over the *Pennsylvania Driver's Manual*. Meanwhile, with the youngest daughter playing quietly in her room, Rhoda and Pebbles the cat were the only ones downstairs.

Rhoda liked the Kraybill home for more than its niceties. She was fairly content living with James and Martha, helping with the cleaning and tending to her niece and nephews. But after being surrounded by all the bustle and noise of her brother's house, she enjoyed the relative quiet of the Kraybills'.

Stretching out on the long tufted sofa, Rhoda closed the magazine and imagined how trim she could be in a matter of weeks if she stuck to her plan. Could she do it? Oh, she dearly loved to eat. Ever since Suzy's death, she had found such solace in eating — especially sweets, which the article said was the worst possible fare for a person like her, already in need of a serious change in her diet.

She daydreamed about what sort of handsome fellow might come along to court her. Would he find her pretty in every way? What about her beautiful car?

There were several good-looking boys at the Beachy meetinghouse. She supposed if she continued attending and began going to the various youth activities, she might just get to know one or two of them.

She rose and headed to the kitchen to peer out the window at her LeSabre, parked in the snow. Having the black-and-white beauty within sight made her as happy as tasting one of Nellie's shoofly pies. Truth was, she dreamed of the day when she could take it for a spin. After her ill-fated "driving lesson" with James and cousin Jonathan, she realized she had a great deal to learn. But she loved having the car near, a symbol of the direction her life was taking.

Soon, very soon, she would drive wherever she wanted to go, thanks to Mrs. Kraybill, James, and Jonathan — they'd all offered to give her the instruction needed to put her in the driver's seat.

Come the spring thaw, she thought, eager for ice-free roads.

Right now, though, she had more on her mind than obtaining her license. The Kraybills' unmarried nephew, Ken, was coming to supper next Sunday night. Mrs. Kraybill had invited Rhoda, as well — insisted upon it, really. But Rhoda felt odd about it, even though Mrs. Kraybill said that this was not to be a "blind date," whatever that was.

Rhoda would think about it and hope to lose a few more pounds before then, maybe.

What if I didn't wear my Plain dress and apron, for once?

Rosie simply would not stop crying, no matter what comfort Rosanna gave her. She wailed as if her heart were breaking, her little tongue curled back in the wide opening of her mouth. The more Rosanna walked her and rubbed her back — even offering an additional warm bottle — the more inconsolable Rosie seemed.

Her crying made Rosanna want to be strong for her precious baby daughter, but it was nigh to impossible to swallow back her own sobs.

When Elias arrived at last, she fell into his arms, weeping as she held Rosie near. "Kate's taken our Eli away."

Such a look of shock came to his dear face. "What do ya mean, Rosanna?"

She explained the sequence of the day, beginning with all the talk of the Old Ways and the word that had obviously traveled about the New Order church service they'd attended. "Kate — well, John, too — they want Eli raised in the old church."

Misery masked his features. "Well, we shouldn't be surprised. They're prob'ly upset at us."

"Kate said as much."

He pulled on his beard. "Rosanna . . . love, where were you when this happened?"

Her heart stopped. "Down in the cellar, doin' the washing . . . with Rosie."

"And where was Kate?"

"With Eli, in the front room . . . nursing him."

He shook his head slowly. "You've been through this before . . . you should've put a stop to it."

She nodded her head, covering her trembling lips.

Then Elias took Rosie from her. "No . . . no, I'm sorry. You aren't to blame." Gently he led her to the table, where he pulled out a chair for her. "I'll head right over there . . . as soon as Rosie here settles down." Their little daughter was snuggling close to Elias now.

She surely senses his strength. . . .

And in a few short minutes, Rosie was sound asleep.

"What about your dinner, love?"

"Food is the last thing on my mind."

"Oh, Elias . . . what're we goin' to do?"

"We'll trust the Good Lord. What else is there?" His eyes softened. "How long ago did Kate leave?"

She told him, and he kissed her cheek and laid Rosie down in her playpen. Then he turned toward the back door with another wave over his shoulder. Oh, how weary she felt. Too fatigued to get up and see him out.

Instead of eating anything herself, she glanced at the now sleeping Rosie and went to the back door to lock it — something she'd never done before in this house, nor in any other. Quite unnecessary amongst the People. Nevertheless it was essential, this day, for her own sanity.

She rushed downstairs to check on the clothes hanging in the cellar — far warmer than outside, where they'd surely freeze. The clothes remained quite soggy, so most likely the makeshift clothesline would be laden with her family's clothing come tomorrow.

Good thing Elias has an extra shirt and trousers.

She touched Eli's tiny sleeping gowns and booties and wept again. If God had called Cousin Kate to give up Eli and Rosie, how was it possible she'd changed her mind?

CHAPTER 27

Chris Yoder was ecstatic Monday afternoon when he saw the 97 percent on his calculus test. The teacher tapped him on the shoulder as he returned to his desk from distributing the exams. "Fine work, Mr. Yoder."

Truth was, he'd hardly cracked open the textbook, but thanks to what he assumed were his genes, he was a natural in all things related to mathematics. His father had noticed this ability early on, which was one of the reasons why he was a shoo-in to run the family's landscaping business if he wanted, keeping the books.

Yes, numbers Chris could understand, but Zach was another matter. His greatest concern at present was his younger brother's seeming inability to get over his obsession with Suzy Fisher. And now he had something new to be preoccupied with — the gold bracelet they'd found at the lake. He'd spent hours yesterday lying on his bed, arm outstretched, staring at the bracelet, letting it dangle as it caught the sunlight. *Strange,* thought Chris, and he was worried enough to pause right there and silently ask God to help Zach.

He'd tried to talk Zach out of keeping the bracelet. Why not give it away to someone, as a gift? After all, it had a terrific Scripture inscribed on it, one that Suzy had chosen herself. Zach had told her he wanted to purchase something special, asking her for a life-changing verse. Her favorite.

Life-changing is right, Chris thought, recalling his brother's excited talk about the gift last June, and seeing Suzy's delight when Zach had placed it on her wrist that terrible Saturday.

Now the bracelet was back, and Chris feared his brother would spend a lifetime gazing at this sad reminder of the first love Zach had embraced fully — and still did.

Caleb located his father in the barn, knowing it was best to get a discussion started . . . not let things just hang and fester. He knew he was taking a big risk, what with Rebekah being told to leave home last night.

He found Daed spreading straw on the floor, and immediately Caleb was handed a rake to help. He set to work, realizing now was not going to be the time after all. His father's scowl was hardly an invitation to begin the much-needed conversation, so he raked for the next hour, finishing the chore while Daed oiled the harnesses.

Later, around four o'clock, when they were spraying the cows' teats in preparation for milking, he said, "I'd like to talk to you, Daed."

His father's head bobbed up. "What's on your mind, son?"

Caleb swallowed, consciously raising himself to his full stature. "I did your bidding."

"What's that?"

"Susannah Lapp. I made a point of seeing her at the Singing last night." He resisted the memory of Nellie's observing them. "Frankly, she's of no interest to me, Daed."

Now it was his father who straightened, putting a hand on the rump of the Holstein. "You speak nonsense, Caleb. Any young man would find her . . . completely appealing."

"She's beautiful, I'll give you that." He would not continue with this line of talk. "This may not be what you want to hear, but I hope to be marryin' someone else come next fall."

A knowing look passed between them. Typically this announcement would be met with congratulations, marriage being the prerequisite for Caleb's receiving the land.

Daed exhaled forcefully. "Thought by now you would've put *that* girl out of your mind."

Caleb paused, stunned at Daed's disregard. "Nellie Mae's who I want for my bride."

"Well, then, you ain't thinking straight."

Caleb held back lest he speak disrespectfully.

"How can ya dare to think she's the one for you?"

"I love her."

His father scoffed, making a sweeping gesture. "Love, you say? So you'd give up our plans — your future here?"

Caleb crouched down to wash the next cow's udder. He hadn't said anything of the kind. He was not interested in giving up the chance to provide well for his bride and their children someday. He didn't know all the ins and outs of this sticky situation, but he *did* know that Nellie Mae would be a wonderful-good wife, and he cared deeply for her.

"I love Nellie Mae," he repeated. This was the most awkward discussion ever. His father had no right to even know whom he was seeing, let alone his intended — at least not until closer to the wedding season, nearly ten months away yet.

"I forbid you to marry a Fisher!"

Fury rose in Caleb's chest, and he stood up. "I best be goin'." He rushed toward the barn door.

"Caleb . . . son!"

It went against everything Caleb knew to be respectful and good, but he ignored his father and strode straight to the house, leaving the milking wholly to him.

As Nellie, Nan, and Rebekah closed up the bakery shop for the day, they talked about the "sad, sad story" Mamma had relayed to Nellie, who couldn't imagine how her friend Rosanna must be feeling.

"You'd think Kate would've had more sense," said Rebekah as she wiped down the display case.

"Taking one twin, you mean?" Nan asked.

Rebekah nodded. "That and giving the babies away in the first place."

"Jah . . . seems strange, ain't?"

Nellie spoke up. "Well, the way I understand it, the Lord God supposedly impressed on John and Kate to give their twins to the Kings. I don't understand all that, but it seems some folk tend to hear from God more than others."

"Well, I can't imagine the heavenly Father directing Kate to take back her son now," Nan said. "Such a cruel thing."

Silently Nellie agreed. She couldn't help but wonder whether Jehovah God was indeed responsible for the initial decision. And, if so, what about Kate's change of heart *now?* Nellie herself had always feared something like this might happen, though she had never voiced it to Rosanna, not wanting to spoil her friend's excitement over the babies.

As Nellie pondered this, she refused to fret about the fact that Caleb's own sister was right now in their home, redding up her bakery shop, of all things. According to Rebekah, her brother had brought her here late last night in the wee hours. So it was Caleb who'd done the good deed for his outcast sister, in spite of David Yoder's having sent her away — such a willful thing for her beau to do, considering he was already on shaky footing at home.

As he is with me.

But no, she could not dwell much on Caleb, or she would feel as despairing as she had following their brief encounter at the barn Singing last night. She did not want to relive that scene with her beau and Susannah looking so cozy together.

Nellie fixed her thoughts instead on dear Rosanna, whom she wanted to visit and comfort as soon as she could get away.

Half asleep, Rosanna held Rosie while sitting in the rocker in the kitchen, expecting Elias any minute. Her husband had been gone much too long for her liking, though she'd had plenty of time to practice her praying — talking aloud to God.

She glanced at her sleeping daughter, who'd struggled yet again after her bottle, refusing to give in to sleep. Could Rosie sense her twin brother wasn't there?

Getting up, she placed Rosie in the playpen, gently tucking her blanket around her and looking fondly at Eli's matching one. Running her hand over it, she wanted to trust the Lord God to return her son to them somehow. Today? Tomorrow?

She fought a battle of wills — what she knew she wanted, and what God had allowed. Was this His sovereign will? She'd been taught her whole life not to question His doing. But with all of her heart she wanted Eli back. Even so, if Elias did not succeed in getting Kate to change her mind, Rosanna must not allow herself to be bitter. At all costs, they must show Kate the love of the Lord. *Somehow.*

When Elias finally returned, he was red in the face — whether from his encounter with the Beilers or from the cold wind, Rosanna wasn't sure.

Rosanna said little as she warmed up his supper. She hurried to get the food on the table, sitting with him, watching him eat. He prayed an extra-long prayer of thanksgiving, both for the food and for "every good and blessed gift."

Before he began to eat, he said thoughtfully, "I spoke at length with John, who certainly supports Kate's taking Eli. They both feel it's necessary to have their son raised under the Ordnung."

She listened, taking in his every word.

"I had a mighty good opportunity to talk about our recent experience at the new church, 'bout seeking a relationship with God's Son. But John washed his hands of it, said he wants nothin' to do with such things."

"Rosie . . . what'll happen to her?" She held her breath.

"They'll let us keep her without a fight. That's what they said."

Rosanna let out a whoosh of air. "They don't mind if Rosie's raised in the more progressive church?"

"I guess they're hopin' she'll marry an Old Order boy, when the time comes. Honestly, I think they just assume the new church will lose its steam eventually, and those who've left will come to their senses and return. I don't see that happening, though."

She didn't, either. The groundswell was strong. Freedom to worship, to study Scripture — well, it was too powerful to stop.

Elias pulled his suspenders, looking at her. "But the way things are with Kate, I guess we can't count on anything."

"You mean she could go even more ferhoodled and come take Rosie away, too?"

"As John kept sayin', 'Things are different now.'"

Something she could not contain rose up in her. "It's wrong, Elias! Wrong as anything! Eli and Rosie must grow up *together.*" Shaking now, she described Rosie's crying nearly all afternoon as if her little heart was aware of the separation. "I won't stand by and let Kate do this!"

"I know how you feel, but getting worked up won't help." His gaze lingered on her. Then slowly, deliberately, he put his hands to his face and covered his eyes for the longest time. He, too, was weeping.

"Aw, Elias . . . love. You want your son back, same as I do."

He nodded, his face still buried in his burly hands. "Jah, more than I dare say."

CHAPTER 28

After supper, while Nellie, Nan, and Rebekah were redding up the dishes, Nan asked Rebekah, "So, did you like helpin' out at Nellie's Simple Sweets?"

Rebekah nodded, drying a platter before handing it to Nellie to put away. "The Englischers are so friendly and chatty, jah? I was surprised how many asked for recipes."

"And I don't mind," Nellie said. "Here lately we're getting all kinds of new folk in the shop. Repeat customers, too." She hoped she wasn't boasting.

"Oh! About that," said Rebekah. "I almost forgot! You'll never guess who's responsible for all the fancy folk makin' a path to your door."

Nellie exchanged glances with Nan.

"Who?" asked Nan.

"Susannah Lapp."

Nan's mouth fell open. "You don't mean it."

Rebekah nodded. "It's true. Caleb mentioned it last night. She all but admitted she's been spending her egg money on newspaper ads. Appears she's intent on stirring up the staunchest Old Order folk."

Nellie was befuddled. "Why on earth?"

"Well, finally. One mystery solved!" Nan said, laughing. "What a schemer."

Nellie didn't feel any too kindly toward Susannah for the boost in sales. It seemed clear the girl was trying to build a wedge between herself and Caleb. And after last night, she'd accomplished it, too.

"Well, her plan didn't work exactly as she hoped, now, did it?" Nan went on more gently, perhaps recalling what Nellie had confided. "The ads have helped more than the tittle-tattle hurt us."

Nellie wasn't so sure. Truth was, she found Susannah's trick to be downright conniving, in spite of the beneficial influx of customers.

Wait a minute . . . could that be what Caleb was talking to Susannah about at yesterday's Singing?

Without even a glance out the window, Caleb knew there was a racket in the barn. It sounded like the driving horses had gotten out — galloping off — and he dashed outside to investigate, leaving *The Budget* behind on the kitchen table.

Caleb checked the barn and confirmed his suspicion, then went promptly to search for the horses in the deep pinewood, hoping to use the newly fallen snow to his best advantage by following the fresh horseshoe prints.

Something had obviously spooked the spirited horses, and he hoped they might soon be noticed by another farmer. He'd known of horses sprinting off into the cold and, having a mind of their own, being found dead in the snow the next day. For this reason he persevered, continuing his search through the knee-high snow, wishing he'd taken time to at least put on an extra layer of socks.

What caused them to run off in this weather? Eventually he turned back toward the house, where his father stood out on the front porch, waiting.

"I couldn't catch 'em," he called. "What do you want me to do?"

"You should've thought of that before leaving the stable door open, son."

So he *hadn't* latched the gate. . . .

But it was not the runaway horses that his father wanted to address as he headed down the steps and around the side of the house to the back door. "Come with me, Caleb."

He followed his father inside to the kitchen, where Mamm was pushing wood into the belly of the old cookstove. He was told to "sit awhile," and he did, though not at his usual spot at the table. Instead he purposely sat at the foot, down where Rebekah had always sat.

"What's on your mind, Daed?" He was taking the lead, an impertinent thing to do.

"Your sister Rebekah." Stopping for a second, Daed looked at Mamm. "Your mother and I want to know where you took her last night."

He's asking only now?

Caleb inhaled. "Rebekah wanted to go to the Fishers' . . . so that's where she is." He wouldn't reveal that she'd slipped into the house unknown to anyone. Surely Nan and Nellie welcomed her with open arms.

Mamm sat to the right of Daed, her hair a bit unkempt as it sometimes was this late in the day. Her eyes seemed all washed out, almost gray where there was usually color, and the wrinkles in her face were deeper than he remembered, settling hard on her laugh lines. "Was she . . ." Mamm paused, reaching up her sleeve for a handkerchief. "Was Rebekah terribly upset?"

He nodded slowly.

"Weeping, I s'pose?" Mamm's lower lip quivered uncontrollably.

"No . . . not that."

She stared at the tablecloth, tears spilling over the knobs of her cheeks.

It was obvious how worried Mamm was — and how angry Daed was, too.

"She'll be fine over there with Nan . . . and Nellie Mae," he added, thinking of the letter he must write to Nellie. He had hoped the conversation with Daed would have made their predicament less dire, enabling him to offer her some word of hope along with his woeful attempt to explain.

"That's the last place you should've taken her, son."

"Where, then? It was awful late," he protested. "And so cold . . ."

Daed shook his head emphatically. "Reuben Fisher's house was not the place, and you know it. That's two misdeeds in less than a day's time."

Caleb cringed, chafing under his father's rebuke. He was glad when Daed headed upstairs to retire for the night, Mamm following dutifully behind. Caleb poured himself a glass of milk, downing it quickly. As he set the glass on the counter, he was amazed to hear the muted sounds of wayward horses galloping on the snow-packed lane, heading toward the barnyard.

"They're back!" Caleb dashed outside to thank their neighbor to the south, who had driven them in, then made sure the horses had no gashes or scrapes. When he was satisfied they were in good shape, he muttered his own disgust at his second transgression, as Daed had declared it, and latched the barn door, this time double-checking.

As soon as Nellie finished setting up the display case Tuesday morning, she left Nan and Rebekah in charge of Nellie's Simple Sweets and rode over to see Rosanna.

Entering the King home, she unloaded her baked goods onto the kitchen table and then threw her arms around Rosanna. Her friend seemed to have shrunk since Nellie had last seen her. Teary-eyed and frightened, Rosanna looked young and lost, and Nellie suddenly felt the older of the two, though Rosanna was nearly four years her senior.

"I am so sorry, Rosanna. Awful sorry," Nellie said softly. "Mamma's completely aghast at Kate's behavior. And Dat, too."

"We shouldn't hold anything against her." Rosanna helped Nellie off with her heaviest coat and two scarves. "Kate's not herself."

"How are you and Elias holding up?"

She shrugged. "It still doesn't seem real.

I keep thinking I'll turn around and there he'll be, in the playpen."

"Kate hasn't changed her mind, then?"

Rosanna shook her head. "Elias went over there yesterday afternoon, but . . ." She bit her lip, unable to continue.

Tears filled Nellie's eyes and she squeezed her friend's hand.

Rosanna turned to warm a bottle for Rosie, and Nellie offered to feed her. Holding the little one in her arms near the corner stove, Nellie relished Rosie's sweetness as she took her bottle. Smiling, she glanced up from Rosie's face and saw the heartbroken look in Rosanna's eyes.

She could imagine how quickly one grew attached to a baby like Rosie. *What a loss!* She was tempted to remind Rosanna that it wasn't as if she'd never see Eli again — she wasn't losing him to death the way her family had Suzy. But Nellie thought better of it.

"I don't see how we can go on this way, without our baby boy." Rosanna's words tore at Nellie's heart. "Surely, the Lord will bring Eli back to us. . . ."

Nellie didn't know what to say.

Rosie had slowed her anxious sucking now, eyes mighty droopy, and she began to succumb to sleep.

Rosanna took Rosie from her, going to lay her down in the playpen. When she returned, Nellie gave her another long hug.

"I hope your son comes home to you very soon," she whispered.

"Thank you, Nellie Mae." Rosanna smiled through her tears. "From your lips to God's ear."

CHAPTER 29

Following Tuesday supper, Reuben headed to John and Kate Beiler's, wishing he'd had an opportunity to do so when Betsy had first told of the dismaying news. Yesterday's horse buyer had remained into the evening, staying on for supper after purchasing several fine Morgans. Thankful as Reuben was for the business, his mind had been elsewhere. Oh, but goodness, he felt someone ought to have a man-to-man talk with John, even though John was known to have a will like a wolf trap.

Reuben couldn't help but wonder if John had been influenced solely by Kate. Or was there more to it?

Navigating the horse along the icy roads, he wondered about his own son James, out learning to drive a fancy car in such treacherous conditions. How awful spoiled a body could become in short order — so much comfort on four wheels — especially on a miserable night like this.

Holding the reins with both hands now, Reuben rode past one farm after another. It was a bright yet freezing night. Following the area's recent heavy snows, livestock were safely stabled in all the farms up and down Beaver Dam Road. Passing Deacon Lapp's place, it looked to him as if the deacon's pasture gates and horse fences were nearly buried in white drifts.

He could see in his mind the deacon swaying from side to side as he walked, something like a grandfather clock. The kind and hardworking man had survived several farming accidents over the years. Despite the many changes of the past months, Reuben still considered the former ministerial brethren as his own, even though he assumed that eventually his brother would cease to oversee the New Order group.

Old things are passed away . . . all things are become new. Thankful for that Scriptural promise, he clucked his tongue to spur the horse along, wishing the Amish brotherhood might eventually see the light of divine grace.

In God's own way . . . and time.

Now that he was out alone in the darkness, Reuben realized he hadn't eaten his fill, and he was sorry he'd refused the tasty coconut cream pie. It certainly had tempted him, but he'd excused himself, pushing away from the fine turkey and stuffing dinner — practically a holiday feast, thanks to dear Betsy. But the wonderful-good pie was all Nellie's doing.

Seeing John Beiler's house, he made the turn into the driveway and wondered how the conversation might go. It wasn't his place to tell John and Kate what to do, but he'd come on Betsy's persuasion, and, well, here he was. Too late to turn back now.

Won't the bishop have something to say about Kate's wicked deed? He'd heard his elder brother had permitted John and Kate to give their babies to the Kings in the first place.

Reuben contemplated the man of God who had been wise enough to suspend the Bann for nearly three months, though that time was rapidly coming to a close. Nearly everyone had marked the date in red on their calendars — February eleventh. Well, everyone safely settled in the new churches had.

But tonight it wasn't so much the church split on Reuben's heart as two little babies being pulled apart from each other . . . and the family raising them.

Unbelievable.

He'd suffered enough loss for the rest of his life, with Suzy's drowning the worst blow of all. But what about Elias and Rosanna . . . all the unborn babies they had lost, only to come to this? Wasn't anyone willing to speak on their behalf? This went much deeper than two women squabbling over babies, he felt certain. The way Betsy had described it, Rosanna could have Eli back, but only if she renounced her interest in the New Order church.

But she hadn't, and now he had appointed himself to defend Elias King, brand-new convert that he was.

One by one, people are coming to Christ. . . .

Hastily Reuben tied up his horse, glancing at the old stone farmhouse where the Beilers resided. With a prayer on his lips, he walked to the back door.

Caleb slid his long legs under the desk in his room, tuckered out from single-handedly unloading more than three tons of hay for a neighbor whose supply was running low due to last summer's drought. Tomorrow would bring more of the same. He leaned back in the sturdy chair, relaxing at last.

He eyed the pulled-down green window shades that blocked the moon's white radiance. The shades were like the shadows on his soul. Never before had he felt so hemmed in there, in the very place he stood to inherit, assuming he bowed to Daed's demands. Caleb thought he had done so — had jeopardized his relationship with Nellie in doing it — but the end result was not to his father's liking.

Did Daed think Susannah could actually beguile me . . . change my mind about Nellie Mae? If so, what sort of man would I be? And what sort of husband?

He felt ensnared, trapped by his father's impossible expectations, yet unwilling to abandon his love for Nellie. His frustration gnawed at him. *I have to find a way to make this work!*

But first things first. Picking up his pen, Caleb began to write to his sweetheart.

Dear Nellie Mae,
I hope you're all right, even though by the looks of your sad eyes Sunday night I fear you aren't. Frankly, neither am I. To think I might lose you because of this ridiculous deed . . . well, I simply can't stand by and let you think the worst of me.
Truth be told, I went against my better judgment. My father insisted I spend time with Susannah Lapp, hoping I would regard her as a future bride. Now, I realize you have merely my word on this, but what

I'm telling you is true.

Talking once with Susannah was the only way for me to say I'd obeyed my father's bidding, something I was anxious to be done with. Then you came into the barn and saw us together, when she and I were already in disagreement, to put it mildly. That girl is more trouble than I ever suspected.

I want nothing more than to see you again, Nellie. Will you meet me at our special place this Saturday night?

I'll bring my courting buggy, so we can at least ride a bit. Please hear me out. Won't you give me a second chance?

Until then.

With all my love,
Caleb Yoder

Satisfied he had explained things adequately to his darling, he slid the letter into his bureau drawer to mail later.

Mamma appeared absolutely chagrined at the news of who'd placed the ad. "Susannah, you say? Why, that schemer!"

"Nan thought so, too." Nellie cut generous wedges of coconut cream pie for Mamma, Rebekah, and Nan as they gathered around the table. Dat was out paying someone a visit.

"Sure would be nice to have Rhoda home," said Nan, changing the subject. Nellie and Mamma muttered their agreement.

"It was your sister I'd set out to see yesterday when I felt impressed to stop in and visit Rosanna instead," Mamma mentioned. She didn't bring up again the heartbreak Rosanna was enduring, yet Nellie knew it was on all of their minds.

They sat quietly, savoring their pie for a while before Rebekah said, "It's been awful nice of you to let me stay here for the time being."

"Won't your father ask you to return home?" Nellie asked gently. Was David Yoder so hard as to forbid his daughter to ever come home?

"I doubt it." Rebekah took another bite of pie, her face serious.

"Well, girls," Mamma said, "let's not forget God does impossible things. He's surely at work in your father's heart, jah?" Mamma's eyes were suddenly bright with tears. "You're welcome to stay with us as long as you wish, Rebekah dear."

Rebekah reached for Mamma's hand. "Will ya remember my family in your prayers? I'd be so grateful," she said, surprising Nellie — Nan, too, apparently, because her eyes looked like big blue buttons.

"How about right now?" Mamma opened a hand to Nan, as well, and Nellie slowly put hers out, too. They all bowed heads. "Our heavenly Father, will you look over our broken hearts — each one — and mend and heal those who are in need of mercy? Please give your grace to Rebekah. Watch over her parents and her brothers and sisters and their families . . . and give her peace this night."

Mamma paused as if to keep from breaking down, releasing Nellie's hand to blow her nose. Nan and Rebekah kept their eyes closed, evidently waiting for the amen, which was only slightly delayed by Mamma's addition of "poor Rosanna and Elias" to her prayer, as well as "dear Rhoda." When she said Rhoda's name, her voice cracked.

Nellie wondered what Rebekah thought of such fervency, but Caleb's sister seemed unfazed and actually inquired about what Mamma thought was the "best way to pray."

"Anyone can talk to God," Mamma explained, looking at Nellie now — "like you would to a close friend or family member." Mamma was undoubtedly hoping to win her over yet.

Sighing, Nellie wondered if she shouldn't

get Suzy's diary out of hiding again. She'd felt so tenderhearted after reading the last third of it. Suddenly she recalled Rhoda's request for it. She'd refused, afraid of what Rhoda would think after reading of Suzy's wild months in the world. But with Rhoda gone, Nellie wondered whether it might have done her oldest sister some good to see Suzy's path to transformation. If Rhoda had read the journal through to its sweet end, maybe she'd still be here with them now.

She looked at Mamma, who had endured such painful losses in the past year. Presently her mother was talking about "trusting in our Savior, even when people around us disappoint."

"Sometimes it's terribly hard, though." Rebekah sniffled.

"Well, sure it is. But it's not so much how we manage to get through the hard things as it is being willing to cling to God's promises while we're gettin' there, ya know?"

Nellie was surprised at the way her mother described things. She couldn't deny being somewhat curious about her parents' loyalty to their newfound faith . . . a faith shared by Nan and Rebekah. *Elias and Rosanna, too.* And to think the Kings' choosing the New Order had taken little Eli from them and put him back in Kate's arms!

When Reuben knocked on the Beilers' back door, he was quickly met by John, who did not usher him inside with his formerly cheerful welcome. Rather, he gave a single nod and stepped aside awkwardly to let Reuben pass.

Immediately it was clear Eli was the center of attention that evening. A doting Kate held him, surrounded by all the children.

Reuben's heart sank but he didn't dare let on. As pleasant as the scene before him was, he could think only of grieving Rosanna King. How was he to broach that thorny subject over the soft buzz of voices?

Kate tenderly kissed Eli's cheek, and the two youngest children leaned in on either side of the rocking chair, kissing him, too. John moved to his wife's side, leaving Reuben to merely observe.

For a moment he almost forgot why he'd come, but Eli began to cry as if he was downright hungry. The oldest girls shushed and made over him, but nothing seemed to work. "What do ya think's wrong?" asked the older of the two. "He just ate, and he's wearin' a fresh diaper."

The domestic peace broken, John finally turned his attention back to Reuben. "What's brought you out on such a wintry night?"

Normally by now Reuben would have been offered a seat at the table and a slice of pie, but there was no sign of hospitality from either John or Kate, and Reuben felt increasingly disconcerted.

Lord, please keep a rein on my temper. Help me to know how to bring up Kate's heartless deed.

Just then someone pounded on the back door, and John hurried to see who it was.

There stood Elias King, his face ashen. "Hullo, John . . . Reuben." Elias's expression registered surprise.

"Elias . . . good to see ya." Reuben's throat tightened up. He felt for this fine young man; it was obvious Elias had come to beg for the child's return, as awkward as it seemed.

Kate rose and wordlessly walked out of the room with Eli, who was still wailing. All six children followed, like ducklings scurrying after their mamma.

When John waved them toward the table, Elias eased himself onto the bench, pain on his face. He folded his hands on the table and eyed Reuben. "I'm glad you're here," he said. "You're witness to the things I mean to say." He then directed his gaze at John.

"Elias, you won't be changin' our minds,

no matter how many times you come over here." John reached for his coffee.

"Now, wait a minute," Reuben spoke up. "Look at this man. Hear him out, for pity's sake."

John's posture stiffened. "Eli is my son."

"That he is, though I feel as though he is mine, too." Elias took in a long breath and offered a thin smile before becoming more solemn. "But hear me out. A baby girl is cryin' without end for her brother, over yonder." He glanced toward the window. "And my wife's pining for Eli, too."

"Eli will be raised here," John stated. "With God-fearin' people."

"We *are* God-fearing people, John. And in the fear of the Lord, you gave Rosanna and me a son . . . and a daughter. They belong together."

John's neck and face were red, although thus far he appeared stubbornly in control of himself. "My son belongs with us, here, where he will grow up in the Old Ways."

"What Eli needs is to grow up knowin' the saving grace of the Lord," Elias stated, his voice firm but calm.

The tension in the air was palpable. It was agonizing to watch this exchange over a single baby — a man-child. It seemed to

Reuben there was no satisfying either person, and he again beseeched the living God for aid.

A flickering thought crossed his mind that a third party was needed, someone to guide them in the right direction. *In the same direction.* "Bishop Joseph should decide," Reuben said suddenly.

"No, I've already made up my mind. I won't allow my boy to be raised by folk professin' an alien gospel."

"But surely you trust the bishop? The wisdom of the Old Order?"

John looked at Reuben, as did Elias. A mutual hope filled both men's eyes. "If that's what it'll take," John said, and Elias nodded in agreement.

"Then I'll speak to my brother on your behalf."

Surprisingly, John reached over to shake Reuben's hand as all three men stood.

"I'll let Rosanna know," Elias said gratefully to Reuben as he made his way toward the back door.

"And I'll tell Kate," said John with confidence.

Reuben bid John good-night and headed home to Betsy. He wondered if what he'd proposed had been divinely dropped into his heart, perhaps.

Rosanna had been walking the floor with fussy Rosie for more than an hour, not understanding how such a tired baby could simply refuse to give in to sleep. So she held her near, talking softly during the short intervals when Rosie would let up to catch a breath, only to begin howling again. Rosanna tried humming, cajoling, rubbing her back, her tummy — everything that had always helped in the past, but to no avail.

When Elias finally arrived home, she was ever so glad. He took Rosie from her, kissing her little forehead, then the top of her head. Even so, she continued to cry.

"What do you s'pose is wrong?"

"Could it be she senses Eli is gone?"

She'd considered that earlier. "Could be, jah. We'll simply give her more attention . . . till her brother's home again."

Elias's face sagged; he must have been dead tired. But she knew it was more than that.

"Kate might not bring Eli back, Rosanna. You must know this."

"No . . . no, let's not think that way."

"Well, the decision's not ours anymore. Nor is it John and Kate's."

"What do you mean?"

344

He paused as Rosie gave in to sleep. "Where Eli should grow up is the bishop's choice to make now," he told Rosanna, who followed when he carried Rosie upstairs to her cradle.

"But no! Bishop Joseph will surely rule in their favor." She began to cry.

He reached for her, tenderly pulling her into his arms. "Come here."

She felt the strength of him, the great affection he had for her, in the gentle brush of his lips against her cheek and then her mouth. "Oh, Elias . . . I've worried so."

He took her hand, leading her to their room. "We must trust God for Eli's future. Not a speck of worry will change a thing."

She agreed, trying to focus on her darling as he sat on the bed, drawing her to him.

"You're so perty, love."

She forced a smile as she sat next to him, his arms around her now. His kisses were ever so light, comforting her, if only for this moment.

"I love you, Mrs. King." He often said this somewhat comically during their most intimate moments, but tonight his tone was wholly serious. "Let me ease your sadness . . . for now." He cupped

Rosanna's chin as his kisses grew more fervent. Their tears of joy and sadness mingled as they comforted each other with their love.

CHAPTER 30

By nine o'clock Wednesday morning, the bakery shop was filled to capacity and abuzz with fancy talk. Nellie was glad for the extra help as Mamma served up warm muffins and sticky buns oozing with icing and glazed sugar.

Nan and Rebekah periodically delivered more freshly baked goodies to the bakery shop from the kitchen at the house. Soon, though, the most requested items on the "menu" were hot coffee and cocoa, which were plenty easy to make on the hot plate Dat had rigged up to a small gas-powered generator.

Next thing, he'll want to put in an oven, Nellie thought with a smile. More and more of the People were having electricity installed, along with phones — her own brother James and family were among the latter. So far, though, there was no talk of such happening under Dat's roof. Nellie was secretly glad, although there was no reason now to worry over whether Caleb and his family approved of them — not after what she'd witnessed last Sunday evening. She truly wanted to look on the bright side of things, as Mamma often encouraged her children to do, but she was consciously bracing herself for a breakup letter from Caleb.

Several regulars were sitting at the table farthest away, where Miss Bachman was indulging in her usual treat — peanut butter fudge — saying nothing else could quite compare. Laughter cascaded from the middle table, where all four chairs were occupied, as was also the case at the first. Twelve customers in all, and every one having a wonderful-good morning together.

Nellie refused to puff up with pride, but she was delighted to see the pleasure they took in enjoying her creations. Oh, she wished she could bottle up some of this happiness and carry it over to Rosanna. If Kate Beiler hadn't seen the light and returned Eli by now, there was surely great sorrow in the Kings' house again today. Sadness seemed to abound in any number of hearts here lately, including poor, displaced Rebekah's.

Even so, David Yoder's loss is Nan's and my gain, she thought, glad they could receive Rebekah during her plight. Spending so much time with Caleb's dearest sister was an unexpected gift.

Sudden hilarity sprang from the second table as a customer told of putting up elderberries for the first time. "I made such a mess. I kept finding purple stains on tea towels and my clothes for months," the woman confessed.

More ladies chimed in about harvesting and canning "like Plain folk."

Nellie headed to the door to meet Nan, who was arriving with yet another basket of cookies — hopefully snickerdoodles and chocolate chip.

"Word has it twin babies were separated near here," one woman said rather loudly, nearly stopping Nellie in her tracks. "The baby boy was taken from his adoptive mother by the biological mom, no less."

"I heard that, too," said Miss Bachman. "Evidently the birth mother changed her mind and took the boy back."

"How awful!" exclaimed another woman.

Nellie felt awkward eavesdropping and was glad for the momentary distraction Nan provided. "Would you mind tending the store with Mamma, following the noon meal?" Nellie asked as they worked side by side behind the counter to unload the basket.

"I'll have plenty of time, jah." Nan explained that Rebekah had gone on foot to her job as a mother's helper for the Amish family less than a mile away.

"What do you think'll happen with her?" Nellie asked.

Nan looked sober. "You know David Yoder as well as anybody."

Nodding, Nellie Mae squeezed her sister's hand, grateful she'd confided her woes to Nan earlier.

Nan returned to the house to put the finishing touches on dinner when the crowd of customers emptied out, closer to the noon hour. Nellie Mae was happy to have a few moments alone with Mamma.

Smoothing her apron, Mamma slipped her hand into her pocket, pulling out two Kapp strings. "I found these on the floor in the cellar, near the wringer washer."

Ever so sheepish, Nellie was reluctant to own up. "What on earth?"

"You snipped 'em off your sister's Kapp, ain't?"

So Mamma knew already. "Jah." She braced herself for the reprimand. "That's my doing."

"Oh, Nellie Mae, you loved Suzy so. Here, keep them close to your heart, or wherever you'd like."

Wiping tears, she put the Kapp strings

safely in her own dress pocket. She would be more careful with them, not wanting to raise eyebrows with Nan or Dat . . . or even Rebekah. "Denki, Mamma," she whispered, reaching to embrace her. "Denki, ever so much."

When Chris and Zach arrived home from school, Zach headed up to their room while Chris made his way to the kitchen. He found his dad sitting at the table, listening to the radio and drinking a cup of coffee.

"Where's Mom?" Chris set down his books and opened the old Frigidaire.

"We're out of milk." Dad glanced toward the stairwell. "Zach barely said a word to me. Everything okay?"

Chris closed the refrigerator, empty-handed, and sat heavily in the chair across from his father. *He knows Zach's still taking Suzy's loss hard. . . .*

Neither spoke for a while. Finally Dad set his coffee cup on the saucer. "Things any better these days?"

"Sometimes," Chris hedged. "Sometimes not."

Dad took another sip of coffee. "Your mother's quite worried. She thinks maybe Zach should see our pastor."

Chris nodded. "He'll be okay."

"Do the two of you . . . talk about it?"

"Now and then." Chris shrugged. "Hasn't helped much, though."

His father smiled. "I've attempted a few conversations, but Zach seems so closed."

"He's always been . . . oh, I don't know."

"Independent?" his father chuckled. "And stubborn?" Another moment passed as he drained his cup. Then he got up and went to the sink. Coming back, he placed his hand on Chris's shoulder. "Listen, the two of you have always been close. More than anything, you've been the best for him, Chris."

"His faith is strong."

"I don't doubt that."

Dad headed toward the back door and turned. "He'll pull out, stronger than before. I'm praying that way."

"Yeah." *I hope Zach gets past the worst soon.*

A half hour later, Chris was still sitting at the table, thinking . . . praying. Zach came wandering down just as he was about to head upstairs to change into sweats.

"Wondered what happened to you." Zach pulled some ice cream from the freezer. "Want some?"

Chris gestured toward the seat his father had vacated.

"What?"

"I've been thinking . . . about Suzy Fisher."

Zach dipped into the half-gallon container. "That's my job." He scooped ice cream into a bowl. "Last call. Double fudge dip."

"Seriously, Zach."

Frowning now, Zach sat down.

Chris took a deep breath. "I need to play older brother for a sec."

Zach groaned. "Not this again."

Not wanting to start off on the wrong foot, he paused. Then, he said, "We're all starting to worry about you."

"Who? Dad? Worry about what?"

Chris sighed. This wasn't going so well. He rubbed his chin. "Look, Zach . . . do we really believe the Good News?"

"C'mon, Chris."

"I mean, sometimes we act like what we believe doesn't hold up in a world where suffering's real. Like the Gospel works as long as things are going well, you know?"

Zach's frown deepened, his jaw clenched. "But you weren't in love with her, Chris."

Chris felt the familiar tension between them. He thought of Suzy's picture, the one Zach continually stared at. "Suzy was a simple Amish girl, right? How do you think she'd feel about that big photo hanging on your bulletin board?"

Zach nodded, glancing out the window. "She wasn't going to stay Amish."

"Maybe not. But it's like you've created a shrine or something."

"I just don't want to forget her."

Chris leaned toward his brother and Zach looked away. "Did it ever occur to you that pictures are forbidden by Amish *because* they can become like idols?" Chris locked eyes with his brother. "Maybe you've done that with Suzy."

Zach clenched his teeth again. "I feel *guilty*, okay? That's not going to go away. She was a lousy swimmer, Chris. We messed up."

Chris swallowed hard. "Yeah, I know."

"Well, then — what do you want from me?"

"To do what we ask others to do."

"What?"

"To accept God's forgiveness."

Zach blew out a breath and looked down, shaking his head. At last he nodded, tears falling freely. "All right. I get it. And I'm trying, okay? I'm trying. . . ."

Chris cuffed his brother's wrist. "Well, don't try so hard, goof. Stop fighting it. Let God work it out."

"I need more time," Zach whispered, swallowing. "It's not easy."

"Take all the time you need, but don't

shut me out. And don't push Mom and Dad away, either."

Zach sniffed, wiping his eyes. A long moment passed until a trace of a smile crossed his lips. "You know, you can be really annoying sometimes."

Chris grinned. " 'Cuz I'm right?"

"No, 'cuz you're annoying."

"It's my birthright, you know. The older brother thing?"

Zach sighed again, his smile fading. "Okay. I'll take the picture down."

Chris nodded. "Hey, I just want my brother back."

Staring hard at his ice cream, Zach said softly, "It's hard to feel forgiven."

"I know, man. I know."

Zach finished eating and then the two of them trudged up the stairs. Chris carried no illusions. Things weren't going to change overnight, but for the first time in a long time, he sensed a glimmer of hope. The old Zach was definitely not gone for good.

Nellie Mae visited Rosanna again that afternoon and could tell her friend hadn't slept much, if at all. Her eyes were swollen and red, and the apples of her cheeks were puffy, too.

Rosanna helped Nellie off with her coat.

Then Nellie embraced Rosanna and encouraged her to sit down.

Rosanna complied, sitting in one of the chairs near the stove. "Elias went over there again last night. Your father, too, I understand . . ." Her voice was weary.

Nellie nodded.

"Kate and John won't change their minds. We're going to wait and see what the bishop says now."

They sat quietly for a few minutes while Nellie got warmed up. She didn't want to hold tiny Rosie with such cold hands. Besides, Rosie was sound asleep, and Rosanna was saying how she'd struggled to get her settled since Monday morning, when Kate had left with Eli.

"It's not like her," Rosanna said. "Could it be she senses my grief?"

"Guess she might." *I sure do,* Nellie thought sadly.

"You know I lost babies before, Nellie Mae . . . before they were even born. But this . . ." She sniffled. "Oh, this is the hardest thing, havin' a babe taken away after he's been in my arms for nearly two months."

Nellie's eyes filled with tears, and she reached over and squeezed Rosanna's hand. Then she said, "And to hear Mamma's stories about Thomas and Jeremiah — twins are ever so close. Could be Rosie misses Eli, too."

"Jah, I think so. Growin' in the womb together must make them closer than other siblings."

Nellie remembered all the talk among the English customers earlier. "Some folk say it's unhealthy to separate twins." The words slipped out before she could stop them.

"Oh, I believe I know as much." Rosanna glanced toward the playpen, which was just out of reach of the woodstove. "You don't have to tell me Rosie's missin' Eli, in her own way. Either that, or she's got one fierce case of colic."

It felt so good to spend time with Rosanna two days in a row, like they had as girls. Under different circumstances, of course, they would be working on a quilt or sewing dresses and aprons all afternoon. She didn't dare ask if Rosanna had a quilt in the frame, or if the frame was even set up. She knew better. Lately Rosanna's time had been wholly spent tending to Eli and Rosie.

Nellie had an idea. "I'll make supper for you and Elias, if you'd like to go up and rest a bit."

Rosanna brightened. "Oh, would ya?"

"Whatever I can do to help."

Rosanna smiled, nodding. She showed her

where Rosie's next bottle was kept in the refrigerator. "The formula is all ready. Just shake it up a bit and warm it on the stove if she wakes up."

"I'll look after Rosie. Not to worry." Shooing her dear friend off for a nap, Nellie watched her amble over to the stairs and climb them slowly. *She's clearly exhausted.*

If her coming could provide Rosanna even a small respite, Nellie was ever so glad.

When Nellie returned home from Rosanna's that evening, Nan and Rebekah were curled up near the cookstove, reading the Bible Nan and Rhoda had purchased some time ago. Nan encouraged Nellie to join them, but Nellie declined, using as her excuse the recent circle letter. Then, when she had finished updating her cousins on recent happenings, she wrote a private letter to Cousin Treva, as well, hoping to mail both at the same time.

That done, she looked up and found solace in observing Dat and Mamma, their heads together as they read Scripture, like two lovebirds. Dat still read aloud to all of them every night, but increasingly he and Mamma took extra time to study further.

At moments like this, Nellie missed Rhoda the most. Things were out of kilter here without her oldest sister. It seemed strange knowing Rhoda was staying at James and Martha's, though Nellie was glad Rhoda was living with family, even if that family had "fallen into the world," as Dat complained.

She hoped the rumor mill was mistaken and that James hadn't bought a car like Rhoda had. *If Caleb's heard there are two cars in the Fisher family, no wonder he's pursuing Susannah!*

CHAPTER 31

By midmorning the next day, the fertile farmland, long since buried beneath more than a foot of snow, looked hemmed in by heavy clouds. Nellie Mae pulled on long johns beneath her dress and wore boots and several layers for the jaunt out to get the day's mail. She breathed ever so lightly on the walk back to the house so that her lungs wouldn't ache with the below-zero temperatures.

When will all this ice and snow begin to thaw?

Spring would arrive eventually, but a thaw in the attitudes of the People seemed less likely. The impending fate of many still hung in the balance, and they all knew what was coming. Would the split succeed in destroying the unity of families and the community despite Uncle Bishop's decision to temporarily stay the Bann?

Nellie glanced through the letters as she

carried the thick stack of mail toward the house. Her heart leapt up, then sank nearly as fast when she saw Caleb's handwriting. A sad little groan escaped her. Was he writing to break things off? She must hasten to read this, not waiting as she sometimes had before, wanting to savor his words of devotion.

She looked to see if Mamma might need her at the bakery shop. For a change customers were scarce, so she went to the house and tugged off her boots. Still wearing her coat and scarf, she ran up to her room and closed the door before opening the letter. She scanned it quickly and was relieved to see it was a letter of explanation.

So the encounter with Susannah Lapp had been a requirement of his father's? What sort of man demanded such things, especially when aware of his son's love for another?

Despite Caleb's attempt to explain, she couldn't dismiss the troubling realization that her beau would do nearly anything for his father's land. He'd taken a terrible chance with their love, even though things must not have gone well with Susannah or he would have invited her to ride home. Instead it was Caleb's sister Rebekah by his side following the Singing that night, not the flirtatious Susannah.

She read the telling line again: *Talking once with Susannah was the only way for me to say I'd obeyed my father's bidding, something I was anxious to be done with.*

As skeptical as she felt about Caleb's motives, she tried not to cry. She'd spent enough time weeping over Caleb Yoder; loving someone so deeply seemed to involve pain. *Just look at Nan's mess with her former beau.*

For sure and for certain, love and falling into it could bring a profound measure of sorrow. Who could argue that? *Except maybe Mamma, who got the pick of the crop with Dat.*

Nellie refolded the bewildering letter and placed it under the mattress, alongside Suzy's diary, and went downstairs to don her boots. Making her way back to the bakery shop, she was hesitant about her decision. She felt as bleak as could be, thinking about the wedge Caleb had created between them — all in the name of obedience to his father. She continued to deliberate. Should she give Caleb another chance? Was their love strong enough to weather this gale?

She must stop second-guessing and make up her mind. *Jah, maybe it's a gut idea to hear him out.* Once again she would brave the wretched cold to meet her beau, though this time her enthusiasm would not help to keep her warm.

Rhoda enjoyed Mrs. Kraybill's attempt to suppress her laughter. "Well? What do you think?" Turning around twice, Rhoda stopped and stood still. She was modeling a chocolate brown midi-skirt, ginger-colored fashion boots, and a gold satin long-sleeved blouse with a fitted deep chocolate velveteen vest — the most striking outfit she'd ever seen. Rhoda had purchased it only yesterday in Lancaster, on the square at Watt and Shand's Department Store, after deeming it the perfect look for this Sunday night at the Kraybills' beautiful home — the night she was to meet Ken.

The enterprising store clerk had also tried to steer her in the direction of the makeup counter, saying how very "mod" false eyelashes were now, to which Rhoda thought the ones the Lord God had given her were thick enough. It was easy to see that the clerk herself had false lashes pasted on her own eyes, because a glob of glue showed on her eyelid. Rhoda had barely managed to keep from smirking. *Mod indeed!* That was one mistake she could easily avoid making.

"I suppose from your turning around repeatedly, you're hoping I'll say I like it, is that it?" Mrs. Kraybill smiled and touched the fabric of Rhoda's soft sleeve.

"You're teasin' me?" Rhoda asked, suddenly less sure of her purchase.

Mrs. Kraybill stepped back. "Rhoda Fisher, you are quite stylish. Our nephew will be pleased . . . and that *is* your desired goal, isn't it?"

Rhoda blushed uncontrollably. She wouldn't come right out and admit to wanting to look pretty — fancy, too. But she knew the cut of this outfit hid a multitude of pounds while emphasizing her best features, and that was more her objective than anything. "I don't want to embarrass myself . . . is all."

"Oh, Rhoda, you surely don't worry about that, do you?"

"Well, I don't really fit in round here with your family. I'm like a kernel off its cob."

The way her words tumbled out made Mrs. Kraybill smile yet again, and soon Rhoda's own silly laugh was mixed with her employer's wholehearted amusement. Such a good time they were having!

Mrs. Kraybill motioned for her to sit on the living room sofa. "You're lovely as you are, Rhoda, even when you dress Plain. Never forget to be yourself. No need to mimic anyone else."

Mrs. Kraybill must not sense how dissatisfied Rhoda was with her weight, her looks, and her life in particular. All that aside, she wouldn't pump for more compliments, which only made her feel more self-conscious.

Folding her arms, Mrs. Kraybill continued to regard Rhoda, obviously pleased with the skirt, blouse, and vest combination. "If you wear that or your regular Amish attire — either one — you'll be fine. It's your decision alone."

Rhoda felt wonderful-good, hearing that. There weren't many areas of life where she had been encouraged to show such confidence, especially by another woman. Mrs. Kraybill's remarks were foreign to be sure. The women she knew best, Mamma included, curtailed all inclinations toward independent thinking.

"I'll wear this outfit, then." With a flair, she adjusted her glasses. "Maybe I'll take off my Kapp and get some new eyewear, too."

"So it's settled."

"Thanks for givin' me your opinion," Rhoda said, glad she'd asked. James would soon return to take her over to his place, where Martha could use her help with the children.

Rhoda considered how Mamma had trained her in the ways of submission and total respect for authority. Beachy Amish though she now was, Martha's daughter, Emma, would be raised in a similar, though less strict, fashion. Plain girls grew up to become compliant young women, knowing nothing else.

Why must I crave something different, then?

Even though Martha was becoming more progressive with each passing day, Rhoda knew exactly what both Martha and Mamma would think of her fetching outfit and bold plan to snag a man. She knew . . . and cringed.

Between brushing down the foals — growing before his eyes — and forking hay to freshen the stall bedding, Reuben managed to slip away to pay a quick visit to his brother Bishop Joseph.

He found him slumped over with sleep in his chair near the woodstove, his big German Bible lying open on his lap. The bishop looked up when Reuben was led into the kitchen by Joseph's eldest granddaughter, who quickly made herself scarce. She headed into the front room, returning to the quilting frame, where she sat with Anna.

He waited as Joseph made an excuse for reading the Good Book in the middle of the day. "And not studying it, mind you," the bishop said before closing it. "What brings you out in such inclement weather?"

Reuben pulled up a chair — no sense stalling. "S'pose you're aware of the Beilers' change of mind and heart 'bout their youngest son, Eli — one of the twins they gave to the Kings."

Joseph narrowed his already-squinting gaze behind his spectacles. "Heard as much."

"Then you must know Kate's taken Eli back?"

Joseph nodded slowly.

Reuben sighed, not sure he was getting anywhere with his brother, whose eyes appeared to long for the remaining forty winks. "I was over talkin' with John about it the other day when Elias showed up, beside himself. In the end I spent some time with both of them, and finally I suggested bringing this matter to you."

"I see." His brother looked as serious as Reuben had ever seen him.

"Rosanna's in deep mournin' for the baby boy she was all set to raise, and Kate's equally set on keepin' him. As for Elias, I witnessed his sorrow myself."

"I gave my blessing for the Beilers to give up their children months ago, jah?"

"Must've taken some deliberating on your

part, Bishop," he offered.

Joseph rose and walked to the sink for a glass of water. "Seems you're talking now 'bout the present time . . . and the future."

"The present is fraught with sadness and pain for Elias and Rosanna."

Joseph turned, holding his tumbler of water. "And the future of the children?"

"That's why I'm here . . . hopin' you might have some wisdom in the matter. The People are torn. Not just over the church split, but a good many are takin' sides concerning the twins, too." He shook his head.

"Siblings bein' raised in different families?"

"At least for the time bein'."

Joseph scratched his gray head. "Till when?"

"Until you intervene in this tomfoolery. John and Elias are in agreement on that. They'll do your bidding, seems."

Joseph shrugged, smacking his lips. "Very well. I'll meet with 'em next week."

Reuben hated to question his bishop brother. "That long?"

"I say, leave plenty of time for it to work itself out."

Again he felt obliged to speak up. "A whole week will seem like an eternity to Rosanna."

"And to the wee twins?"

Reuben hadn't quite looked at it that way, but he supposed that was also true. He nodded. "Seems there's great sorrow in the little ones' hearts. Both of them."

Joseph bunched up his wrinkled forehead into a deep, searing scowl. He tugged hard on his beard, the length of it seeming to grow. "Mighty prickly situation, I'll say that."

Not wanting to press the issue, Reuben chose not to ask yet again for an earlier meeting. His brother was known to rule on the side of mercy and usually had a sensible approach to the conflicts amongst them. They'd simply have to wait. "So next week it is," Reuben stated.

Joseph gave a quick head bob. "Jah. Tell them I'll see to it then."

He thanked Joseph and hurried out the back door. Hopefully he'd gained some ground for both families, though he couldn't begin to guess how Bishop Joseph would decide.

'Tis not for us to know the times and the seasons, nor the hearts of men . . . but to simply trust.

During the ride home Reuben prayed for a satisfactory and pleasing outcome for both parties, one that would allow Eli and Rosie to grow up as siblings, not as cousins. But what Reuben prayed most of all was for them to come to know their Savior, however the Lord willed it.

CHAPTER 32

Her father was out hitching up the family carriage to the horse on Saturday evening as Nellie made her way out the back door after supper. Not wanting to be noticed, she hurried down the lane toward Beaver Dam Road.

"Where ya headed, Nellie Mae?" Dat called after her.

"Oh, just out for a bit."

"Why not ride with me, then?" he offered. "I'm heading over to visit Elias King. That the direction you're going?"

Altogether baffled, she accepted, welcoming the chance to be warmer when she arrived at the stone mill. "Denki, that'd be right nice."

He tightened the girth and checked the straps. Once he was seated and holding the reins, he said, "Hop in, Nellie."

She'd never felt so awkward before, riding alone with her father on the night meant for pairing up with a beau.

"This here cloud cover's goin' to bring us more snow," Dat said, making conversation.

"Can't say I'm eager for more."

"Me neither, tellin' the truth." They rode for a distance and then he added, "Weatherman says there's a change comin', starting tomorrow."

"Really?" Nellie was surprised her father would be privy to such news.

"Heard it over at James's."

She tensed up. "My brother's got himself a radio?"

Dat seemed reluctant to talk more on the subject. "Appears he's facing in the wrong direction, least for now. No telling if he'll keep heading thataway. He's just itchin' to be somewhere he's never been." Dat sighed. "Make sense?"

"I think so." She assumed her father was saying James wasn't solidly on the wrong path, only toying with it. "There are some who have to find out for themselves that what they've been missin' ain't what they want."

Dat turned to her, smiling. "That's exactly what I mean, Nellie Mae."

No wonder Mamma found Dat so interesting. With her many siblings, Nellie had rarely gotten time with him all to herself.

"I have to say there's plenty of hope to go around." He leaned forward, looking up at the sky.

She didn't say more, and neither did Dat. His last words merely floated between them.

Hope . . .

Soon, when Elias's drive came into view, Dat stopped on the road and offered to let her out there. She got out and waved at him, thankful he hadn't asked where she was heading. With no moon to guide her, she was glad the old mill was only a short distance away.

Nellie spied the back of Caleb's open buggy as she made the bend in the road and experienced again the torrent of sadness she'd felt at seeing him with Susannah Lapp. There he was, waiting for her, parked around the corner from the mill.

She willed herself not to cry and kept walking. She would not make a fool of herself running to him, though she was hungry for his embrace, longing for the good Caleb she knew and loved.

"Nellie Mae . . . over here," he called, stepping down from his courting buggy. He must've heard her boots on the snow.

"I see you, Caleb!"

He moved swiftly toward her. "I'm so glad you came." He wrapped his arms tightly around her.

After a time, she stepped away.

"Ach, you've been walkin' a long ways." He reached for her hand and led her to the buggy. Then, lifting her up like a doll, he settled her in his buggy and hopped up to join her.

"I was fortunate to get a ride with my father." She explained that Dat was going to visit Elias King. "Such a sad story *that* is."

"But the Kings made a poor choice, ain't?"

Nellie bristled. She recalled comforting Rosanna. "'Tis true Elias has moved away from the Ordnung. That's made John and Kate furious."

"S'pose it's understandable."

This night was starting out on the wrong foot. Why had he continued in this vein when his letter had indicated he wanted to patch things up?

"I'd say a promise is a promise . . . and it must be kept." She'd said what she truly thought about the Beilers' offering their twins to Elias and Rosanna — what she thought about Caleb, too.

She stuck her neck out even further. "Along

the same lines, how am I to understand what you and Susannah Lapp were doin' together last Sunday night?"

"Nellie Mae . . . honey, surely you read my letter." He slipped his arm around her. "That's why you're here, jah?"

"I'm here 'cause I want you to tell me how you could go back on your word, being with another girl. We're betrothed, Caleb."

"I told you . . ." He paused. "If I could do it all over again, I'd stand up to Daed and not seek out Susannah."

She stared at him, not yet sure whether to believe him.

"Susannah's nothin' but trouble," he said.

"I'd hate to think where you'd be if you *had* defied your father."

"Out on my ear, like Rebekah." He looked at her. "And I'd lose the land."

"And where would you go if your father kicked you out?"

He was silent for a time. Then he sighed loudly. "I don't know. Maybe Mamma's folks — they have a vacant Dawdi Haus."

She couldn't see his eyes, nor all of his face. His reply made her wonder. Was he merely throwing out an option to sound persuasive?

Fact was, she had no way of knowing, because he had already *made* the choice to follow his father's bidding. He'd flirted with Susannah, trying to . . . what? But no, Nellie wouldn't ask what he'd had in mind, or what his father had hoped might come of the encounter. Too painful.

Caleb broke the stillness, reaching around her to pull her close. "Ya sure you're warm enough? You're shiverin' so. I'd hate for you to get sick again. What if we stopped off and got warmed up at my grandparents' place? I could show you the Dawdi Haus I'm talkin' about."

"Ach . . . I don't know, Caleb."

"It's where my Daed's parents will move once you and I are married. Mamma's folk live in the main house . . . so the Dawdi Haus is empty."

"Empty?"

"Jah. There's even a second smaller addition built on to that one, too . . . both vacant, though only for the time being. Someday it'll be all filled up with our aging relatives — yours and mine."

She'd seen as many as four additions attached to a farmhouse, all graduated in size, so this was no surprise. It was his suggestion about spending time there that surprised her.

"Well, are you sure it's all right?" she asked.

"What better place to pass the time on a freezin' cold night? Courting in an open buggy in the dead of winter is downright silly, don't ya think?"

She heartily agreed, beginning to shiver already.

"No one'll know," he said. "If that's what you're worried 'bout."

Before she could challenge him further, he added, "It's not as if we haven't been alone before. As a courting couple, we could even spend time in your bedroom, too."

Nellie was well aware of that — she had a special courting loveseat for just such an occasion — but she wasn't sure why he was so quick to mention the latter now. All the same, he was quite right. No matter where they went, they'd be alone, so why not take shelter from the cold beside a nice fire?

A golden light streamed from Rosanna's kitchen as Reuben lifted the woolen blanket off his driving horse, preparing to head home. He would never forget the look of innocent anticipation on both Elias's and Rosanna's faces. He'd offered a brief prayer for them, asking God to protect and keep the young twins safe, as well. Elias had offered his own request for "wisdom from above" at the tail end, which gave Reuben hope. The youthful couple had grown in the knowledge of the Lord in a very short time, and already they were being tested beyond what Reuben himself thought he might be able to bear.

He and his Betsy had never had trouble conceiving or birthing their nine children. There was something particularly tragic about having your first son offered under the guise of a heaven-sent gift, only to have him stolen away.

Martha had asked Rhoda to read a selection from *Uncle Arthur's Bedtime Stories* to Emma and Matty while Benny and Jimmy were having a shared bath. Feeling quite obliged to her brother and sister-in-law for offering her a place to stay, Rhoda was eager to do whatever she could to ease Martha's nearly endless duties. Tonight Emma and Matty were clean and cozy in their nightclothes, ready for *Aendi* Rhoda to read the "Susie and the Scissors" story.

Matty curled up next to her on the bed while Emma sat nearby, legs crossed beneath her long cotton nightgown and bathrobe. Midway through the story, Matty decided he wanted Mamma reading instead, and soon Emma was mimicking him. "Mamma, Mamma . . ." Rhoda realized she was a poor substitute for their mother.

"How about I sing a song?" Rhoda asked.

"Sing 'bout Jesus," Emma suggested, smiling.

Rhoda didn't know what sort of songs she meant. "You sing one, sweetie."

"Yesus liebt mich . . ." Emma sang in her childish voice, Matty joining in as best he could. When they'd finished, Emma grinned and looked her full in the face. "'Tis true, ain't so?"

Rhoda scarcely knew what to say. Till now, she hadn't thought of Jesus loving her. The preacher at the meetinghouse talked that way to be sure, but Rhoda had never thought of it so casually.

Martha appeared in the doorway and came to kiss the children, signaling bedtime. Rhoda likewise said good-night and kissed their soft foreheads and said, "Don't let the bedbugs bite."

"If they do . . . squeeze 'em tight." Martha chuckled.

Rhoda had to smile as she looked over her shoulder at them before closing the door. Such cute little ones. Now it was her turn to bathe, but she wanted to share tomorrow's plans with Martha first, so she followed her down the hall, pausing at Martha and James's bedroom door. "Do ya mind if I come in?"

"Sure, Rhoda."

"Mind if I close the door, too?"

Martha's face brightened. "Ah, secrets?"

"Not really." But she thought again. "Jah, I guess 'tis." She began to tell about Ken Kraybill and her supper plans for tomorrow night. "What do ya think?"

"Sounds like you're inchin' away from the People mighty quick, jah?"

That she was, and with little remorse.

"My mother always said you should only date the kind of man you'd want to marry." Martha went to sit near the foot of the bed.

"I can see the benefit of that," Rhoda said.

"So what would ya want with an English fella?"

"He ain't Amish, that's what." Her words probably sounded brazen.

Martha scrutinized her. "You're ready to leave the Plain life behind?"

"'Tis a puzzle." Rhoda sighed. "Some days I think I am. Others, no."

Martha had a big talk on. "I s'pose you'll discover some good out there in the world — look at us, we've got ourselves a radio . . . and a car, for goodness' sake. James says we can spread the Gospel better because of it — gives us a way to see more believers and whatnot, too."

"So are ya saying you're staying Plain, even though in some ways ya ain't?"

"We're set apart but keen on traveling to church more than twice a month. With a car, we'll get to the meetinghouse more quickly, maybe pick up others along the way. To us it's simply a better buggy, not somethin' to take pride in."

"It's all so confusing," admitted Rhoda.

"The way James sees it, it's hard to say you know you're saved and still be Amish."

"You'll dress Plain but drive a car and dial up folk on a telephone, ya mean?"

"Why not?"

Rhoda thought on that. It sure seemed like Martha had this figured out. If only she herself could be just as certain.

Nellie felt awkward, even shy, as Caleb led her into the darkened house, pushing the door open for her and swiftly closing it behind him. He leaned back against it, gently pulling her into his arms. "Come here, love. . . ."

They scarcely moved as their eyes grew accustomed to the dimness, even though if she were to admit it, she kept her own mostly closed. In spite of herself, in spite of all that had happened — all the forces that threatened to keep them apart — she savored how wonderfully near he was. Her broken heart seemed to mend in his reassuring embrace, and she pushed away the memory of all the sad hours after last Sunday's scare, hoping . . . wishing what she'd seen with Susannah Lapp was a bad dream.

"I'm sorry," he whispered against her ear. "Forgive me?"

Could she? She felt herself starting to cry.

"I had a choice, and I made the wrong one, I know now." He caressed her face with the back of his hand. "I didn't need to talk with Susannah to know she's not who I want."

Nellie could scarcely speak for her tears. "I wish to believe ya . . . I do."

"I'll make it up to you, love."

"Jah, I forgive you." She wiped away her tears.

He nodded. She could see him faintly in what little light reflected from the snow outside. The black silhouette of the barn, where he'd put his courting buggy and unhitched horse, filled much of the view through the back window of the Dawdi Haus.

"You're sure this is a good idea . . . being here, Caleb?"

He kissed her cheek, then the tip of her nose. "We're together now. Someday soon we'll always be."

Should she give in to his ardent affection and simply enjoy his nearness — this almost too-special closeness?

"I love *you,* Nellie Mae." He pulled her still closer.

An unfamiliar, nearly delirious feeling swept over her. It was probably wrong to yield, but, oh, she wanted to. "My Caleb . . ." She wrapped her arms around his neck.

He kissed her hairline, bumping back her Kapp in his enthusiasm. "I was scared I'd lost you."

Nellie tried to breathe, her face against his. Something clicked in her, like an alarm somewhere in the distance. Their fondness for each other was far too powerful to be given much rein. They shouldn't linger here in this tantalizing seclusion. Slowly, consciously, she pulled back, holding him at arm's length. "We . . . shouldn't stay. . . ."

"Why not?"

She inched back. Being this close to Caleb made her all ferhoodled. "I think we'd best be goin', truly."

"Let's just talk awhile. Come, I'll build a fire."

Even without the woodstove fired up, the kitchen of this snug Dawdi Haus was far warmer than Caleb's open carriage. She shivered at the thought of returning to the elements for the long ride home.

"What is it?" He gently tugged her back to him. "Are you frightened?"

"A little, jah."

"There's nothing to fear. I promise." He led her through the darkness of the small kitchen to the equally cozy sitting area, where an upholstered settee was positioned near a black stove.

She let him kiss her hand, unsure how long he planned for them to remain. "Caleb . . . I . . ."

He pressed his finger on her lips. "You're worrying needlessly. Let's just enjoy this evening."

She longed to do exactly that . . . but without realizing it, she'd stepped away from him.

Caleb pursued her. "Just pretend we're riding in my courting buggy, Nellie Mae . . . how 'bout that?" He kissed her cheek. "Can you think of our time here like that?"

Can I? This setting was far different than a ride in his open buggy, or even sitting beside him on the wrought-iron bench by the millstream. Anybody knew that.

This time Caleb trembled as he held her near, and her only thought was how much she liked being this close to him.

"Jah . . . I can," Nellie said at last, her worry fading as she surrendered again to his tender embrace.

CHAPTER 33

The settee was nearly too small for the two of them, yet she and Caleb had been whispering for nearly an hour now, reveling in the warmth of the fire and each other. Her feet were tucked beneath her and she leaned on his chest.

After a time, she stretched her legs and went to stand closer to the woodstove. "I like this little house. It's perfect for two, jah?"

"Well, too small for the family we'll have someday."

He was right, of course — she wanted as many babies as the Good Lord saw fit to give them.

Caleb patted the settee. "Come sit with me again, Nellie Mae."

She found her way back to him in the firelight, and he reached for her hand. Snuggling again, they talked for a while longer of the family they longed to have someday. Then Caleb gently caressed her face. "You're ever so lovely. I can't imagine a prettier wife. . . ." He paused, reaching up to touch her Kapp, letting his hand rest there momentarily. "Would you think poorly of me if I asked you to take your hair down, love?"

Nellie was startled. Wasn't it enough that they'd hugged so intimately?

"I've seen it down before, remember?"

She did recall the night he'd seen it unwound, long and flowing. The night she'd rushed to the door, sure he'd come to ask her to marry him in the privacy of her room. She had been robbed of that special time. They both had.

Unexpectedly, she thought of Susannah. Wouldn't *she* do Caleb's bidding if the tables were turned? A jealous fury rose in her at a vision of Susannah reaching for Caleb.

Slowly reaching up, she removed her head covering, slipping it off with ease. Then she began to slide the hair pins out, one by one.

Caleb leaned over and, before she could respond, his hands mingled with hers, as together they undid her long, thick hair.

He turned her face to him, and he cupped her face in his hands. His touch took her breath away. Was he going to lip-kiss her, their first real kiss?

"You're mine, Nellie Mae, no matter what

my father says."

Nellie fought her senses. The distant alarm she'd sensed earlier had returned. What she knew was right — what Mamma had taught her — clashed against what she wanted to do with all of her heart. Suzy had written about feeling the same way in her diary, including a Scripture about despising what was evil and clinging to the good.

But Caleb was miles different from other boys. She believed that much even as his hand slid down the full length of her hair. "I can't count the times I've imagined this moment, Nellie."

She raised her face to him.

He ran his thumbs lightly over her eyebrows before leaning near to kiss her lips softly. Lingering there, he backed away for a moment, looking longingly into her eyes. Then his lips found hers again with such fervency she felt dizzy. But she did not wince or move away, delighting in this new thrill.

"Nellie . . . we'll be together soon. Married. I promise."

She nodded slowly and then leaned forward and kissed him back.

"Oh, love . . ." Caleb's voice was husky as he rose to put out the gas lamp.

Still nestled in Caleb's arms, Nellie Mae

fought hard the sleep that threatened to overtake her. Caleb had already succumbed, his head back against the settee, his chest rising and falling slowly.

Nellie had always thought she'd wait to lip-kiss till after she'd said her wedding vows, but the warmth of the room and the tempting privacy here, in this tranquil place, were more than she'd bargained for.

Glancing again at Caleb, she slipped her hand into his limp one. How long should she let him sleep before they headed back into the blistering cold? She must not stay out all night; nor did she want to worry Mamma, most of all.

Nellie wished she might pin up her hair again, for she felt worldly with it cascading all over her, caught between her back and the settee and Caleb's shoulder. Yet lest she awaken him too soon, she decided to let her hair remain long and flowing, trapped between her desire to fully embrace this night and the reality of the passing hours.

No longer able to keep her eyes open, Nellie eventually gave in to the heaviness behind them. *Just for a few minutes,* she told herself.

"Wake up, Caleb! Wake up, I say!"

Someone was shaking him, and when he

opened his eyes, Caleb looked into the glowering face of his grandfather.

"*Du muscht mir here!* Hearken to me!"

Gradually he became aware of his surroundings — the Dawdi Haus . . . and Nellie Mae asleep on his shoulder. And his grandfather, who was staring at Nellie, too, with her lovely hair strewn over her shoulders.

Caleb sat up quickly.

"I'll be havin' a word with ya, son. Upstairs."

Caleb rose without speaking, first releasing Nellie, who must also have slept through much of the night on the settee. The old stove was now as cold as it had been warm earlier. Nervously he followed up the narrow steps. Without a doubt, he would catch what for.

Were the private hours alone with his beloved worth the tongue-lashing he was sure to receive? As Dawdi closed the door to the front bedroom, Caleb was suddenly concerned for Nellie Mae, who was all alone now. Would Mammi go in and speak straight to her, too?

Her hair being down is an abomination.

He recalled how responsive Nellie had been last evening. How, once he'd assured her there was nothing to fear, she had seemingly enjoyed his touch, leaning toward him as they kissed. But there was plenty to fear, he knew. *What have I done?*

Wide awake now, he sat down on the cane chair as Dawdi instructed. "Listen here, Caleb, if I were your father, I'd be out and out *angscht* — concerned."

Eyes cast down, he nodded. He knew better than to speak too soon, if at all. He must wait till Dawdi had his say and only then offer an apology. He had to do something to keep this mum, though. *What a foolish thing . . . not counting the cost beforehand.* Nellie was far more prudent than he — she'd asked repeatedly if they were taking unnecessary risks, and her fears had been proven true. For putting her in such a bad light, he was most sorry.

"You ain't turning out to be like your big brother Abe, are ya?" Dawdi bellowed.

At the mention of Abe's name, Caleb blanched. Abe was the family's black sheep, as his father had called him for a full year following — that and so much worse. No, Caleb was nothing like that brother.

"I'm waitin' for your answer, Caleb." Dawdi's eyes were black as stones.

"My intentions toward Nellie Mae have nothin' to do with Abe's mistake." Caleb swallowed his dread and considered how shallow his defense would sound. After all, his grandfather had found the two of them asleep together.

"Well, my guess is that you'll be marryin' this girl, jah?"

"This year."

"The sooner the better, ain't that right?" Dawdi's eyes narrowed, growing more solemn. "I'll let you in on a secret, Caleb. What you feel for Nellie Mae has nothin' at all to do with marriage or a future together. Not commitment, neither."

Inwardly, Caleb disagreed. He loved holding Nellie in his arms, kissing her — he'd scarcely been able to stop. She was to be his bride, after all.

Dawdi rose and stood in the window, his outline dark in the predawn light. "You like this girl a lot, that's apparent. But if you love her, you'll make sure she's pure on your weddin' night."

Caleb cringed. This Dawdi was more plainspoken than his own father, who had never talked about the birds and the bees or suchlike. "We did not sin as you believe," he spoke up.

Dawdi made a vague gesture in the dim light. "I don't mean to run this into the ground, but hear me out. The first kiss opens the door. You begin to crave more kissin' and whatnot, and soon you yearn to have all of her." His brow furrowed as he pulled on his long gray beard.

Dawdi walked toward him, paused, frowning, and sat down again. "There's more, Caleb."

He shifted in his seat. When would this stream of criticism cease?

"That's Reuben Fisher's daughter downstairs, jah?"

Caleb felt goose bumps down his back. "Jah, Nellie Mae is Reuben's."

A deafening silence, then — "I think you know your father's stand on courting a girl from Preacher Manny's bunch."

"Jah, I do."

"Yet you deliberately spent the night with her?" Dawdi harrumphed. "How do you think your father will react to this?"

My father? He stood up to protest. "I promise you, Dawdi, this will never happen again."

His grandfather rose, eyes glaring. "That is for certain, and your father will see to it."

Caleb groaned. "But, Dawdi . . ."

"How could you risk your land for a girl from the Fisher family? Haven't you heard the stories — how Suzy died in the arms of an Englischer?"

Caleb dropped his gaze.

"Your inheritance hangs in the balance.

Don't be a fool." Dawdi eyed him, his meaning all too clear to Caleb.

Too stunned to speak, Caleb left the room.

Downstairs, he found Nellie weeping, her hair wound up in a makeshift bun, eyes red and swollen. Mammi sat erect in a wooden chair.

Because he'd brought all of this upon her, Caleb fought the lump in his throat as he helped her into her long woolen coat. Mammi gave them both a sour look as he ushered Nellie Mae out of the front room and toward the back door without another word.

Nellie could not speak for her embarrassment, not only for herself but for the dreadful things Caleb's grandfather had presumed of them. Pressing her lips together to keep from crying, she shivered in the morning cold as she recalled the shouting concerning Abe Yoder, Caleb's oldest married brother. Had Abe pushed the sacred boundaries as a youth? If so, to think David Yoder and his family had kept that secret till now.

Her thoughts whirled as Caleb hurried the horse, recalling how he'd shown such grave concern over Suzy's sowing wild oats . . . over *her* suspected indiscretions — mere hearsay at the time. Yet, all the while, he'd been privy to his own brother's very real sin.

It appeared no one was good enough. No matter how hard she strived, it was impossible to completely measure up. Preacher Manny had said so quite clearly the time she'd gone to the New Order church, adding that God's Son did for us what we couldn't do for ourselves.

With the way she'd longed for Caleb last night, Nellie was a sinner, too. She'd wanted him enough to prematurely push past the courtship boundaries, letting down her hair.

Even so, she mustn't fret over what might come of her and Caleb's recklessness. She'd made a poor choice, and now she must live with the consequences. She and Caleb had set themselves up for being found out, and that's exactly what had transpired.

She shouldn't have allowed her jealousy over Susannah Lapp to fuel her vulnerability. Yet she had no excuse. Nellie knew that she, and not Susannah, was responsible for her actions.

Knowing the truth as she did, she could easily let herself be disgusted with Caleb and his family. She thought of Caleb's brother Abe and found herself grinding her teeth.

The Yoders were the biggest hypocrites she'd ever known!

Presently Caleb's breathing was rapid, as fast as when suddenly they'd pushed apart last night, ceasing their kissing. But he also wore a look of both determination and frustration, one she had not witnessed before.

Truly, they were equally at fault. After all, hadn't she encouraged his affection . . . giving hers so gladly?

Her emotions flew back and forth between love and sheer disappointment — with Caleb and with herself. She sat straight as a board as the horse galloped all the way back to Beaver Dam Road, coming to a halt at the end of her lane.

"When the dust settles, we must talk." Caleb jumped out of the buggy and came around to help her down.

She needed no help and wished to go inside quickly. Nonetheless, he pulled her up close and, before she could object, kissed her soundly on the lips. Nothing like the sweet yet passionate kisses earlier, this kiss felt reckless, even possessive. Slipping free, she stepped back and appraised her beau. "It was impossible not to hear what your Dawdi said 'bout your brother Abe."

He looked her square in the eyes. "This doesn't change anything for us, does it?"

She stared past him to the pale horizon. There was precious little time before her father would make his way to the barn. Mamma would be getting up, too, setting the table for breakfast.

I spent all night with Caleb, and now it is the Lord's Day.

"Next time, we'll play it smart and stay at the millstream," he said quietly.

She looked back at the house, relieved the windows were still dark. "Next time? *What* next time? Didn't you hear your Dawdi?"

"Oh, Nellie, have I wronged you so?" He reached for her hand.

"We can't take back what we've already given." She felt as guilty as if she'd lost her virtue. "Our first kisses will never be new again." She whimpered in his arms, her face pressed against the harsh weave of his wool coat.

"No matter what Dawdi said, I can't be sorry for what we've shared, Nellie Mae. I just can't."

She understood that. Oh, how she did! She loved him desperately, yet she was more afraid than ever for their future.

"I best be goin'." Nellie made a move toward the door, but Caleb quickly seized her shoulders, turning her around.

"Nellie, wait . . ." He sighed loudly. "We

may have gotten a bit carried away. I'm sorry for that."

"So am I." She turned and walked toward the house.

"This doesn't change my love for you." Caleb's words hung in the air like frost clinging hard to a tree.

Nellie whispered his name with each snowy step . . . as guilt engulfed her.

CHAPTER 34

Nellie plodded out to the carriage bright and early to squeeze in along with Dat, Mamma, Nan, and Rebekah. This day she would be counted among those missing from the old church.

As dreadful as she felt over last night, she tried to dismiss Caleb from her thoughts while the buggy headed into the sun. All down the shimmering road, she wondered if the remorse she carried in her heart showed on her face. She'd peered into the small hand mirror in her room, searching for the slightest hint, fearing the People would suspect what she'd done.

A single moment had the power to alter one's life, Mama had once told her. She'd thought the same of Suzy's reckless living — her sister had learned of the perils of first love the hard way. Sometimes such affection was as short-lived as the morning dew. Mamma had always said it was old love —

long love — that was best in the end.

Presently Mamma was commenting on how much warmer it was today than it had been for weeks.

Dat spoke up. "Months, it seems."

Sitting behind her parents, Nellie tuned out the occasional remarks from Nan and Rebekah next to her, wishing for solitude. She was nearly too tired to sit up.

The fields were dazzling white as far as she could see. Thanks to the unexpected sunshine, the day was brighter in all respects — a welcome change from the many gray weeks.

Nan and Rebekah continued their pleasant prattle, and Nellie went deep within herself, where the truth hurt most. She'd thought more highly of herself than she ought. She was all puffed up, as Dat would say — filled with the pride of life, *her* life . . . thinking she could withstand temptation and putting herself right in the middle of it last night. She had tempted Caleb and herself, believing she was invulnerable to sin. According to Suzy's diary — which she'd opened and read part of again this morning — it was far better to be repentant than to continually try to be good enough . . . on her own strength.

Nellie in that moment realized why she'd attempted to be good and failed: She'd wanted to do things her way. *That's pride, pure and simple,* Suzy had scrawled across the top of one diary page, when considering her desire to forge her own path.

Nellie and her younger sister had quite a lot in common.

Caleb stood outside the preacher's farmhouse, dog tired. He looked around, aware that Nellie Mae was not present. Had he offended her beyond her ability to forgive him? Certainly she'd not been herself when he'd taken her home before dawn — and no wonder. He could kick himself now for setting them up for his grandfather's accusations.

Today, following the common meal, Dawdi would seek out Daed and the hammer would drop. It was not possible to brace himself for a calamitous response from his father, but he would not hesitate to say that Nellie and he were actually innocent, no matter how things may have looked to Dawdi.

Looking now at Abe, where his brother stood in the lineup of men waiting to go into the house for worship, he noticed the set of his jaw. Was Abe always this solemn on the Lord's Day? Or was he merely reverent, and nothing more? Not till today had Caleb paid much mind to Abe, who already had five children and another on the way. Was he content with his lot in life, without an inheritance?

I must get Daed to hear me out, he thought. *If only I can get him to see the light . . . that Nellie Mae is still Old Order through and through.*

It was foolish, perhaps, to hope, but after last night, Caleb was convinced he must have Nellie Mae for his bride at any cost.

In spite of a lack of appetite, Caleb forced himself to eat. He kept his eye on his grandfather in mute dread as the older man set down his coffee and rose unsteadily to his feet. Caleb watched over the rim of his own cup as Dawdi lumbered across the room with grim determination. Standing before Caleb's father, Dawdi tilted his head to the side, beckoning Caleb to follow. At least the whole room wouldn't be privy to the confrontation to come.

Realizing it was futile to avoid the impending clash, Caleb rose from the bench and followed his father and grandfather out of the room, pausing only long enough to squeeze his mother's hand as he passed.

In the utility room, he pulled on his coat. From the small window, he glimpsed his father and grandfather already in the yard, their breath rising and mingling over their heads at the heated force of their words.

There was no mistaking the reddening of Daed's cheeks above his beard.

Caleb sighed and headed out to meet his fate.

His grandfather passed him on his way back toward the warmth of the house, his expression worrisome, though regretful nonetheless. Daed remained several yards off, hands on his hips.

"Son," his father began, "I would not have believed it if your own grandfather hadn't told me. Did I not forbid you to see that Fisher girl? That's bad enough. But to carry on with her in your Dawdi's house? What kind of —"

"We did nothing wrong."

"All night, with her hair down — not wrong? What kind of son have I raised? And you wanted me to believe you loved this girl, respected her?!"

"I do, Daed, I plan to —"

"Were you hoping to force my hand? Well, you're dreadfully mistaken if you think I would give you my land, my life's blood, just so you can have your way with that loose girl!"

"Daed, please —"

"Do you reckon me ignorant? Just because you are — thinking with your body instead of your brain! New church indeed — a woman up to Eve's old tricks, if you ask me!"

"I don't deny I was foolish to take her to the Dawdi Haus. But that was my doing. On my word, Nellie is as innocent today as she ever was."

"And how can that be?"

"It's my fault, Daed, not hers. I bear the full responsibility."

"Indeed you will, Caleb. A mighty heavy price you'll pay. I demand you abandon your relationship with Reuben's daughter and repent . . . to me. Then, and only then, will I consider handing over my land. Meanwhile, you have a single hour to pack your things and get out of my house."

The words — and the cold calculation in which they were delivered — were a knife to his soul. He assumed his father would be angry, but he hadn't expected this. Nor had Caleb expected to feel his father's rejection so deeply. Still, this man was his Daed, his pillar and strength since boyhood. How could it not hurt to be condemned so mercilessly?

Since it was such a sunny, nearly balmy day, Rebekah suggested she visit the Old Order Amish family where she helped each week with the little ones. Nan offered to take her and invited Nellie Mae along.

"Let's get some fresh air."

Even though Nellie had gone on the long ride to church, she jumped at the chance to ride with Nan and her friend. She felt disconnected and anxious for companionship.

It turned out Rebekah was invited to stay with the family, who offered to come by the Fishers' later for her things. Nan and Nellie rode back home together, talking for a while about Rebekah's eagerness to influence all of her old church friends toward saving grace. "She views livin' with them as a way to witness . . . hopin' to lead them to the Lord."

Nellie Mae hardly knew what to think. Caleb's sister had become a zealous soul in only a short time, a transformation she'd also observed in both Dat and Mamma, as well as in Nan. "God's Word has amazing power to divide and to heal," Preacher Manny had said that very morning. "Allow it to renew your mind . . . and your heart." He'd quoted a Scripture, too, one she'd never heard. *"Let this mind be in you, which was also in Christ Jesus."*

Renew her heart? Would that remove the sting of her guilt?

I can be forgiven, she thought. *Made clean — like new?*

Looking out at the stark black trees as she rode, Nellie knew her goose was cooked, and by her own hand — just as Caleb's was, only for a different reason. If she continued to soothe her conscience by going to the new church, which had pleased her family today, then Caleb would not want to court her.

How will he ever convince his father to relent now?

Deacon Lapp's house came into view as they rounded a bend, and she saw Susannah outside with several of her sisters, playing with their dogs. Nellie's heart sank at the sight of her.

Nan looked over at Nellie from the driver's seat. "You're so quiet all of a sudden."

"S'pose I am."

"*Was ist letz? —* What's the matter?"

Nellie hesitated to tell Nan all that had transpired in the past twenty-four hours, yet here was Nan, wanting to chat, her face reflecting genuine concern.

Nellie took a breath, hoping she wasn't handing off a burden to Nan. "Did you ever let your hair down for a beau? Ever even think of it?"

"Why *would* I?" Nan was staring at her. "Why'd ya ask such a thing?"

"Just wonderin'."

"Well, I know some girls who do. But from what I've heard, it ain't such a good idea. Leads to . . . well, worse things."

Quickly Nellie changed the subject to Rhoda, and thankfully Nan latched on to that. "Should we stop over at James's to visit? You miss her as much as I do, I'm sure," Nellie Mae said.

"More than she prob'ly realizes."

"We could drop in right quick."

"Not today," Nan said.

Nellie paused. "Surely she's sorry she left, wouldn't you think?"

Nan sighed and urged the horse onward. "She seemed bent on leaving, and we haven't seen her since."

A wave of renewed sadness swept over Nellie. "We can only hope she gets her fill of the fancy . . . and soon," she replied.

It was a bit chilly in the Kraybills' formal dining room, and Rhoda was glad to be offered some tea. When it was served, piping hot, the steam floated above the dainty cup. She tried to hold it just so, the way she'd seen Mrs. Kraybill do. Mr. Kraybill, on the other hand, was having black coffee, as was Ken Kraybill, their blue-eyed nephew. His eyes weren't the only appealing thing about him as he sat tall in his chair across from her, frequently singling her out with his friendly gaze.

The tea gradually warmed her, and when

it came time for Mrs. Kraybill to serve her homemade strawberry cheesecake pie, Rhoda noticed both Ken and Mr. Kraybill waited until Mrs. Kraybill picked up her small fork — the only one left at each place setting — before reaching for theirs.

She felt rather ignorant, though relieved at having managed to somehow make it through the meal this far. The multiple forks and spoons on either side of the lovely china plates, the neatly pressed white linen napkins, and the crystal vase of flowers that graced the center of the table — all of it was a wholly new experience.

Even knowing when to speak was a challenge. She'd taken small bites, like Nan and Nellie Mae always did, to make sure it didn't take long to quickly chew and swallow before replying when someone spoke to her. Thankfully the food was just delicious, all made from scratch, as she knew Mrs. Kraybill enjoyed doing.

Self-conscious in her outfit, despite Mrs. Kraybill's — and even Martha's — assurances that she looked very nice, Rhoda had to remind herself to breathe. Especially when she looked up only slightly to ask for the sugar and felt Ken's eyes on her. Did he think she looked like a Plain girl masquerading in an Englischer's getup? Or did he even know she was Amish?

Thank goodness for Mr. Kraybill, who had carried the conversation nearly the entire meal. Presently it was Mrs. Kraybill who was telling an amusing story about having gone to the pantry and realizing one of the children had removed most of the labels on the soup cans. They'd had what she called "mystery meals" for weeks on end.

Ken chuckled, and Rhoda watched the corners of his mouth turn up, accentuating his handsome features.

Rhoda took another little bite of the pie and was reaching for her teacup when Ken addressed her. "Have you lived in this area long?"

"My whole life."

Mrs. Kraybill intervened. "Rhoda's father raises horses not far from here."

Not a peep about her Amish background. Was that purposely left out? Try as she might, Rhoda did not recall Mrs. Kraybill ever saying that Ken was aware of her being Plain. But now that she was here, flaunting fine and fancy clothes and a loose, English-style bun, she guessed it might not be such a good idea to come right out and spoil things — not with the admiring way Ken looked at her.

Pushing away the memory of another Englischer's gaze, she asked, "How long have you lived in Strasburg?"

"Nearly three years. My family lived and farmed in the Georgetown area, southeast of Strasburg, where I grew up." He paused to take a sip of his coffee before continuing. "I purchased an old house listed on the National Registry of Historical Buildings, right on Main Street. It's something of a real-estate investment. I live on the third story and rent out the first and second floors."

"Like a bed and breakfast?" Rhoda blushed, realizing he probably was not a cook, unless he hired someone to do that.

His smile lingered and she had to look away. "Interesting you mentioned that, because I've thought I might want to go that route someday."

She wondered suddenly if he was looking for a cook, perhaps. But no, surely that was not why he was sitting here at the Kraybills' candlelit table. His presence was, after all, Mrs. Kraybill's doing, or so Rhoda assumed.

"Shall we move somewhere more comfortable?" Mrs. Kraybill asked, getting up.

Rhoda rose as well, reaching for her plate and the teacup, thinking she would help by carrying them into the kitchen.

"Leave everything on the table," instructed

Mrs. Kraybill in a near whisper.

The adjournment into the front room, or living room as Mrs. Kraybill was fond of calling it, was more relaxing for the three of *them* than it was for Rhoda, who was seated next to Ken on the sofa.

Glancing occasionally at Mrs. Kraybill, who seemed very pleased with herself, Rhoda put two and two together. Here was a young man who looked to be in his mid- to late-twenties, yet with possibly no prospects for a wife. Had he, too, been passed over for some reason? She studied Mrs. Kraybill's demeanor, wondering.

The talk turned from Ken's favorite movie star, Sean Connery — whoever that was — to Mr. Kraybill's obvious concern over the cost of the war in Vietnam. "Over twenty-five billion dollars a year. Imagine that!" he said with a fierce frown.

Well, Rhoda certainly couldn't begin to. She wasn't even certain how to *write* a number that big, let alone comprehend how it might otherwise be spent. Mr. Kraybill obviously had no such difficulty himself as he sat with one leg balanced on his other knee. "Really," he said, leaning forward as if to emphasize his next point, "this war has become too personal for LBJ."

Rhoda listened carefully, concerned that

Ken might think she was a bump on a log. She'd heard the president referred to by his initials before, but she didn't know enough about politics to express an opinion.

Just now she felt like a fish flopping on dry land. How might she ever fit in with fancy folk, really? It was one thing to work for them, but to socialize? She must start reading the newspaper more carefully, during her morning break. More interaction with English folk was key if she truly wanted to be part of their world.

When it came time for the Kraybills to put their children to bed, Rhoda and Ken found themselves alone. Unexpectedly, he asked if he might call her sometime, and she felt terribly shy. He seemed very gentlemanlike — nothing like the dreadful Glenn Miller — and Rhoda thought it might be nice to spend more time with him. *Another way to get better acquainted with the English world.* Demurely, she nodded and smiled before giving him James and Martha's new phone number.

"I'll look forward to it." Ken smiled a most pleasant smile.

"So will I," she replied, glad she hadn't said "jah."

Chapter 35

All six of them, including babies Eli and Rosie, were situated in the bishop's front room Wednesday afternoon. The two couples faced each other, Rosanna cradling Rosie as she sat beside Elias, and Kate holding Eli, next to John.

Bishop Joseph stood before them, all in black, except his white shirt. He explained to them the purpose of the meeting, his expression grave. Swallowing hard, Rosanna could hardly keep her eyes off little Eli, sound asleep in Kate's arms. Oh, but if he hadn't grown in the past week! She longed to hold him again, to breathe in his sweet baby scent, but she refused a single tear, determined to keep a sober face, no matter what might result from this most awkward and difficult gathering.

"Are the four of you in unity?" the bishop asked.

John and Kate shook their heads no.

"Elias and Rosanna?"

"We pray only for God's will." Elias's voice was steadfast.

"The outcome, then, is not your concern?" asked the bishop, singling out Elias.

"We desire what is best for these little ones" was his confident reply, and Rosanna regarded him with a healthy dose of pride.

"And you, John? What is your answer to that?"

John's face turned red. "This here's my son, and Rosanna has our daughter . . . over there with her." He breathed slowly and Kate momentarily put a hand on his arm. "We'll be raisin' the twins as cousins, if you see fit, Bishop. 'Tis how we look at it."

Everything within Rosanna began to churn. "No . . ." The word slipped out before she could stop it. She looked to Elias for support, groaning inwardly.

"My wife thinks of Eli as her own — we both do. We love him just as we love Rosie and intend to follow through with our agreement to raise them both." Elias looked across at Kate. "You've broken your cousin's heart, Kate. Truly you have."

The bishop cleared his throat. "No stone throwing, Elias."

A strike against them; the air went out of

Rosanna. Bishop was leaning toward the Beilers, it seemed.

"Kate, you'll have your say-so now." The bishop gestured to her.

"Eli's the fruit of my womb. He belongs in the church of his forefathers."

"Jah, growin' up in the Old Ways," John spoke up. "We can't think of our son learnin' heresy!"

Elias rose to his feet. "Did not the Son of Man come to show us the way to the Father? Aren't we all sinners, in need of redemption? You call that heresy, to be counted among the saved?"

John leapt from his chair. "Our son should be shielded from the lies of Satan. Declarin' you're saved? That's the worst of it!"

"And Rosie?" The bishop stepped forward. "Is it right for *her* to know and embrace such teachings?" He eyed John and Elias. Making a motion toward the chairs, he said, "Please sit."

Both men took their seats. The room became hushed once again.

The bishop shook his head. "No amount of reasoning will solve this knotty problem. I see it as being a bone of contention all the days of these youngsters' lives . . . and yours." He scrutinized each couple.

Rosanna prayed silently, trembling within

and without. *Show mercy, dear Lord . . . give us your grace.*

Bishop Joseph continued, "There will be no end to the strife 'tween your families." Alternating his gaze between the couples, he pulled on his long beard. "I'll leave the four of you to have one last chance to hash this out. When I return, I want you *cousins* to have come to a reasonable solution." Turning, the bishop left the room.

Rosanna looked down at darling Rosie — her tuft of light brown hair was so thin and silky. Somehow she managed to rest peacefully amidst this storm of wills.

Elias sat stiffly, tension emanating as he spoke suddenly. "John and Kate, don't you see what we bear . . . the pain we have lived with these few days without Eli? We love that little boy dearly." Elias paused as if trying to maintain his grip on his emotions. "His sister Rosie has been cryin' all week without him next to her in the playpen. Multiply that by all the years ahead . . . it ain't right."

The silence was broken only by Eli's quick gurgle as he moved in his sleep.

"Kate, won't you take pity on your cousin? On Rosie?" Elias asked.

"We've said our piece," John replied. "You've made a poor choice, leaving the church of your baptism . . . and we're takin' back our gift."

Kate spoke up. "Out of the kindness of our hearts, we'll allow you to keep Rosie as your own. That's more than fair."

"Aw, Kate," Elias said, his voice quavering. "Can't ya see? That's awful wrong."

The bishop returned, wearing a deep frown. "Is there no resolution, then?"

"We've offered Rosie, but they want both babies," John told the bishop.

"Well, then. I have no choice but to rule in this unspeakable situation." The man of God straightened to his full height.

Rosanna noticed the room brighten as unexpected sunshine streamed in from behind a cloud, filling the front windows with light. They'd gathered in this large room many times over the years for Preaching, blending their voices in one accord with their kinfolk . . . including John and Kate.

"The Lord God created these young ones as unique and separate people, yet they are bound fast by unseen cords." Going to Eli first, the bishop touched his head, lingering there. Then he moved across to Rosanna and placed his hand on sleeping Rosie's head.

Kate scowled at Rosanna, who remained silent.

Looking helplessly at her husband, Rosanna

held back her tears. *All the happy days and years ahead . . .*

Then, though her heart was breaking, she could no longer keep still. "Bishop?"

He looked at her tenderly, his eyes filled with understanding, as if he knew what she was compelled to say. "Speak your piece, Rosanna King," he urged her.

"Ach, the babies shouldn't be torn apart." Her chin trembled. "Eli and Rosie must grow up as brother and sister, as the Lord God created them in their mother's womb."

"Rosanna . . ." Elias touched her arm. "Love . . ."

She dared not look at her dear husband or she might lose heart. Continuing, she said, "I believe it is better for John and Kate to raise both babies." With that, she rose and carried Rosie to John and placed her in his arms, blanket and all. Then, faltering as she went, Rosanna returned to Elias, who took her hand as she sat down again without saying more.

The bishop wiped his own tears. For more than a minute, silence reigned. "You, Rosanna, are a true and faithful mother," he pronounced. "I pray you might birth many-a wee babe, should the Lord God see fit."

Ashen, Elias looked at her. But there was

no protest in him as they stood in unison and made their way through the kitchen toward the back door, neither looking back.

Dear Lord, please give me strength, thought Rosanna, suppressing a flood of tears till she was safely in the carriage.

Much to Nellie Mae's delight, the sun was making a steady reappearance, and the glossy white acres stretched out to touch the brilliant blue of the sky. She had been hankering for a walk all morning, so when Nan offered to stay at the bakery shop with Mamma, Nellie stepped out for some air.

I feel much lighter without all those layers. Making her way toward the one-lane bridge, she headed east on the narrow strip of road. It wouldn't be long till the creek was running free. She smiled at the memory of splashing its waters on her face one long-ago spring morning at Suzy's suggestion. How surprised she'd been at dipping her hands into its cold — like liquid ice. Suzy had delighted in its freshness, claiming, "It wakes a body up clean to the quick."

She hadn't been walking for more than fifteen minutes when a car came toward her and slowed to a crawl. A man who looked about her age rolled down his window. "Excuse me, miss . . . you must live around here. I think I'm lost."

She hadn't had much contact with English men, so she was leery of going near the car. Even so, she stopped.

"I'm trying to locate a particular Amish family," he went on. "I've already counted more than a dozen Fishers on the mailboxes. Like looking for a needle —"

"In a haystack?"

He laughed merrily, his gaze softening.

"Which Fishers?" she asked, keeping to her side of the road.

"They had a daughter Suzy, who drowned last year."

The air went out of her. Surely she was staring at this stranger. What could this be about? she wondered. "Suzy was my younger sister," she admitted ever so slowly.

His eyes registered momentary sadness. "Then . . . you must be Nellie Mae."

She nodded, wondering how he knew.

He opened the door and stepped out. "I'm Christian Yoder . . . my younger brother, Zachary, was your sister's boyfriend."

Startled, she noted a slight resemblance to Caleb as he drew near. How long ago was it that she'd determined to search for Suzy's friends, and here one of them was smiling at her?

"This is a surprise," she managed to say.

"It sure is — all those Fishers, and I run into you."

He was taller than Dat, and his hair looked nearly golden in the sunlight. In a burst of memory, she recalled Suzy saying this brother had invited her rowboating the day she'd drowned.

Christian reached into his jacket and pulled out a photograph. "Zach wanted Suzy's closest sister to have this. That's you, I guess." Slowly he handed it to her, as if uncertain whether she'd take it.

She gasped to see Suzy's familiar freckles, warm smile, and pretty blue eyes looking back at her. Behind her sister, sunbeams danced on the water of a lake. Tears sprang to Nellie's eyes. "Oh, Denki, it's wonderful-gut to see Suzy again." She brushed back her tears.

"I realize your loss is still raw for you . . . for all of your family." He paused, glancing down at his feet in the snow before lifting his gaze again. "Suzy talked of you often, Nellie Mae."

A little sob escaped her. "Ach, I'm ever so sorry. . . ."

"Don't apologize. I can't imagine losing Zach or any of my brothers." He dug into his jacket pocket again. "Here's something else." He held out a gold bracelet. "Zach gave this to Suzy not long before . . ." His voice trailed off.

Nellie stared at the bracelet. "Suzy must have loved it."

"My brother was going to ask her to go steady that day." Christian hesitated momentarily. "Zach's young, but he loved her. Everyone noticed the special something they had. An amazing pair . . . they would have been great in marriage someday . . . in ministry, too."

"Ministry?"

He nodded. "Yeah. Zach loves to preach, and Suzy was encouraging him in that direction."

Suzy was in love with a preacher?

She listened, soaking up every word. Again, she studied the bracelet, noting its inscription: *Not by works of righteousness but by His mercy He saved us.*

"Based on the first verse Suzy ever memorized," Christian explained.

She couldn't believe he was offering the bracelet. "Doesn't your brother want to keep it?"

"Not anymore. The bracelet's for you or your family."

"Thank you ever so much." She didn't know what more to say, though she cherished both gifts. She found herself looking at the forbidden picture again, knowing she would treasure it most of all. A far better reminder of Suzy than her Kapp strings!

"It's nice to finally meet you, Nellie Mae Fisher," Christian said, smiling a little.

She felt nearly too embarrassed to speak, yet she knew he was only being friendly. "Will you tell Zach how much this means to me?"

He smiled again. "I'll do it. He'll be glad to hear you liked them." He leaned slightly forward. "Please extend our condolences to the rest of your family, especially from Zach."

"So kind of you . . ."

He seemed reluctant to leave, or at least she sensed as much. "Were you heading somewhere?" he asked.

"No," she said quickly, lest he offer her a ride. "Just out getting some sun."

He nodded, gave a half wave, and headed back to his car.

Nellie turned, walking swiftly as she carried Suzy's bracelet and picture. As Christian Yoder's tan car pulled away, she dared to raise her eyes to follow it all the way down the road, toward Route 10, till it became a shiny dot in the distance.

CHAPTER 36

Upon their return from the bishop's, Rosanna washed away her tears and dried her face. She asked Elias to help her set up her quilting frame, determined to return to making quilts for sale, just as before. Keeping her hands as busy as possible was the best way to keep from breaking down and weeping. Her two sisters-in-law might not be interested in helping anymore, now that she and Elias were attending the new church. But Elias reminded her that the Lord both gives and takes away, and His name was to be praised, no matter.

Before today, she'd feared how their jumping the fence might affect extended family relationships. Yet despite the hard events of this morning, peace prevailed in her heart. Who besides the Lord could possibly know the future?

Returning without the twins to this house, the place where she and Elias had intended to raise Eli and Rosie, was the second most difficult thing she'd done today. The first was placing precious Rosie in John Beiler's arms. Now she must relinquish the babies in every way, praying for the strength to do so . . . and for the ability to forgive.

The loving gift Kate offered me is gone.

Unable to hold back her tears, Rosanna folded up the playpen in the sitting room. At least her darlings were together, and she and Elias would surround them daily with prayer.

Caleb counted his possessions, glad at least to own a good, spirited driving horse and the courting carriage his father had given him back when he'd turned sixteen. He had gathered his few personal belongings and carried them into the Dawdi Haus where he and Nellie Mae had spent their blissful, forbidden hours. Banished by his father, he would live there, laboring for his maternal grandfather.

Daed planned to drop by at the end of the week, to talk man to man. His father seemed certain Caleb would come to his senses by then, as he put it. Yet as long as it meant giving up Nellie Mae, Caleb was unwilling to relent.

Eyeing the little house she had liked so much, he began to unpack. He could kick himself for the mess he'd made. He *did* respect and love Nellie Mae, even though both his Daed and his Dawdi doubted it. A few kisses were nothing to be embarrassed about, were they? He hadn't thought so until he'd seen in Nellie's eyes the weight of guilt she carried. Given enough time, he would make it all up to her, just as he promised. For now, though, he must work off his debt of sin here, knowing that when he'd saved up enough money, he could make his next move.

The strange encounter with Christian Yoder stood out in Nellie's mind as she went about her daily routine, baking enough pastries to supply the increasing demand. Although the ad had disappeared, a host of customers were still coming, especially since the weather was more promising. Any leisure moments were spent reading the Bible Nan had offered to her weeks earlier. Nellie also found herself rereading the final sections of Suzy's diary.

While she knew better than to reveal the picture of Suzy to anyone else, the gold bracelet could not be kept a secret. She'd shown it first to Mamma, who had merely looked at it, not making much over it, except for the inscribed verse. Nan, too, cared little about jewelry, though she touched it gently. Nellie was glad to have it, placing it carefully on the dainty blue dish on her dresser — the cherished gift from Suzy so long ago. Each time she walked past, she remembered what Christian had said about the verse being Suzy's favorite.

Not by works of righteousness . . .

Could she rest in God's love and not continually blame herself for being too affectionate with Caleb? She'd tried for days to assuage her guilt, rationalizing their intimate behavior, but each time she came up short, feeling even more disgraceful. Giving away even a single kiss had been too much.

Reuben glanced toward the bakery shop, noticing Nellie Mae's Closed sign hanging on the door. For some odd reason, no one had bothered to get the mail earlier, so he lumbered through the snow, the scent of woodsmoke in the afternoon air.

Out on the road, he opened the mailbox, spotting a single envelope inside addressed to him.

The name and address of the sender was nowhere to be seen. *Well, what the world?*

Tearing open the envelope, he began to read.

Dear Mr. Fisher,

My name is Zachary Yoder, and I've waited too long to send this. I'm writing to ask your forgiveness.

I know you only through your daughter Suzy. We dated for a short time late last spring, and I was with her when she drowned. She wasn't wearing a life jacket, and I bear the blame for that.

I hope it helps to know Suzy was happy that day. She loved you and talked so fondly of her family. I don't know how you might feel about this, but she was a new Christian, having just found a relationship with her Savior, Jesus Christ. I hope this news brings you some comfort.

Every morning I pray for you and for your family.

I will miss Suzy for the rest of my life.

Most sincerely,
Zachary Yoder

Tears sprang to Reuben's eyes as he stared in wonder at the short letter. So this Zachary fellow was a believer, too, just like their Suzy. . . .

He folded the letter, somewhat curious

about the young man who'd written it. Thoughtful as the gesture was, he decided then and there not to share this note of apology with Betsy, fearing it might stir up her grief.

Sunday morning, Nellie was the first one ready after Dat, who'd gone out to hitch the carriage to their best driving horse. At church, when Preacher Manny quoted the verse etched on Suzy's bracelet as his sermon text, she let out an involuntary gasp. All during the preaching, she felt a familiar tug, wanting to bow her head in prayer. She recalled having felt the same way the first time she'd attended here. Oh, the strong urge to confess each and every one of her sins!

She listened intently as Preacher Manny went on to speak out against "worldly things" before the final prayer. "There are some who would push the limits. Such things may have their place, but not here." She assumed he was attempting to separate the chaff from the wheat, those who fancied the modern from those who desired only the Gospel, as he'd mentioned in today's message to the People.

Folk were eager to discuss the sermon during the common meal — the usual old church menu of bread, butter, jelly, cheese, red beet eggs, pickles, coffee, and many pies. Nellie found some things to be comfortingly similar.

By the time they returned home, Nellie was even more tender toward the Lord and the words she'd heard this day. It was impossible now to ignore what she knew to be true.

Without telling Mamma where she was heading, Nellie hurried to the barn, where she slipped inside her father's woodworking shop and closed the door. It was a well-isolated spot on the Lord's Day, and she briefly wondered about the Nazareth shop where Jesus had worked as a carpenter.

Standing near the table saw, she gazed out through the windows to the sky. It wouldn't be too many more weeks before she would help Mamma and Nan clean out their corners, from the attic all the way down to the cold cellar, with its many shelves for hundreds of canned goods and jams. Dat, for his part, would rake out the lawns and plow and cultivate the fields, preparing for another season of growth . . . and harvest. Spring would soon bring new life for all the People of Honey Brook.

Sighing now, she thought how quickly the grace period had come and gone. Tomorrow the Bann began anew, but that was not her concern. Wholly ready to follow in Suzy's footsteps, Nellie knelt in the sawdust and released the burden she'd carried inside, as well as her guilt over Caleb. She offered them up to the Lord God, whose will and gift of grace she'd rejected far too long. "O dear Lord," she began, "will you receive me as I am, with my black heart a-tickin' ever so hard just now? Please wash me as clean as new snow." She paused, thinking of Caleb. "Will you also call my beau? May he take your hand, just as I am now. . . ."

Jehovah God had led her — nearly all of her family, really — to this wondrous place of peace. Feeling spotless and clean, Nellie Mae rose and hurried to the house.

Before sunset on Sunday, Caleb headed to the Fishers' home. He steered his horse into the lane with a bit of trepidation, having violated courting custom, coming here to Nellie's father's house. When he'd tied up the mare, he walked to the back of the house and knocked soundly on the door.

As he waited, he considered his plight. *So much at stake now . . .*

Moments passed, and he heard the sound of rustling from inside. Then the door opened, and there stood Nellie, wearing her blue *for good* dress. In the dying sun, she looked radiant, until her eyes met his.

"Ach, Caleb?" Nellie looked shocked. "What are you doin' here?"

He said quietly, "Is there someplace we can talk?"

Glancing over her shoulder, she hesitated. "Uh, wait here." Then she disappeared inside.

His heart was pounding as he waited. She seemed startled to see him, and he sensed her uneasiness. The intimacy of last weekend was exacting a heavy price from both of them. To think all of this could have been avoided.

He looked over at Reuben's barn and the outbuildings surrounding it. The vast corral stretched out nearly as far as he could see. Surely Reuben's youngest son, Benjamin, would receive this land one day. Caleb did not begrudge him this blessing.

He considered yesterday's difficult conversation with Daed, and the one he now planned to have with Nellie. He'd rehearsed it repeatedly.

Wondering why Nellie Mae hadn't returned to the door, he turned to look in and saw her pulling on her coat and scarf.

When at last she stepped out, she looked downright pale. "I can't believe you've come here, Caleb. In broad daylight and all." She was clearly unsettled. "I s'pose we can talk in the bakery shop."

He nodded, recalling the first time he'd gone to Nellie's Simple Sweets last September, bringing her an invitation to ride after the Singing. Their first evening together . . .

They walked in silence, and then she turned toward him. "I was wonderin' how to tell you something . . . and now, well, you're here." She avoided his gaze.

"Jah, and I've got something to say, too."

She glanced back toward the house. "Best wait till we're inside." She picked up her pace, and he wondered if she'd told her father he'd come unannounced.

Once she'd closed the door behind him, they went to sit at a small round table. In the near twilight, she looked as pretty as she had on their first date. "You go first, love," he said.

She touched her neck. "I don't know how to begin." She paused to look hard at him, the first time she'd truly looked at him tonight. "I'm sure you'll be surprised at what I have to say."

"Go on."

"I'm going to join church."

He nodded. "'Tis a gut thing, jah?"

Her face paled again, and she closed her

eyes for a moment. "I mean the *new* church, Caleb."

New church? He groaned.

"I gave my heart away today. I can't begin to describe it, really." She looked up at him, tears streaming down her lovely face. "I'm saved, Caleb. I've never felt anything like this."

He shook his head, stunned. "This happened at Preacher Manny's?"

"No."

Jah, gut. Maybe it wasn't too late. Maybe he could still talk her back to good sense.

She pointed toward the barn. "Over there."

He was confused. "Over where?"

Her words formed slowly. "I opened my heart to God's Son in our woodworking shop."

Ach, she's spoiling everything. Everything! "Oh, Nellie, love . . . you know I'm opposed to this salvation talk. I thought you were, too."

"I wish you could know what I know . . . what I'm feelin'."

"Manny's church won't keep you for long," he declared.

"But this isn't about choosin' a church. I'm choosin' a relationship with my Savior, Jesus."

"Ach, Nellie Mae —"

"No, please listen." She grabbed his arm. "It's all in God's Word. We've clearly missed it. Don't you see?"

Perplexed by her strange exuberance, he removed his black hat and ran both hands through his hair. She was making things difficult, if not impossible. "I want to marry you before the wedding season next fall."

She frowned, pursing her lips. "But your father's land?"

"I've given it up — for *you*. There's nothing to keep us from marryin' now."

Her eyes became sad. "Ach, but it's your birthright, after all."

Nodding, he said, "What's done is done. Daed has no say about us any longer."

She seemed to ponder his words, then brightened as she reached across the table for him. "You honestly did that . . . for us?"

He rose and went to her. "I know I can make you happy." He pulled her to her feet. "I promised I'd find a way."

She raised her eyes to his. "Jah, and I do love ya, but . . ."

"But what?" His heart nearly stopped. "This strange gospel can't be what you truly want. Don't let them take you away from me."

She wiped her eyes.

"They've brainwashed you, Nellie."

She looked as beautiful and innocent as the day he'd first smiled at her, back last summer at market.

"You're as stubborn as I was, Caleb. Remember when I was so embarrassed 'bout my parents' interest in Preacher Manny's group? I told you I could never be like that."

"And I believed you."

"But now . . . now I see things more clearly." Her expression was earnest. "Won't you jump the fence with me? Please, won't you come to Preacher Manny's church?"

He shook his head, his heart sinking. "Aw, Nellie, you know I can't do that. And I've got it all worked out — we'll wed in the springtime and then go to Sugarcreek, Ohio, or wherever you want to live. We'll run away together."

Her mouth trembled. "You see only this life, but it's as short as a wisp of breath in the cold air. You see it and then it's gone. Think of Suzy." Her voice sounded sad.

He took Nellie's hand, so small in his. "I know life is short, love — that's why I want to spend it with you."

"What do I have to do to help you see?" Her eyes pierced him. "Suzy died to get my family's attention on heaven."

"Don't say such a thing."

"Truth is, heaven's got a face, and not just Suzy's."

Releasing her hand, he pulled her into his arms. "You scare me, the way you talk."

She clung to him, her cheek wet against his. "You can give up your land for me, but not your heart . . . to the Savior?"

He was weary of her reckoning his future. What had happened to the girl who was willing to do anything for him? "I've given up the land — everything, really — for you, Nellie."

"But you can't just walk away from your land," she protested. "You'll come to resent me for it . . . and for refusing to stay in the Old Ways. Won't you always wonder why I didn't love you enough to join the old church?" She was sobbing now.

Even so, he held her near, hoping his precious girl might change her mind — about Preacher Manny's church . . . and about him.

Dat and Mamma's joint decision to leave behind the Old Ways before the Bann was reinstated tomorrow meant their family would be spared the shunning, something for which Nellie Mae was truly grateful. Come fall, she and Nan would join the New Order church on baptism Sunday. As for Rhoda, it was hard to know what she would ultimately decide; she continued in her Rumschpringe, free from any fear of the Bann.

But the way things were going, Nellie wondered if Rhoda might not leave the Plain community and fully embrace the world. Nellie had such a hankering to see her oldest sister, so she borrowed Dat's horse and buggy. Daily she would pray for both Rhoda and Caleb. To think she'd let her beloved beau walk out of the bakery shop and out of her life. There was no turning back now, not with him so set against the Savior.

Rhoda was already in her nightgown and bathrobe when Nellie arrived at James and Martha's. She seemed happy to see her and took Nellie to her room.

"I've brought you something," Nellie said as she presented her sister with Suzy's diary. "I was wrong to keep this to myself. She was your sister, too." She placed the journal on the bed quilt. "Read it for yourself, if you want. Like a good story, the surprise is at the end, though of course you already know something of that."

Rhoda's face lit up. "Well, I never thought I'd see the likes of this. Denki, sister."

"There's more." She reached into her pocket. "Close your eyes and hold out your hand." Nellie placed the gold bracelet in Rhoda's outstretched palm. "Now open."

Rhoda's eyes sparkled through her glasses. "Ach, what's this lovely thing?"

She explained how the brother of Suzy's boyfriend had bumped into her on the road while trying to locate their family. "You're the one who loves perty things, jah? It makes the most sense for you to have it."

She glanced right then at the dresser mirror adorned with various necklaces, and they laughed in unison. "This is so dear of you, Nellie Mae. Truly it is." Turning the bracelet over in her hand, Rhoda again murmured her delight. Then she put it on, fastening it into place before eyeing it close up. "Looks to be some etching on it."

"Jah. Ever so special, really."

Rhoda invited her to visit anytime, and Nellie sensed she was discontented there. "Tell Nan I miss her, won't ya?" Rhoda said, her eyes sad.

"And all of us miss *you,* 'specially Nan." She looked around the room and then shook her head. "I'd be lyin' if I didn't say I hope you'll consider comin' home . . . real soon."

"Well, I can't let you think that." Rhoda rose and they walked together past the sunroom and toward the back door, where they stood and looked out at the night sky.

Rhoda sniffled as Nellie reached to hug her. *"Da Herr sei mit du* — the Lord be with you, Rhoda."

On the ride home, Nellie fought back tears as her thoughts returned to Caleb and their many nighttime drives together. Oh, but she wished she could somehow influence him away from the grip of the ordinance. But that was his choice to make — or not make. If he jumped the fence eventually, he'd have a dear price to pay. Even though he'd said he had given up everything for her, she knew Caleb could never walk away from his family. David Yoder's hooks were in him but good — just as Caleb supposed Preacher Manny's were in her.

The stars on this clear night twinkled and beckoned against the darkness. Nellie Mae remembered all the times she and Suzy had laughed together under the canopy of twilight, imagining whom they'd marry and what their children might look like. The long jaunts through nearby woods . . .

She hadn't gone to the woods Suzy had so loved since the winter snows, but she would return. Often she had found a reassuring solace there.

The horse drew the carriage along, and the stone mill came into view. Her eyes lingered on the wrought-iron bench near the still-frozen stream, the place where she and Caleb had sat enjoying love's finest hours.

Please, God, help me not regret letting him go. . . .

EPILOGUE

With the dawning of February eleventh, nearly one hundred and fifty people withdrew from the Honey Brook Old Order church, forming two new distinct local congregations. Word has it, according to Dat, that almost a hundred Lancaster County families have left for the New Order, which is beginning to spread to other states, too. I can't help but wonder about the courting couples sure to be caught betwixt and between, as Caleb and I sadly were.

Such a splintering of families and relationships. It's hard to understand how the grace of God can both mend hearts and break them. Belonging to Jesus is often a thorny road.

Mamma is heartsick because Rhoda's taken a second job as a waitress at the Honey Brook Restaurant. Seems my sister needs more money than the Kraybills are able to pay, although Rhoda's still there three days a week. By the looks of her, wearing fancy clothes more often than not, I'd guess she's got herself an English beau, though she's mum on that.

Nan and I have become ever so close, sharing nearly everything, as she used to with Rhoda . . . and I with Suzy. Nan knows Caleb wanted me to run off with him. She knows my answer, as well. There *are* times when I miss him nearly more than I can bear, until I remember his adamant stand against saving grace, and the Scripture warning against being unequally yoked comes to mind. Such a splintering apart it would be had I agreed — our marriage torn in two directions, our children ferhoodled between their mamma's faith and their Dat's Old Ways.

Thankfully Rosanna had the wisdom to see that little Eli and Rosie did not experience a similarly traumatic separation. Tears spring to her eyes when I visit nearly every week, though. Rosanna's quilt sales are thriving once again, and I daresay she has no time for raising babies. She and Elias will get through this murky, painful tunnel, but for now it is one step at a time.

Here lately Preacher Manny's church is jam-packed every Sunday. It's so nice having Rosanna there. She's confided that Elias hasn't talked further about tractors recently, not since his conversion. Wish that were true of my brothers, but Thomas and Jeremiah are planning to get one to share, of all things. When word reached his ears, Dat groaned and said, "Where's all this goin' to end?"

I'd say it's better to soak up Scripture and share a tractor with your twin than to plow behind a mule team and be in bondage to the Ordnung.

There's much to be thankful for, even though my greatest regret, when I consider it now, is my failure with Caleb. I know I'm forgiven, but I gave away my first-ever kisses to him . . . and he saw my hair down, too. There's no way to ever forget that.

I can only wonder how he's doing since our final encounter at Nellie's Simple Sweets. The grapevine's tendrils haven't reached my ears, so evidently he's still in Honey Brook working for his Dawdi.

Occasionally I've wandered down to Cambridge Road and the woodsy atmosphere of the old mill — Caleb's and my private haven. Right or wrong, I allow myself to relive our courtship days . . . and pray the Lord will call him to the truth.

ACKNOWLEDGMENTS

Along this journey, I've met a number of lovely people — research assistants who tirelessly gave of their knowledge, their memories, and their own unique stories. Several who contributed time and energy, digging for hard answers, are the following: Dale and Barbara Birch, Dave and Janet Buchwalter, Frank Casatelli, Nick Curtachio, Fay Landis, Jake and Ruth Bare, and Priscilla Stoltzfus. I am so grateful.

Sincerest appreciation to my first-class editors — David Horton, Julie Klassen, and Rochelle Glöege — and to all of the Bethany House team.

Ongoing gratitude to my husband, Dave, who helps plot every story and makes my writing days less lonely. And to our daughter Julie, who reads the first draft with enthusiasm.

To the people that time forgot, I offer my earnest thanks.

With joy, I offer up this story to the greatest storyteller of all, our Lord Jesus Christ.

ABOUT THE AUTHOR

Beverly Lewis, born in the heart of Pennsylvania Dutch country, fondly recalls her growing-up years. A keen interest in her mother's Plain family heritage has inspired Beverly to set many of her popular stories in Amish country, beginning with her inaugural novel, *The Shunning*.

A former schoolteacher and accomplished pianist, Beverly has written over eighty books for adults and children. Her novels regularly appear on *The New York Times* and *USA Today* bestseller lists, and *The Brethren* won a 2007 Christy Award.

Beverly and her husband, David, make their home in Colorado, where they enjoy hiking, biking, reading, writing, making music, and spending time with their three grandchildren.